FELDHEYM CENTRAL LIBRARY

WITHDRAWN

W9-AVC-308

3 9876 00350 5086

M

Lutz, John

Oops!

03/19/98
FELDHEYM

c1998

19 1/02
25 v 5/14

10/27/98

damage
noted

10

OOPS!

OTHER NUDGER BOOKS BY JOHN LUTZ

Death by Jury
Thicker than Blood
Diamond Eyes
Time Exposure
Dancer's Debt
Ride the Lightning
The Right to Sing the Blues
Nightlines
Buyer Beware

ALSO BY JOHN LUTZ

SWF Seeks Same
Dancing with the Dead
Better Mousetraps

OOPS!

A NUDGER MYSTERY

JOHN LUTZ

ST. MARTIN'S PRESS
NEW YORK

A THOMAS DUNNE BOOK.
An imprint of St. Martin's Press.

OOPS! Copyright © 1998 by John Lutz. All rights reserved.
Printed in the United States of America. No part of this book
may be used or reproduced in any manner whatsoever
without written permission except in the case of brief
quotations embodied in critical articles or reviews. For
information, address St. Martin's Press, 175 Fifth Avenue,
New York, N.Y. 10010.

Production Editor: David Stanford Burr

Library of Congress Cataloging-in-Publication Data
Lutz, John,
        Oops!:a Nudger mystery/John Lutz—1st ed.
            p.   cm.
        "A Thomas Dunne book."
        ISBN 0-312-18152-3
        1. Nudger, Alo (Fictitious character)—Fiction.
        I. Title.
    PS3562.U854057   1998
    813'.54—dc21   97-36529
                                                CIP

First Edition: February 1998

10 9 8 7 6 5 4 3 2 1

03/19/98
FELD

FOR ELLIOTT

Looking the right way while going the wrong way

OOPS!

CHAPTER ONE

What I want you to do," she said, "is climb in through my bedroom window wearing dark clothes and a ski mask, like a real burglar, then I'll seduce you and you'll spend the night."

Nudger was astounded. "Uh, no, I think I'll pass." He took a long sip of iced tea. "Did I hear you right?"

"Sure," said Lacy Tumulty. She was an attractive, dark-haired woman in her early thirties. Her eyes were brown, her mouth wide and mobile, with large, perfect white teeth. Her petite yet muscular build, her shaggy hairdo, and the way she habitually cocked her head to the side when she talked reminded Nudger of wire-haired terriers he had known.

"I'm not a burglar," Nudger said, rather defensively. "Not even a pretend one." He didn't know quite what to say about the second part of her proposition.

"That doesn't matter," she said. "What I have in mind is a fantasy thing. I'll pretend to be asleep, but I'll be watching you and—"

"Wait! Stop!" Nudger held up both hands, palms out. "We're not going to do this, Lacy."

She cocked her head to the side and stared at him in amiable confusion. "Why not?"

"I don't even want to discuss it. This is supposed to be a business meeting. Besides, I'm . . . attached."

Lacy raised her eyebrows. "Married again? You?"

"Not married. Attached."

Lacy sat back in her chair. They were in Tippin's restaurant on Watson Road, a ten-minute drive from Nudger's office. She was seated with her back to a wide window that looked out on a parking area and some sort of medical facility with elderly people coming and going. Nudger was only in his mid-forties, but sitting here with Lacy, he felt elderly himself.

"I'm still involved with Claudia Bettencourt," he said.

"Ah, that one!" Lacy nodded vigorously. "Well, good for you. And for her. I remember meeting her a couple of times. I liked her. But you know, maybe she wouldn't mind what she wouldn't find out. I've always known you kind of like me in that way, Nudger."

"Not quite in *that* way," Nudger said. "You're not much older than some of my ties. You could be my daughter."

Lacy sipped her diet cola then shook her head. "DNA would prove otherwise, even if my mother had no alibi." She grinned and shoved away her half-eaten chicken-salad sandwich. "You do realize all I'm suggesting here is a kind of harmless foreplay. You afraid I'm going to double-cross you for some reason and have you arrested for burglary and rape?"

"No, it's not that."

"Then you really *are* one of those faithful guys?"

" 'Fraid so." For an unguarded moment Nudger did speculate as he looked across the table at the young and burstingly healthy Lacy. He did like her, though not in *that* way. They were in the same line of work. Lacy had started with a downtown security firm, and last year had begun her own private investigation business. They had bumped into each other several times, and gone to lunch once when Lacy was working up her nerve to go into business on her own. Nudger hadn't painted a very attractive picture of the self-employed private investigator. Lacy hadn't been discouraged. In fact, she hadn't seemed to be paying much attention to him. Hmm, maybe she'd been interested in him in a way he hadn't suspected. Nudger couldn't help feeling flattered. He took another sip of his tea, tilting back his head and causing ice cubes to shift in the glass and bump his nose. "You need to be careful about who you make those kinds of propositions to," he said.

"Oh, I am careful."

"Then you've changed. I've never known you to be careful about anything. Which means that one of these days you might trust some guy who really *does* steal from you and rape you. Or worse."

"I doubt that. I'm a shrewd judge of people."

"But anyone can be wrong about anyone else. That's why we get clients. And you seem to be doing well, Lacy. That's dangerous."

"Dangerous?"

"Yes. When you're doing well, that's just when you're strutting along, maybe even enjoying tempting fate, and then *Oops!*—you slip on a banana peel. Life works like that, with a wink and a bruise."

"You're no banana peel, Nudger."

"Business," he reminded her. "On the phone you said you had a business proposition for me. And since your fantasy is erotic burglary and not prostitution . . ."

"Maybe some other time, prostitution," Lacy said thoughtfully. "Does Claudia know she's a lucky woman?"

Nudger sometimes wondered, but he said that yes, Claudia knew.

Lacy sat up straighter, her wide mouth set in a serious arc. Obviously, small talk had ended. "So here's the business deal, Nudger. A man named Loren Almer hired me last week to investigate his daughter's allegedly accidental death."

"There's that troublesome *A* word."

"Almer? Accidental?"

" 'Allegedly,' " Nudger said wearily.

"Yep. Almer thinks she was murdered. He wants me to find proof."

Nudger was uneasy. He tried to stay away from murder cases. They made him afraid. They made his nervous stomach a fiery furnace. Murder was one of the most contagious of crimes and could become personal in a hurry. "Do the cops think the daughter was murdered? Are they investigating?"

Lacy made a backhand motion of dismissal. "Screw the cops, Nudger. They say it was accidental death, and they're investigating nothing."

"How'd it happen?"

"Betty Almer—that's the daughter—fell down the basement steps of her house and fractured her skull on the concrete floor."

"Who else was in the house?"

"Nobody. And it was locked from the inside. It looks like Betty got out of bed in the middle of the night, probably to check on her furnace, and took a tumble."

"Why her furnace?"

"It had been acting up. She'd mentioned that to her father and her fiancé."

4

"Fiancé?"

"Guy named Brad Millman. Part owner of a company that installs swimming pools. He and Betty Almer were going to be married in the spring."

"Were they living together?"

"No, he's got an apartment on a lease out near the airport. Betty lived alone and died alone. Supposedly."

"What, other than that she was locked inside the house, makes the police call her death an accident?" Nudger asked.

Lacy cocked her head and stared at him as if he might be insane. Just like a terrier when Nudger had tossed a stick and actually expected a member of another species to run fetch it. Where was the logic in that? "Why, there's no sign of foul play," Lacy said.

Nudger thought there must be something he was missing. "Then why does Almer think his daughter was murdered?"

"I have no idea."

"Didn't you ask?"

"Not specifically," Lacy said. "I don't care why. He hired me to prove it was murder, and I told him I'd look into the possibility. You know . . . see if she had any enemies, owed anyone money. That kinda thing."

Now Nudger was catching on. "And you want to bring me in on the case."

"That's the favor I want to do you," Lacy said.

Nudger stared out at the gray sky and the puddles from last night's storm. Life could change people, make them cynical. Gray, like the weather. "Are you doing nothing but taking this man's money, Lacy?"

"Don't think that, Nudger. The reason I want to split

the fee with you is because I know you'll do a thorough job."

"Even if you know it'll lead nowhere. A woman in a locked house tripped and fell down the steps and died. That seems pretty straightforward. Had to be an accident."

"I figure her father's got a right to have that confirmed. But I honestly don't have time to do the legwork right now."

"And you didn't want to turn down business."

"Right," she said. "I thought of you right away."

Coming in your bedroom window, Nudger mused.

"I appreciate you considering me," he said, "but no thanks this time."

She gave him her wide, bright smile. He knew how she thought she could convince anyone of anything. She was 90 percent right. "C'mon, Nudger. I'd do it if I could, but I've got this divorce case that's taking up all my hours. Just me sitting all alone on stakeout in my car with my Porta Potti. And the husband kind of likes me."

"You're frightening, Lacy."

"Do it for me as a favor, please. I know you can use the money."

She was right about that. Bills were unpaid, and Nudger's former wife Eileen was stalking him with her lawyer, the despicable Henry Mercato. They were haunting the periphery of his life, threatening to haul him back into court, squeeze him for more alimony. He could indeed use the money. And he certainly had the time. Too much time.

He sighed. "Okay, send me the Almer file. I can give it a few days."

Lacy's dark eyes glowed and her smile seemed about to fly from her face. "You're a wonderful guy, Nudger!"

"Sure. That's why you chose me to be your burglar."

"Right on the mark," she said, standing and drawing a yellow file folder from the briefcase she'd set on the floor by her chair. "I don't have to send you the file. I brought it with me."

"You're always sure of yourself," Nudger said.

"You should be sure of me, too." She leaned over the table and kissed him on the cheek. "Give me a call when you find out anything," she said as she walked away.

"If I find out anything," he called after her.

He watched her walk from the restaurant, still worrying about her. She was smart and resourceful, and considering she only weighed about 110 pounds, she could take care of herself physically. But she was ungodly daring and over-confident, which could lead to catastrophe. To Lacy it was a given that she was a step ahead of the other guy, which wasn't always true.

The waitress approached the table and gave the check to Nudger.

CHAPTER TWO

Nudger had phoned ahead, so when he walked through the Third District station house the next morning, the desk sergeant didn't try to stop him but merely nodded hello.

The station house on the corner of Tucker and Lynch was a low, brick building with a tiled floor, always full of echoes. Today the usual smell of sweat and desperation was disguised by the scent of what might be insecticide or a strong cleaning solvent. Whatever it was, it stung Nudger's nose and made his stomach queasy. Someone back in the holdover cells was singing what sounded like a hymn with unintelligible words. Three plainclothes detectives at the door to the Squad Room were huddled with their heads close together, comparing notes. A phone was ringing over and over. Somewhere a police radio was transmitting a static-filled, metallic voice as cars were directed over the crime-plagued grid of city streets. Police world. Nudger didn't miss it.

St. Louis Police lieutenant Jack Hammersmith's office door was open, so Nudger gave a perfunctory knock on the doorjamb and entered. He shut the door behind him, blocking most of the noise, most of the past.

Hammersmith, an obese man with receding white hair, slate-gray eyes, and a pale, smooth complexion, was seated behind his desk, the phone pressed to his ear. His clean-shaven jowls spilled over his collar and jiggled as he talked. He smelled like too much Old Spice aftershave, which was better than the insecticide smell out in the hall.

"Sure, sure," he was saying into the phone, not breaking cadence with his conversation as he glanced at Nudger and nodded a greeting. "Sure, sure. I got yours, too." He hung up abruptly. Just like Hammersmith to do that. He had a thing about always being the one to break off a phone conversation and hang up. Some kind of control fixation, Nudger figured. And it manifested itself sometimes in other ways.

"Have a seat, Nudger," Hammersmith said, gesturing with a flesh-padded hand toward the hard oak chair in front of his desk. Nudger knew the uncomfortable chair had been chosen for the office deliberately; Hammersmith had no time to waste and didn't like visitors staying longer than was necessary.

As Nudger sat, Hammersmith floated his fleshy hand up to the foul green cigars aligned in his shirt pocket like cellophane-wrapped missiles ready to be launched. He merely touched the tips of the cigars. He wasn't going to light one now, but he might, if Nudger outstayed his welcome. He just might. They both knew what the noxious cigars could do to Nudger's delicate stomach.

"I got the information you asked about," Hammersmith said, opening a file folder much like the one Lacy Tumulty had given Nudger yesterday in the restaurant. "A tumble down the steps and fatal bump on the head. I don't see what's to investigate here. "Who's your client?"

"The dead woman's father."

"Father, huh? I suppose he has reason to suspect his daughter's death wasn't an accident."

"So I've been told."

"You sure it's not just one of those deals where the family can't cope with the death, can't accept reality yet?"

"I'm not sure of anything," Nudger said.

"Well, you never were, Nudge." Hammersmith put on a dainty pair of rimless reading glasses and gazed down at the open folder on his desk. "Betty Almer, single white female, thirty-three years old, apparently got up in the middle of the night and tripped down the basement stairs, fractured her skull. Broke a wrist, too, on the way down, according to the autopsy."

"Why was there an autopsy?" Nudger asked.

Hammersmith squinted at him from behind the rimless lenses. "The father—Loren Almer, it says here—requested it. But there was nothing suspicious, according to the ME." Hammersmith flipped a page and continued to read. "House was locked from the inside. The father found the body himself. Betty Almer didn't meet him for breakfast that morning at Uncle Bill's Pancake House as planned, didn't answer her phone, so he went to find out why. He let himself in with his key. Found out why. I love those German pancakes at Uncle Bill's, but I've gotta watch my weight."

"Police question the father?"

"Sure. Nothing suspicious about him, any more than there was about the daughter's death. He was grief-stricken, according to the report. Need his address and phone number?"

"I've already got them," Nudger said.

Hammersmith glanced at his wristwatch. It was silver and had military time marked in red beneath the numerals. "Pancakes for lunch, I don't guess they'd be any worse than pasta."

"Calories are calories," Nudger agreed.

Hammersmith gazed at the folder's contents again. "We talked to her fiancé, too. Fella named Brad Millman. He didn't seem to care about the autopsy one way or the other. Seemed as upset as you might imagine, but also seemed to accept Betty Almer's death as a tragic accident. As a matter of routine, we questioned the dead woman's friends and employer. There was no suggestion of odd behavior by her or anyone else during the days leading up to her death, no mention of any enemies. She was happy about her impending marriage, happy about life. No suicide here, no murder. An accident. We went over the house thoroughly, Nudge. Not only were the doors locked, but so were the windows."

"Deadbolt locks on the doors?"

"On both the front and back doors. Also chain locks. Betty Almer took the precautions of a woman living alone. Nobody could have gotten in and then left the house and locked the doors behind them. Or the windows."

"What about the door from the basement to the yard?"

"There is no door to outside from the basement. And no old coal chutes or fruit cellars. It was a fairly new house. There was nothing unusual about the basement until the dead body."

"What did Betty Almer trip over?"

"Huh?"

"You said she tripped going down the basement stairs."

"One foot tripped over the other, I guess," Hammersmith said, a bit testily. Nudger had come for a favor, information; was he going to be difficult? Hammersmith touched the ominous cigars again. "Look, Nudge, people trip over nothing but air every day and get killed, somewhere in the world. Why not here? Why not Betty Almer?"

"I guess that's the way we have to convince the father to see it," Nudger said.

Hammersmith raised a thin white eyebrow. "We?"

"Lacy Tumulty and I," Nudger told him.

Hammersmith rolled his eyes and drew a cigar from his pocket. "That young woman has too much carbonation in her blood."

"Not to mention larceny in her soul," Nudger said.

"Is she the one who steered you onto this case?"

"More or less," Nudger said.

"She can be trouble."

"Well, she does have some unsettling ideas."

"Like Hitler did."

"I don't think she's political."

"You better be careful, Nudge. Lacy comes around here now and then. She's dating one of the uniforms in the district. Guy named Dan Kerner."

"Young love," Nudger said.

"Young confidence woman," Hammersmith said. "You ask me, I think she's using Kerner. Dating a cop just so she can wheedle information out of him." Cellophane rattled as he unwrapped the cigar. Nudger knew the conversation was drawing to a close. "Damned pillow talk leads to lots of trouble."

"Maybe they're just friends," Nudger suggested.

Hammersmith fondled the greenish cigar then clamped it between his teeth. "Jush friendsh my ash," he said around the cigar. "She even comesh here and bringsh him preshents."

"Presh—er, presents? Like what?"

Hammersmith removed the cigar and studied its wet tip. "Little trinkets and toys. And sometimes things that embarrass him in front of the other guys. Tiger-stripped bikini underwear once. Her idea of a joke. Another time a black ski mask."

"Ski mask?"

"Yeah, like he's a criminal and not a cop. I guess that was the idea. Who the hell knows what a woman like that is thinking?"

"Who the hell," Nudger agreed.

Gazing at Nudger with his calm gray eyes, Hammersmith nodded slightly as if in approval or agreement. "Calories are calories," he said.

"Just go easy on the syrup."

Hammersmith stuck the cigar back in his mouth. "Bishy day ahead of me, Nudge. Crime never shtops."

Nudger stood up and thanked Hammersmith for his help.

Hammersmith nodded and found a book of matches. He struck one and fired up the cigar.

Nudger got out of there fast.

CHAPTER THREE

Nudger was hungry. All that talk about pancakes, maybe.

Before leaving the Third District station, he used the pay phone to call Claudia Bettencourt and see if she wanted to meet him for lunch at Uncle Bill's. She was teaching freshman English this year, and she had some kind of alternating schedule Nudger hadn't yet figured out.

Claudia was home, but she told him she was busy grading papers and didn't have time for a long lunch. She suggested he pick up some White Castle hamburgers and bring them over to her apartment. It was only eleven o'clock. Kind of early for hamburgers, Nudger's delicate stomach was warning him. But he wanted to see Claudia.

Chewing antacid tablets as a precaution, he zipped up his jacket, then walked from the station out into the cool air and crossed the gritty, puddled lot to where he'd parked his Granada.

The old car, like Nudger, seemed to be suffering already in the slide toward another St. Louis winter. It was red, so the considerable rust wasn't too noticeable until you got up close, but it needed shock absorbers, which caused the front end to sag and made the car bound somewhat like a gazelle over rough roads. And more and more often, Nudger had to raise the hood and insert a screwdriver down the mouth of the carburetor to get the engine started. At least the heater worked. Sometimes. That was a necessity in St. Louis.

Nudger got in and was relieved when the engine turned right over. He hadn't been inside the station house very long, so the heater began to blow warm air immediately. And White Castle had a drive-through window, which meant he wouldn't have to turn off the engine and try to restart it before continuing on his way to Claudia's apartment. Things were breaking right. Now he was comfortably warm and on his way to a long afternoon with Claudia. Maybe his luck would hold.

"I think I've developed a yeast infection," Claudia said.

Nudger's heart plunged. They weren't married and

14

didn't even talk much about marriage, but they'd been close for several years now and told each other such things.

"Been to the doctor?" he asked, putting the white paper sack of hamburgers on the dining room table.

"Yes. He gave me a prescription. It'll take awhile, like it always does, then things will return to normal." She smiled and kissed him on the cheek.

He watched her move to scoot the papers she'd been grading to the far side of the table. She was a slender woman with lean features, a very straight nose that was slightly too long, shoulder length dark hair, and dark, dark eyes that pulled at him. And she had a way of walking. His choice, even with a yeast infection.

The old steam radiators pinged and clanked comfortably in the second-floor apartment. Beyond the angled venetian blind slats, Nudger could see the upper branches of a big maple tree just outside the window. Most of its leaves had fallen, and the ones that were left were shriveled and brown, ravaged survivors of early fall windstorms.

While Nudger laid out the hamburgers and french fries, Claudia went into the kitchen and got some Diet Pepsi from the refrigerator.

As they sat enjoying the distinctive little square White Castle hamburgers, Nudger told Claudia about Lacy Tumulty and the Almer case. It wasn't so much the case that interested her.

"She actually wanted you to pretend to burglarize her apartment, then sleep with her?" Claudia asked incredulously.

"That sort of thing's not so unlike Lacy," Nudger said. "I

mean, she's probably asked lots of guys to do that. I mean, she's basically a nice kid and not really as promiscuous as this makes it seem. I mean—"

"Shut up, Nudger."

"Sure."

"That girl's got a lot to learn."

"My concern is that she survives the lesson."

"She at least seems to have the instinct for asking the right man to share her fantasy."

"I turned her down," Nudger reminded Claudia, wondering if he should be insulted.

"But you wouldn't have gotten carried away with your role and hurt her."

Now he understood and was reassured. "Most men wouldn't hurt her, but it only takes one who will for things to get out of hand, and for her to get raped or maybe killed."

"So what are you going to do now?" Claudia asked.

"Do? Me? What can I do? If she has this fantasy and is determined to act on it—"

"I meant about the death of Betty Almer."

"Oh. I'll talk to her father, try to convince him that this investigation will probably lead nowhere."

"Didn't Lacy already do that?"

"Yes, but I want to tell him that myself before I take his money, even indirectly, in exchange for my services."

"Maybe he's right and there is something suspicious about his daughter's death. You should allow for that possibility when you go see him."

"The police saw nothing suspicious in it."

16

"The police are busy with deaths where the bodies have knife wounds and bullets in them."

Nudger knew she had a point. And if there was the likelihood of a violent death being accidental or a suicide, it was to everyone's advantage to make it read that way officially. Life and death moved fast and nothing was perfect.

He finished his french fries and wiped his hands and mouth with one of the white paper napkins that had been in the sack with the burgers. Claudia picked up the little cardboard boxes each hamburger had come in, along with the larger french fry boxes, and stuffed them and the napkins and empty soda cans into the sack, then carried it into the kitchen. Nudger heard the *plomp-plomp!* of the foot-pedal-operated rubber wastebasket lid opening and closing.

He got up from the table, patted his stomach, then walked into the living room and sat down on the sofa. It was slightly cooler in there than in the dining room, but still comfortable.

Claudia came in carrying two cups of hot chocolate with miniature marshmallows floating in them. Smiling, she walked across the room and handed a cup to Nudger, then sat down on the sofa next to him. She moved up against him and rested her head on his shoulder.

"You're an honorable man, Nudger."

He sipped hot chocolate, taking in some of the marshmallow. "Sometimes, anyway." He sighed. "What's it ever profitted me?"

"It's why I love you. You're an honorable romantic."

Yeast infection, Nudger thought.

Then he felt guilty. She really did love him, he was sure. Most of the time, anyway. And wasn't she right? Wasn't he, in his own halting way, something of a romantic? Certainly he was in a romantic business—viewed from the outside. Writers like Chandler, Hammett, and Parker had made sure of that, and he was grateful for their efforts. He bowed his head and kissed Claudia's cheek. She placed her slender, graceful hand on top of his. It was surprisingly warm, he guessed from gripping her hot cup with both hands.

"My temporary medical problem is a local one," she said.

Hey, she was right about that, too! His hope soared. He remembered how the Granada's engine had turned right over.

The phone rang.

Claudia unnecessarily told him not to go away, then stood up and hurried out of sight around the dining room archway to answer the phone.

Nudger could hear her voice, but the caller was obviously doing most of the talking. Claudia's voice became even fainter, and he could hear the sharp clacking of her heels on the hardwood floor, then on the tile floor of the kitchen. Apparently she was talking on the cordless phone and could roam.

The clack-clack of her heels came his way suddenly and she appeared from around the corner holding her white Sony cordless phone out toward him. The expression on her face had changed in a way he didn't like.

"It's for you," she said. "It's Lacy Tumulty. She's calling from her hospital bed."

CHAPTER FOUR

Lacy reminded Nudger of bruised fruit. Her face was badly swollen, stretching her skin and giving it an unhealthy gloss even where it wasn't colorfully bruised. Both eyes were narrow, reddened slits, knife wounds that could see. The right side of her mouth was puffed more than the left. When she smiled at Nudger, wincing with sudden pain, he winced with her and saw that some of her front teeth were missing. No wonder she hadn't told Claudia much and had gotten off the phone as soon as possible. It must have been agony for her to speak.

Nudger crossed the pale green hospital room and stood near the bed, where Lacy lay on her back, covered to her neck with a thin sheet. An IV tube from a plastic packet of clear liquid coiled down from a steel rod attached to the bed's headboard and disappeared beneath the sheet. He moved to pat her reassuringly but drew back his hand. Anywhere he touched might hurt her.

He simply looked down at her, feeling his eyes beginning to tear up, and shook his head slowly in sympathy.

"My hair mus' be a horror," she said thickly, barely moving her swollen lips.

"Was it that burglar thing?" Nudger asked. "Did the fantasy get out of hand?"

She shook her head no—moved it, rather—a millimeter left, then right. "I never got injured doin' that, Nudger.

I would ha' been better off spending last night that way than tailing a wayward wife."

"Ah, the divorce case and the husband who likes you. Did the wife hire somebody to do that to you?"

"Don' know. No explanation was given. Huge guy I never saw before did this to me, had a pointy head and ears tha' stuck out like Mickey Mouse, but he looked more like Brutus. He jus' grinned while he was whaling away at me."

"Brutus?"

"Big cartoon bully that used to beat up on Popeye." She almost smiled. "If I'd ha' been able to get my hands on some spinach, it mighta come out different."

"Did the goon say anything at all to you?"

"Uh-uh. Only grunted through his grin whenever he hit or kicked me. Like it was foo' for his soul."

"Foo?"

"Food," she pronounced carefully and with obvious pain around her broken teeth.

"Maybe you shouldn't try to talk."

"Feels okay. Tongue's 'bout the only thing I can move. Got punched in the ear, though. Can't hear very good, so you gotta stay close and talk loud enough."

The wide wooden door swung halfway open, and a severe-looking nurse with pinched features and skinned-back dark hair peered in. Her eyes narrowed as their gaze passed like cold water over Nudger, and she ducked back out of sight into the hall. The door eased shut with a slight hissing from its pneumatic closer. Nudger didn't think his visit was going to last much longer.

"I wan' you to keep goin' on this," Lacy said. It was obviously getting more difficult for her to talk.

20

"The divorce case? Listen, Lacy——"

"Uh-uh," she interrupted. "Betty Almer case. We can't gi' up, Nudger."

"Why not?"

"Money."

Nudger thought about that. His need for money was serious, with the rapacious Eileen and her lover-lawyer the repugnant Henry Mercato pressing harder than usual for additional alimony. But Lacy had been badly beaten, maybe because of the Almer case. Which meant Nudger might be badly beaten. Woe! Maybe they should give up. His stomach twisted and turned, then growled a warning.

"We don't need money that much, Lacy. A delay won't make a lot of difference in an investigation like the Almer case. I know you feel terrible now, but in a few weeks you'll be up and around again. More your old self."

"I'm my ol' self now, Nudger. And it'll take me longer 'n a few weeks to be able to dance again. He cut my——"

The door swung open wide.

Nudger expected to see the severe nurse with the skinned-back hair and accusatory glare. Instead a well-dressed dark-haired man in a brown suit entered the room. He had a pen in the pocket of his white shirt, and a section of black tube was visible inside his suitcoat. He had kind blue eyes and was smiling in a way that made it seem he smiled often.

"I'm Doctor Ryker," he said, nodding to Nudger. "I'm afraid Lacy needs her rest. Visiting hours aren't until later this afternoon."

"I invited him," Lacy said. "He's my fren' an' business 'socciate. It's 'portan'."

Dr. Ryker turned his smile on her. "That doesn't make any difference. Hospital rules. Besides, I'm not so sure you're ready for visitors."

"Jus' a momen' more," Lacy pleaded.

Dr. Ryker hesitated, then nodded. "Only a moment, now. I'll be out in the hall."

When the doctor had left, Lacy gazed pitifully at Nudger with her swollen eyes. "I don' wanna let this fee get 'way, Nudger."

"I can't help you, Lacy. I've talked to Jack Hammersmith. He assured me there's nothing suspicious about Betty Almer's death. It was accidental."

" 'Mersmith doesn' know wha' he's talkin' 'bou'." A wide crack in her upper lip began to seep blood.

Nudger knew Dr. Ryker was right. This was no time for Lacy to have visitors. No time for her to keep talking, wearing herself down.

"I'm sorry, Lacy." He edged toward the door.

"Don' lea' like this!" she pleaded. "Think 'bou it. Please!"

Nudger felt his insides melting. What could he say? How could he answer? He knew he was being manipulated, but it was manipulation out of desperation, as if a bird with a broken wing lay before him beseeching him for a worm. He knew he was the worm. Women were always doing this to him.

"Are you sure it isn't that you have scruples?" Nudger asked. "I'd feel much better telling you I'd think about it if you wanted to continue the investigation because of scruples."

"Money," Lacy affirmed. "Got no med'cal 'surance." Her lip began to bleed profusely.

Nudger sighed.

"Think 'bou' it," Lacy asked again. Her eyes appeared to lose focus.

"I'm thinking," Nudger told her.

"You're mos' kind man I know, to help me. I got a few scruples. You gon' help me?"

"I said I would."

"Prom'se?"

"Sure. I suppose."

She managed a grotesque smile, but a smile. "Than' you."

He moved toward her to kiss her forehead, but there wasn't enough room between cuts and contusions. He gave her a smile he hoped was reassuring, then backed away and quietly left the room. She might not have seen him smile. She might have drifted off to sleep. He hoped she was sleeping, not in pain.

"Mr. Nudger," Dr. Ryker said.

He was standing on the other side of the wide corridor, leaning with his back against the wall, his hands in his pants pockets. Nudger walked over and stood near him.

"She's hurt more seriously than she seems to believe," the doctor said.

"How seriously?"

"Aside from being badly bruised, she sustained damage to her kidneys, and she has several broken ribs."

"What about her hearing? She said she'd been struck in the ear."

"Any hearing loss is temporary."

"She started to tell me about being cut, just before you entered the room."

Dr. Ryker frowned. "Her attacker used a knife on her Achilles tendons, just above the heel. When that tendon is severed, the foot flops more or less independently, detached from the muscles in the leg. He managed to sever one tendon entirely, and sliced halfway through the other."

Nudger felt faint and had to lean against the wall. "My God! Why would he do something like that?"

"He apparently wanted to hobble her. Sadism maybe. Or possibly he wanted to make sure her activities were curtailed."

Nudger felt a rage for Lacy's attacker growing like flame in his stomach. "Will she be able to walk normally again?"

"There'll have to be an operation to reattach the severed tendon and repair the damaged one. Recovery from tendon operations is a slow process. It will be months before she'll be able to get around more or less normally."

"Months?"

"Six, perhaps. She'll be able to walk before that, of course, but with a cane, and then with a limp." He looked distressed. "It's a shame, a young, pretty woman like that. But she might recover faster than most. She seems to have spirit."

Now Nudger understood why Lacy wanted him to take over the Almer case in order to preserve at least part of the fee. She'd be on the shelf for a long time, and was without medical insurance. To say she needed money was an understatement.

Maybe reading Nudger's mind, Dr. Ryker said, "The admissions nurse said she had no relatives. Are you a close friend?"

"A friend, anyway," Nudger said. "We didn't see each other often. Lacy was always more than a little reckless. To know her is to worry about her."

"At least she had the foresight to continue her medical insurance from her previous employer," Dr. Ryker said.

Nudger blinked. "Are you sure?"

"Oh, yes. Admissions always checks those things."

Nudger believed him.

"The nurse will give her a sedative soon," Dr. Ryker said. "She really shouldn't have visitors. We'll be operating on her tomorrow morning."

Nudger gave the doctor one of his cards. "If there's any kind of a problem, will you have someone call me?"

"Of course." The doctor returned the compliment by handing Nudger one of his own cards, which was bordered in blue and gold and looked expensive enough to be a Hallmark.

Dr. Ryker shook Nudger's hand, then walked back into Lacy's room.

Though Lacy had lied to Nudger about not having medical insurance, he couldn't feel angry. It was what he should have expected. A person's character didn't change because of serious injury. Usually.

He stared at the closed door to her room, wondering if he should go back inside after the doctor had left and confront her about the insurance lie.

But he only wondered for a moment. She'd only smile,

wink with a swollen eye, and ask him what was the big deal about a small lie between friends. Her lower lip would probably start to bleed again.

Nudger turned away and walked down the hall toward the elevators, telling himself he'd merely told Lacy he'd think about taking on the Almer case by himself. He hadn't actually said he'd do it.

Or *had* he?

The truth was, he couldn't remember.

He punched the elevator button as if it had punched him first.

This true-to-your-word credo wasn't easy when you couldn't recall what you'd said.

CHAPTER FIVE

Fickle St. Louis weather worked its wiles. Warm air had pushed in from the south, and by evening Nudger could drive with the car windows down. The engine noise was louder that way; and there was a new noise coming from the car, what sounded like the squealing of a fan belt. Or possibly a water pump about to give up and become a costly repair.

Nudger tried to ignore the squealing and listened to the Rams-Giants football game as he drove north on the Inner Belt and exited on Page Avenue. There was a lot of traffic on Page. At red lights the cars lined up and provided a cacophony of sound, music from various radios, the mingled voices of the game being announced—lost in the rising rumble of accelerating engines as the light changed to green.

Nudger drove east to Hanley Road, then wound through side streets and began looking for Loren Almer's address in a neighborhood of modest and well-kept brick homes in the suburb of University City.

Almer, a supervisor with the post office, had been home from work for only a few hours. On the phone with Nudger, he'd seemed aggrieved by the news of Lacy's injuries and agreed to see Nudger immediately. He wanted no time wasted in the investigation of his daughter's death.

Nudger found the house, a small brick home with black shutters and an attached garage with a white overhead door. There was a tall oak tree in front that shaded most of the yard. A large rock with the house's address neatly stenciled on it in black numerals leaned against the tree's thick trunk. Nudger parked the car and made his way along a brick walk to the front porch. Ivy that had remained a rich green grew thickly on both sides of the walk and spread out for a few feet in both directions over the lawn.

Loren Almer answered Nudger's ring within a few minutes and peered out at him through the glass in the aluminum storm door. He was a short man in his fifties, bald and with a scraggly gray Vandyke beard. When Nudger had identified himself and Almer opened the door and invited him inside, Nudger saw him more clearly without the reflecting glass between them. Almer had pained blue eyes and not much in the way of eyebrows to go with the beard.

"I hope Miss Tumulty's recovering okay," he said, motioning Nudger into a small living room with a blue carpet, gray sofa and chair, and a large-screen TV that dwarfed all other furnishings. He had a window open somewhere and sound from outside was sifting in with a warm breeze: a car motor running steadily nearby, kids shouting in the distance, almost certainly the crack of bat on ball. The baseball season never really ended in St. Louis. For a moment Nudger was taken back to his childhood days of sandlot baseball.

"She won't be getting up and around for a while," he said to Almer, pulling himself back to the present. "Which is why I'm here." He found himself staring at the TV, wondering how someone had fit the huge, bulbous object through the door.

"How long will she be incapacitated?" Almer asked, sitting down on the sofa after Nudger had sat in the gray chair.

"Months."

"Oh, dear!" Almer's hand went to his head. He touched his temple lightly with his fingertips, as if checking to see if there might be a hole there. Then he looked with more interest at Nudger. "Are you handling the case now?"

Here was another opportunity for Nudger to say no, he was only here because Lacy couldn't come, and she would be making arrangements about the investigation. That was the sort of answer he knew he should give. This was at least an opportunity to be vague.

But Nudger looked into Almer's agonized eyes. Grief stared back at him like a trapped animal. No one every really got over the death of a child. "It looks that way," he said.

"I had faith in Miss Tumulty," Almer said.

"She has faith in me," Nudger told him, wondering

what kind of persuasion Lacy had used to convince Almer of her investigative abilities.

Almer looked around him as if he'd never before been in his own living room. "I'm alone now, Mr. Nudger. My wife, Betty's mother, died three years ago. Betty was my family, everything to me." His voice quavered and the flesh beneath his right eye began to dance. Then he looked toward a narrow wooden mantle over an obviously fake fireplace on the opposite wall. A framed photo was on the left side of the mantle, a vase of obviously artificial silk flowers on the right. The photograph was a studio portrait of an attractive young woman with an oval face and lots of wavy dark hair. Her eyes were bright and she was smiling as if she'd just heard something that amused and astounded her.

"I assume that's Betty," Nudger said.

"*Was* Betty," Almer corrected forlornly.

"Anyone can have an accident," Nudger said.

Almer gave a sad laugh, almost a whimper. "Let me show you another photograph of Betty," he said, standing up from the sofa.

Almer moved toward a short hall leading to the other rooms in the house. He was much frailer than he'd appeared through the storm door, and he walked with a bent-kneed shuffle, as if his legs were devoid of any strength or spring. Wading through grief, Nudger thought, watching him.

Almer returned within a few minutes carrying not one photo but a handful of snapshots and a yellowed newspaper clipping. He handed them to Nudger, then sat back down on the sofa, still moving as if his legs had been sapped of all strength.

Nudger looked at the photographs, all of the same young woman at different ages. In the first photo she might have been ten years old, with a shaggy haircut and freckles, posed in front of a cactus, a vacation shot. In the others she grew older, became a pretty high school girl in a band costume, holding a clarinet. Then came the graduation photo, posed against backlighting that formed a pale halo around her head, a fixed smile that was nonetheless beautiful.

The last two photographs showed her at about twelve, then in her early teens, in gymnast suits. In one photo she was standing poised on one leg on a balance beam, her other leg stretched out before her and held high, as if she were examining the toes of her bare foot. In the other she was doing a handstand on the parallel bars. A similar photo was in the old newspaper, along with her name and the fact that she'd placed third in the state high school gymnastics championship. Her highest score had been in the balance beam competition.

Almer had risen from the sofa and was standing before Nudger, staring down at him with a hard expression as he bit off his words. "Betty didn't die in an accident. She never tripped over her own two feet in her life. She worked out regularly at a gym the last three years, and she and her fiancé entered dance contests. I never saw her in better physical condition or more graceful and nimble. She didn't fall down those stairs. She was pushed. I believe that, and I think Miss Tumulty believes it."

"Maybe she does," Nudger said.

"The question is, do you?"

Nudger looked down at the newspaper photo, then up again at Almer.

"I believe it enough," he said.

He kept telling himself that over and over while Almer
wrote a two-thousand-dollar check as payment in advance
for his services.

"This wasn't necessary, I would have billed you,"
Nudger told him, accepting the check and tucking it into his
pocket.

Almer smiled grimly. "It's better this way. I want you to
feel obligated, and I know you will feel that way. I sensed
right away that's the kind of person Miss Tumulty is, which
is why I hired her. You're the same kind. With folks like
you, honor's more of a motivation than money."

Fear was a motivation, too, Nudger thought. And grief.
Both of them clouded judgment and lent an urgency that
forced people into mistakes. But he didn't mention this to
Almer.

As he drove away from Loren Almer's house with the
check in his pocket, he wondered if Almer was deceiving
himself about his daughter's death the way he was about
that honor business.

CHAPTER SIX

We dig the hole," Betty Almer's fiancé Brad Millman told
Nudger the next day, "then we put in packed sand, a thick
vinyl liner, and we got us a swimming pool that'll hold up
good as a concrete one and costs half as much."

Nudger watched a huge, awkward piece of equipment Millman had called a backhoe snort and growl and clank as it took gigantic bites out of a South County homeowner's lawn and deposited the dirt in a waiting dump truck.

"Funny time of year to be putting in a swimming pool, isn't it?" Nudger asked. It was unseasonably warm again today, but it was still October.

"Not at all," Millman said. "Swimming pools are like a lot of things for sale—buy them during the off-season and you get the best deal."

That made sense to Nudger, yet if it were true it would make the off-season the prime season, which would mean. . . . He stopped thinking about it.

"You say my office told you I'd be here, Mr. Nudger?" Millman asked, speaking loudly over the lusty noise of the backhoe. He was a tall man, gangly but with muscle, wearing jeans and a faded blue work shirt dark with perspiration. He had unruly straight red hair, and a thin face with the kind of craggy good looks that pudgy yuppies on exercise machines strive to achieve.

"That's right," Nudger said. "A woman named Judith gave me the address."

The two men silently watched the voracious backhoe take another huge bite out of the yard.

"It's about Betty Almer," Nudger said. "I'm investigating her death for her father."

"I thought that Lacy Tumulty woman was doing that. She's some sort of private detective."

"She got hurt. I took over the case."

Millman scraped mud from the soles of his construction

boots onto the concrete edge of the curb. "I already talked to that Lacy woman."

"I wanted to hear for myself what you thought," Nudger said.

Millman glanced at his wristwatch, then at the chugging and clattering backhoe. "It's noisy here," he said, "and it's about lunch time. I can afford to be away for a little while. There's a McDonald's near here."

"I know where it is," Nudger said. "I'll drive."

"No, I better follow you," Millman said. He touched the black beeper on his belt. "Never know when I'm gonna have to jump up and rush back here."

Nudger waited while Millman talked to the backhoe driver, then to a man shoveling dirt in what looked like an effort to define the shape of the pool.

The Granada started right away, continuing its good behavior despite the occasional squeal from beneath the hood, and Nudger drove to McDonald's while Millman followed in a white pickup truck that sat high on oversized, knobby tires.

It was noisier in McDonald's than standing near the backhoe. About a dozen teenage girls in the parochial school uniform of white blouses and plaid skirts were eating lunch, secretly smoking, and practicing how to curse and be catty. They were getting it down pretty well.

Nudger and Millman carried their Big Macs and colas to a far booth and got as comfortable as possible sitting opposite each other on the orange plastic benches.

"Her dad got you convinced Betty's death was suspicious?" Millman asked, when they'd unwrapped their hamburgers and had started to eat.

Nudger had a mouthful of food, so he merely nodded.

"Old Loren," Millman said, "I think he loved Betty as much as I did. That's why he keeps trying to push for a criminal investigation. He can't let her go."

"Can you?"

Millman's eyes filled with tears and he looked away and swiped at them with his knuckles. If he was an actor, he was one who could cry on cue. "Next question," he said, when he'd turned back to face Nudger.

"Do you think her death was an accident?"

"Yeah. I've got no choice but to think so. I mean, something like this happens and automatically you look for someone or something to blame. I reacted that way myself at first, so I know just how Loren feels. But we gotta face facts. Betty was alone in the house. She tripped and fell down the stairs and died. There's nothing to suggest otherwise. Her death was fate, and Loren can't accept that. I can, I guess. I know how it is, you're living good, happy and planning to get married, then suddenly fate does a job on you." He sipped cola through a straw.

"The banana peel theory," Nudger said.

He immediately regretted his words, thinking Millman might think he was trivializing Betty's death and be angered.

But Millman only nodded glumly. "I guess, if the theory is that anything can happen to anyone at any time."

"That's pretty much it," Nudger said.

Millman scrunched up his eyes so they were almost closed and the crow's-feet at their corners deepened. "Betty's dead, and sometimes I feel like I might as well be, too. Fate messed up both of us with that fall down the stairs."

"Her father's a victim of fate, too."

"I know that. But I don't think he knows it. Because he's not ready to know it. He wants somebody or something other than fate to blame."

"How'd you and your prospective father-in-law get along?"

"Just fine. Loren's a good guy, very sincere, with his feelings on his sleeve. Sensitive, I guess you'd say. If he didn't approve of me, he sure put up a good front. My business is doing fine, so I could support his daughter well enough, and he knew we were in love. I've got no problems like alcoholism, gambling, or woman beating or anything, so why should he object to me?"

"Did you object to him?"

"No. He was just Betty's father, that's all. I was marrying her, not him."

"Almer said Betty used to be a gymnast, too graceful to fall down the stairs. Said she and you entered dance contests."

"Yeah, real regular, over at Club Swan. We did Imperial Swing dancing."

"Which is?"

"Something like jitterbug, only more acrobatic." Millman looked over at the cluster of teenage schoolgirls. One of them took an exaggerated drag on her cigarette then blew a dense plume of smoke, sneaking a glance in the direction of the counter where the NO SMOKING sign sat and the manager lurked.

"Like I should *care!*" she said, loudly enough to be overheard, and the other girls giggled.

"I'll tell you though," Millman said, "Betty was a good

gymnast in high school, and she was in great shape. Worked out three times a week at Tabitha's Gym. It really is kind of odd that she'd die the way she did. I mean, tripping over nothing, tumbling down those steps she'd gone down a thousand times before and hitting her . . ." His voice trailed off and he bowed his head, maybe trying to shake the image his own words had conjured up. Betty Almer's death kept reminding him of her, causing fresh pain each time. Death liked to rub it in.

Nudger sat and sipped his soda, hoping Millman wouldn't break and cry. Hoping he wouldn't follow suit himself if that happened. What would the girls in the plaid skirts make of that?

There was a shrill *beeeeep!*

Millman's hand went to his belt immediately in a smooth, practiced move, like a gunslinger reaching for his shooting iron. Only he didn't draw, and the beeper was silenced. He peered at it, then looked up at Nudger. His eyes were moist, but he seemed to be in control.

"I better get back to the job site," he said. "I got a feeling we hit roots."

"Roots?"

"From the neighbor's big maple tree. I told the driver to call me if the backhoe hit roots. Gotta dig up those roots carefully and make sure we don't kill that tree, or there won't be a dime of profit in this job." He hastily rewrapped his half-eaten Big Mac and stood up. Then he drew his wallet from his jeans and pulled out a business card. "Phone me here if you want anything else. Or at home." He unclipped a ballpoint pen from his shirt pocket and scribbled his home number on the back of the card, then laid it on the table next to Nudger's hamburger. "Call me anytime, day or night, if you really do come across something that might mean Betty's death wasn't an accident."

Nudger said that he would, and slipped the card into his shirt pocket.

"Good luck with the roots," Nudger said, as Millman hurried away, carrying his lunch to eat during the drive back to where the pool was being installed.

Nudger watched him through the window as he climbed up into his pickup truck. Millman chomped into his hamburger, then started the engine and drove out of sight. An ambitious, hardworking guy leading a hectic life. And apparently a happy one, until fate played the death card.

Roots, Nudger thought. That's what I'm trying to dig up, too. He wished there were some sort of backhoe that could accomplish that.

Then he realized he was supposed to be the backhoe and took a big bite out of his hamburger.

CHAPTER SEVEN

After leaving McDonald's, Nudger drove to Critendon Savings and Loan, where Betty Almer had worked as a loan officer. It was a ground-hugging, beige brick building on Telegraph Road and had the look of a military bunker, as if there might be some future need to beat back attackers if a run on the banks should occur. The grounds around the building were impeccably kept, with squarely trimmed yews growing around a perimeter bordered by black rubber edging. Narrow horizontal windows looked like positions from which gunfire could be directed to mow down any robbers who dared to approach the beige bunker. Your savings were safe with Critendon.

The inside of Critendon Savings and Loan was cooler than outside, carpeted in the same beige color as the bricks, with dark wood furniture. The tables, where wooden dispensers of deposit and withdrawal slips sat next to interest rate charts, had imitation slate tops. There were half a dozen pens on each table, tethered by thin silver chains to glued-down plastic holders. To Nudger's left, two tellers were stationed behind a waist-high wooden counter. To his right were several desks arranged in a row as precisely as if they were boxcars on rails. A man and woman sat behind two of the desks in back, and a young woman with piles of blonde hair sat at the front desk. The plaque before her said INFORMATION and sure enough she smiled knowingly as Nudger's eyes met hers.

"If you're in the information business," he said, standing before the desk, "I'd like some about Betty Almer."

The smile faded from her pale face. She was attractive in her wan way, but with too much makeup and dark false eyelashes that gave her the look of the geisha girl. "I'm afraid she's—"

"I know," Nudger interrupted. "I'm making some inquiries about her death."

"Maybe you oughta talk to Mrs. Crowther, our branch manager."

"Maybe," Nudger agreed.

She managed another smile, now that she was off the hook when it came to answering questions about Betty Almer; they were in familiar, routine-business territory now and she could handle it. "I'll see if Mrs. Crowther's busy, if you care to wait."

"Please," Nudger said, but he didn't sit down in one of the nearby Danish armchairs.

She spoke for a minute into the phone, then directed Nudger to a cubicle with a door in it along the back wall.

As Nudger walked over the spongy beige carpet toward the door, it opened and a tall, gray-haired woman wearing a dark business suit stood waiting for him. The estimable Mrs. Crowther.

When he got near enough, she extended a hand and introduced herself. They shook, and she invited Nudger into her office. He sat down in one of two black-upholstered small chairs facing the desk. Mrs. Crowther sat down behind her desk. She was in her fifties and had old acne scars and sad brown eyes. Her earrings looked like little gold quarter-moons and gathered and gave back cold sunlight at different angles as she moved.

As soon as she'd sat down, she folded her hands together on her desk and sat waiting for Nudger to speak. He felt as if he were applying for a loan, and that it would turn out the way it always did.

He cleared his throat, then explained who he was and asked her what she could tell him about Betty Almer.

"Betty was a pleasant young woman and a good worker," Mrs. Crowther said. Though her expression remained neutral, her Adam's apple bobbed as she swallowed. Possibly that was all the show of emotion permissible at the Critendon compound. "We were all terribly sorry about what happened. I know that's what you'd expect to hear under the circumstances, but in this case it happens to be true. There weren't very many dry eyes around here for days after Betty's death."

"Did she have any close personal friends among the employees?"

"We were all her friends, but we don't allow a lot of socializing on the job here. One of the tellers, Lucy Bain, was probably closest to her. I think they worked out together at some gym now and then after work."

"How did Betty behave during the days leading up to her death?"

"Normally. That is to say, she was happy, as she'd been for weeks. She was going to be married, you know."

"Yes. Did you ever meet her fiancé?"

"Only briefly. He came in a few times to pick her up after work. Brad, I believe was his name." Mrs. Crowther's somber brown eyes became sadder. "We met again—the young man and I—at Betty's funeral."

"Do you recall Betty having any trouble with anyone? Not necessarily a fellow employee. Maybe a disgruntled customer who argued with her."

"No, nothing like that. Betty was an ordinary, sweet kid, Mr. Nudger. She had a good life ahead of her, then she lost it all in a fall down the stairs. It was unexpected and tragic, and there's really not much else I can tell you."

Nudger stood up, thanked her for her time, and asked if

he could talk for a few minutes with Lucy Bain. Mrs. Crowther said a few minutes wouldn't matter if there were no customers waiting, and as she showed Nudger from her office she pointed to a short, very young brunette behind the tellers' counter, waiting on an elderly man with a cane who was the only customer. She was talking and pointing to a piece of paper on the counter, and the man was nodding at whatever it was she was saying.

When the man had finished his transaction and left, Nudger walked over and introduced himself.

Lucy Bain had the looks of a pretty teenager who hadn't lost her baby fat. Her green eyes were guileless and her bright red lips smiled above a double chin. She had a scattering of freckles across the bridge of her nose, and a complexion that suggested she was a redhead who'd dyed her hair brown. In a high, almost childish voice, she told him pretty much what Mrs. Crowther had said about Betty Almer.

"Betty loved Brad," she added with the certainty of youth. "She really did."

"Did she say so?" Nudger asked.

"More than once. And I met him a few times. He seemed like a real nice guy. Anyone could tell in a minute they were hung up on each other. I told that other man the same thing."

"Other man? The fella with the cane?"

"No. A different man. He came in here this morning and asked me about Betty."

"A cop maybe, investigating the accident?"

"He didn't say he was a policeman. Didn't say who or

what he was, really. He just struck up a conversation about Betty's death while he was getting a hundred-dollar bill broke down to twenties, like he was an account holder who knew her, and started pumping me for information. When he saw I didn't like it, he left."

"Leave a name?"

"No. He was an older man, about your age, average size, with buzz-cut gray hair and a droopy brown mustache."

"Mid-forties, graying hair, brown mustache," Nudger reiterated. "Anything else about him?"

"No. And I don't know about mid-forties. . . . He could have been older."

Stung, Nudger changed the subject.

"I understand you and Betty worked out together."

"That's right. Three times a week after we got off work, right down the street at Tabitha's Gym. Betty was in great shape, and really agile. It's hard to imagine her tripping and falling down some steps."

"Don't you think that's what happened?" Nudger asked.

Her wide green eyes stared at him in wonderment. "Sure that's what happened. That's what everybody said, the police and all. That *has* to be what happened. Doesn't it?"

"Looks that way," Nudger said.

A woman who'd been standing at one of the tables making out a deposit slip had walked over and was waiting for Nudger to finish at the tellers' counter. Possibly the alert and efficient Mrs. Crowther was observing them.

"Time for me to make my withdrawal," Nudger said to Lucy with a smile.

She was still staring at him, obviously puzzled, as he

moved away from the counter. The woman clutching her check and deposit slip quickly stepped up and took his place.

Tabitha's Gym was in a small strip shopping center three blocks east of Critendon Savings and Loan, on the opposite side of Telegraph Road. Nudger parked his car in the closest available slot and walked toward it.

As he approached its entrance, he caught a glimpse through the tinted window of rows of leotard-clad women of various shapes and sizes doing some sort of exercise that caused them to jump from side to side in unison with their hands clasped behind their necks.

As he pushed open the door, loud music assailed him and he saw that the women were moving to the beat of drums. Facing them and leading their motions was a lean woman in her twenties, with short dark hair and amazingly muscular legs. She was wearing a black leotard and fancy workout shoes with white ankle socks, and though she was doing the same exercise as the rows of women, she seemed to be doing it faster and with a smooth and practiced elegance. She glanced over at Nudger, then ignored him.

The music stopped suddenly.

"Squats!" the woman shouted. "Squats!"

Immediately the women placed their hands on their hips and lowered their bodies into squatting positions, their thighs spread wide, then rose and repeated the process. Nudger looked away.

"Cool down! Cool down!" the leader of the pack shouted after a few minutes. She and the other women, standing straight now but still with hands on hips, tilted back their heads as if to howl like wolves, then began breathing deeply and rotating their torsos in slow circles.

"Keep it up! Keep it up!" the leader shouted, but she herself stopped the strange cooling down exercise and walked over to Nudger.

"Help you?" she asked.

Nudger found himself waiting for her to ask again. She'd seemed to say everything twice.

Then he told her who he was, and that he was investigating Betty Almer's death.

She stood for a moment looking down at her incredibly colored and complicated exercise shoes, as if debating whether to talk to him. Then she looked up. "Take ten, Ladies! Take ten!"

The women collapsed onto the padded floor and reclined in various poses of exhaustion.

"I'm Nancy Gritter," she said, shaking his hand. Hurting it a bit. "I own Tabitha's and knew Betty slightly. She used to be part of our evening group."

Nudger followed her into a small office with a desk and two chairs and all kinds of before-and-after photographs of overweight women who'd been transformed into fashion models. Behind the desk was a large framed photograph of Nancy Gritter in an unflattering weightlifter's outfit, holding an impossibly huge barbell high above her head and making a face that suggested she'd just accidentally tasted eggplant.

Nancy Gritter sat down behind the desk. Nudger remained standing. He couldn't help noticing that she had no breasts. He'd heard that happened to women who exercised excessively, but he didn't know if that was true. He had no intimate knowledge of it.

"Betty was serious about exercise," she said. "She made great improvements here and was in excellent physical condition."

"What do you think about her accident?"

"I think you must not be sure it was an accident, or you wouldn't be here. Is there reasonable doubt?"

"Doubt," Nudger said, "but I wouldn't say reasonable. Still, it should be probed."

"I don't see why."

Nudger didn't either, really, but he simply sat and said nothing.

"Freak things happen," Nancy Gritter said, "even to the least likely people."

"Was she among the least likely?"

"Definitely. Betty wasn't just strong, she was quick and agile."

"Did you know she was about to be married?"

"Yeah. I met the guy a few times when he came in here to pick her up after classes. Kind of a jerk."

Nudger was surprised. "Why do you say that?"

"He couldn't help ogling the women. Like you. I was watching you in the mirror."

"Well, you know . . . a natural reaction, I guess."

"Not necessarily."

Nudger didn't know what to say to that. And he was pretty sure he hadn't ogled, but there was no point in arguing.

"Was he the only one who met Betty here?"

"Sure. Other than Lucy Bain, a woman who used to

come in with her. They took the evening aerobics classes together, but I haven't seen Lucy for a while. I think they worked together at a bank in the neighborhood."

Nudger asked a few more perfunctory questions, then thanked Nancy Gritter for her time.

As he stood up he paused, curious, and said, "This is Tabitha's Gym. Is there a Tabitha?"

"My cat."

"Ah, I should have known."

"Remember," she said as he was leaving her office, "Betty was among the least likely to have that kind of accident."

He nodded and went out the door. The women lounging on the floor looked crestfallen as soon as he stepped from the office, then stared at him with obvious relief when they saw he wasn't Nancy Gritter. Their ten-minute break wasn't over.

The Granada acted up in the parking lot. Its starter ground but the engine refused to kick over. Sweating hard beneath his light jacket, Nudger got the screwdriver from the glove compartment and raised the hood. He unscrewed and removed the air filter from the top of the carburetor, careful to get a minimum of oil on his hands, then inserted the long screwdriver down the carburetor's throat so it jammed the butterfly valve open.

When he got back into the car and turned the ignition key, the motor started immediately and roared at full throttle. He leaped out of the car and banged his head on the hood as he hurriedly removed the screwdriver before the engine could shake itself to death.

The roar fell to a smooth if clattering idle. Nudger

looked with dismay at the grease on his hands, then rubbed them together and brushed some of the looser oily particles off of them. He did notice that the squealing he'd heard earlier coming from the car had ceased, but he knew that might only be because he had the hood up and was staring at the engine and might be able to locate the source. Mechanical things taunted him that way.

As he climbed into the car and drove away, he noticed a man sitting in a late-model green Buick watching him. His hair was cut so short it was gray stubble that reflected sunlight, and he had a drooping brown mustache.

After turning onto Telegraph Road and merging with eastbound traffic, Nudger checked periodically in his rearview mirror to make sure he wasn't being followed.

But that kind of stuff was for detectives in books and movies. He knew there was no way to be sure.

CHAPTER EIGHT

Around five that evening, Nudger phoned Lacy from his office to see how she was feeling after the operation on her damaged tendons.

"Everything went okay," she said, "but I feel worse. I'm stretched out here in this hospital bed getting madder and madder."

He filled her in on what he'd learned.

"None of that makes me feel much better," she said

glumly when he was finished. "Except for the two thousand we're going to split."

Nudger hadn't thought about how the advance was to be divided, but he didn't argue. If he'd had a good head for money, he wouldn't be one of the few males left in the civilized world paying alimony. He wouldn't have minded child support, if he and Eileen had parented any children—in fact, he would have been proud to pay it and make sure it actually went to benefit the kids. (He thought he might as well have more than one child, since this was all hypothetical.) As it was, he was helping to support Eileen and the odious Henry Mercato.

"Are you sure the man who beat you wasn't about my age, but with bristly gray hair and a large, droopy brown mustache?"

"I told you, Nudger, the goon who knocked me around was a giant with a head of dark hair that grew so it made his head look like it came to a point, and his ears stuck out like open car doors." She sounded annoyed. Then her tone changed. "But, I'll tell you . . ."

"Tell," Nudger urged, recognizing the uncharacteristically thoughtful tone in Lacy's voice.

"I do think I've seen the guy you just described. And lately. Can't remember where, though."

"He might have been driving a dark green Buick."

"One car looks like another to me, Nudger."

He considered telling her that in her business she should learn to discern one make of car from another, then he thought better of it. She was lying in bed in agony and wouldn't appreciate a lecture.

"I could be wrong about seeing the guy, Nudger. I've got a bad memory for faces."

"Do you need anything?" he asked.

"Couple of good legs," she said with a sad catch in her voice.

"You'll have those again before very long," he assured her.

"That's what the doctors tell me, only they don't sound as certain as you." She paused. "There is something I need, Nudger. For you to come by and see me."

He was surprised. "You lonely?"

"Of course I am."

"I'll get over there soon," he said, feeling a pang of sympathy for her. She sounded so morose and pitiable. His eyes began to sting as if he'd been peeling onions.

"Make sure you bring the thousand in cash," she said. "I can't get to my bank, and a check won't buy me much in this hospital."

He said he'd do that, then told her good-bye politely and hung up. Obviously Lacy's capitalist spirit was unbroken.

Despite the fact that he hadn't had much of substance to report to Lacy, Nudger was getting a feel for the kind of woman Betty Almer had been, and why she was missed.

She'd been a loving and happy daughter to her father Loren; a future understanding life partner and object of desire for Brad Millman; a cooperative and well-liked employee at Critendon Savings and Loan; and a competitive and physically fit client of Tabitha's Gym. Who'd want to take the life of such a woman, other than fate?

The only other aspect of Betty's life Nudger wanted to explore had existed inside the neon-illuminated building he was walking across the blacktop parking lot toward now. Club Swan. It was on Olive Street Road and had once been a hardware emporium, then a restaurant, and for the last five years a dance club. The builders had been thinking of storage space rather than acoustics, so the building was a huge Quonset hut with a domed roof and few windows, a series of hard surfaces supported by overhead steel beams. It magnified sound like a bull horn.

It was late in the evening and loud music was booming with a bass beat from the place. Nudger found himself walking jouncily to the rhythm. The entrance was outlined in flickering red and blue neon, as was the edge of the roof. He'd been told that most of the time the dancing in Club Swan was the usual sort of non-touch self-expression, but on designated nights and weekends, the Imperial Swing dancers took over the floor. This was a designated night.

Nudger paid a cover charge to a tall Black man wearing baggy pleated slacks and a flowered silk shirt. Then he made his way through the barrage of sound and press of people toward a bar with a green neon outline of a frenetically dancing couple suspended above it.

Miraculously, he found an empty stool and wedged himself between a fat man and a woman in a tight blue dress and sat down. He ordered a Pete's Wicked Ale, then managed to swivel on his stool so he could look the place over more carefully.

What he saw mostly were people. No band; the music

wasn't live, but maybe its volume could overcome its synthetic origins. Though the light was dim, it wavered in intensity. From high above, pencil-thin blue laser beams pierced a smoky haze and danced over the revelers. The dance floor was large and crowded. Nudger had seen Sylvester Stallone seek then pursue countless movie bad guys through such places, maelstroms of sound and sight that addled the senses. He didn't feel like Stallone, though. He felt like a mid-forties guy, Lucy Bain's older man, out of place and time.

The dancers weren't traveling around the floor at all, but were doing a kind of swing dance that involved the woman being tossed about or spun wildly. *Wildly* seemed to be the operative word. Nudger could understand why a former athlete like Betty Almer had liked this kind of dancing. It required speed and strength and a measure of endurance. The dancers' ages ranged from teen to middle age. The older dancers were in obviously good physical condition for their ages. Better condition than Nudger, anyway.

As he leaned back against the bar and sipped his ale, wondering what it would feel like to dance with such skill and abandon, a man in jeans and a shirt and tie asked the woman on the next stool to dance. Nudger didn't see how she'd be able to move much in such a tight dress, but she followed the man toward the dance floor as he pushed through the crowd. They found room on the edge of the polished wood floor, and Nudger was amazed to see the woman unzip her skirt up the side almost to her hip. She was wearing blue latex tights beneath it, and she held the man's left hand with her right and began dancing wildly, grinning and doing a step that shifted her weight and jutted her left hip out with every other beat of the music. It was something to see.

That woman's about my age, Nudger was thinking, when he noticed Brad Millman on the dance floor.

Millman was wearing the requisite baggy pleated slacks cut narrow at the cuffs, and had on a cream-colored sport jacket and a green shirt with a band collar. His dance partner was a young girl wearing black tights and an oversized red T-shirt with black and silver sequins scattered over it. They were both among the better dancers on the floor. They even did some sort of move where the girl dropped to the floor and Millman, still holding her hand, spun her around as she rotated on a hip then rose effortlessly into an under-arm turn.

The music stopped. Millman and the girl exchanged a few words, then went their separate ways. The girl strode to a table occupied by half a dozen men and women. Her sequins glittered in the alternating light and exaggerated her movements even when she merely walked. Millman joined a man and another woman at a small table on the opposite side of the dance floor. He picked up a drink and downed half of it before setting it back on the table.

"Ever see that movie where Sylvester Stallone chases the villain through a club like this?" asked the voice of the man who'd occupied the stool the woman in the tight dress had vacated. "The one about the creepy blond guy who's killing people all over New York?"

"I saw it," Nudger said, not turning to look at the man. He was working and didn't want to be drawn into inane conversation.

"I don't see you as Sylvester Stallone," the man said. "More like Sylvester Pussycat."

Nudger swiveled then on his stool and saw the man with the bristly haircut and droopy brown mustache. His heart jumped with fear and his stomach twitched.

A friendly smile formed beneath the awning of a mustache. The man had a kind face despite hard blue eyes. "I know you but you don't know me," he said. He handed Nudger a business card. It said that he was Ollie Bostwick and that he was with First Security Insurance.

Nudger shook Bostwick's hand, which was cool and dry and very strong. "I'm—"

"I told you, I know you," Bostwick said. "I even know why you're asking questions about Betty Almer. Up to a point, anyway."

Nudger took a sip of ale as he studied Bostwick. Though he was average size he looked fit beneath his muted plaid dark sport coat and gray slacks. If he chose to let his hair grow out, it didn't look as if he'd have any on the crown of his head. His pale eyes were intelligent as well as uncompromising. Like Hammersmith's eyes, Nudger thought.

"What's your interest?" Nudger asked.

"Right now, you. You're investigating the possibility that Betty Almer was murdered. I'd like to know why."

"Privileged information," Nudger said.

"What's this? You a priest or a lawyer?"

"Are you?"

"Nope. Only a claims investigator."

And no one to fear, Nudger reminded himself. He willed himself to breathe easier. His stomach relaxed. Still, he didn't like to give away information without getting something in return. Like more information. "Does First Security think Betty was murdered?" he asked.

"We're not to that point. I'm only conducting the sort of routine check that's done whenever there's a sizable settlement due."

"You mean a life insurance payout?"

Bostwick smiled instead of answering Nudger's question. "Quid pro quo. That's Latin. It means something for something. You know any Latin?"

"I know that kind," Nudger said. "Life is a series of trades."

"I never thought of it that way, but by golly you're right."

"Betty's father didn't mention she had life insurance."

"He your client?"

Nudger nodded.

"Her life was insured," Bostwick said. "Her father might not know about it because he isn't the beneficiary."

"Who is the beneficiary?"

"Her fiancé, Brad Millman," Bostwick said. "The fella who was just out there on the dance floor doing the hokey-pokey with the girl that glittered."

Here, Nudger thought, is a guy who knows less about dancing than I do. But he would know a lot about other matters. "Big settlement?"

Bostwick did a funny thing with his lips beneath the mustache and nodded. "A hundred thousand dollars. People have done you-know-what for less than that."

Nudger looked over on the other side of the dance floor but couldn't see Millman now. The table where he and the man and woman had been sitting was unoccupied, the glasses on it empty. "You saying your company suspects Millman of killing Betty Almer?"

"I'm saying we didn't until I came to town and stumbled across folks who acted as if there was some reason for suspicion. First a woman named Lacy Tumulty. Now you."

Nudger explained to Bostwick that Lacy had requested some help in investigating Betty Almer's death, then had been hospitalized and asked Nudger to take over the case entirely while she recuperated.

"Is this Lacy Tumulty the sort who'd take on a case just for the money, knowing there was nothing to find?"

"Maybe," Nudger said hesitantly.

"C'mon, Nudger, I thought we had a two-way exchange of information going here."

"Maybe is an honest answer."

"What about you? Would you accept a case under those circumstances?"

"No. I'm helping a friend in need."

"One who's hospitalized. What happened to Tumulty? She need some kind of operation?"

At least Bostwick didn't know everything, wouldn't be one of those annoying insurance claim snoopers always a step ahead of Nudger.

"Quid pro quo, Nudger," Bostwick reminded him.

"She's had two operations. One for each leg. Somebody beat her up and slashed both Achilles tendons."

"Yeow!" Bostwick said with a wince, suitably impressed in a way that gave Nudger perverse satisfaction.

"She was working on a divorce case, and it apparently got ugly." Nudger massaging the truth.

Bostwick raised his glass of beer to his lips and sipped,

then used the back of his knuckles to wipe foam from his mustache. "Doesn't sound like a party to a divorce case did that to her," he said. "It'd be the wife or husband who'd draw the hate and violence."

"It was apparently some kind of professional goon who did it. He wasn't mad at her at the time, just having fun."

Bostwick looked out at the dancers, then at Nudger. Nudger thought they were the only two motionless people in Club Swan; maybe they'd be asked to leave. "If he cut her tendons," Bostwick said, "he didn't just want to discourage her. The object was to incapacitate her for a long time."

"Like until an insurance settlement was paid?"

"Maybe. You ever hear of a man named Wayne Hart?"

Nudger searched his memory with no result. "No. Why?"

"His name came up a few times, is all," Bostwick said. "Millman made a call to him from his cellular phone; it's a matter of record. But when I mentioned Hart's name to Millman, he acted as if he didn't know him."

"So who is Hart?"

"I have no idea. Maybe Millman doesn't, either. He might have simply called Hart about a minor business matter then forgot his name. The call only stuck in my mind because it didn't in Millman's."

"Cellular phone conversations can be eavesdropped on," Nudger said.

"This one wasn't. Certainly not by my company. It's not allowed, you know, if you eavesdrop deliberately then try to use the information in litigation. I don't know what the conversation was about, only that it occurred. Hart might simply be an employee of a plumbing supply outlet or an equipment lessor that does business with Millman's company. Most likely he is somebody like that. But now and then fortune smiles on me, and I thought you might recognize the name and it might mean something."

"Sorry, but I don't and it doesn't," Nudger said. "What do you make of the grieving fiancé out there dancing with another woman?"

"Not much, tell you the truth," Bostwick said. "I've been tailing him for a while. He doesn't seem to have anything going on the side. He might be here drinking and dancing trying to fight his depression. That's not unusual in a man after a wife or fiancée dies and the really dark period sets in."

"Then you think he'll leave here alone?"

"That'd be my bet. He came here once before and left alone. He knows those other people. He and Betty Almer were regulars here." He raised a hand and twirled the long mustache so that one side of it twisted up slightly like a handlebar. "So far, Nudger, I haven't found any reason not to recommend that my company pay the settlement. Which leads me to present you with a proposition."

"I'm all ears, which is a problem in a place like this."

"You let me know if you find a reason the settlement shouldn't be paid, and I'll let you know if I find one."

Nudger agreed, and they shook hands on the arrangement.

The music paused for five seconds then began again, even louder than before. The lights dimmed, and the blue laser beams started darting around like fingers of fate. Even more people flooded onto the dance floor and began moving to the hard beat of a woman with a piercing voice screaming in rhythm with what sounded like a thousand drums and screeching guitars. Nudger liked most kinds of music and had once owned an impressive collection of classic blues. But this number tested even his eclectic taste. His empty beer mug began to dance on the bar.

"What the devil are they doing out there now?" Bostwick asked incredulously, staring at the dancers.

"I don't know," Nudger said, "but it's not the hokey-pokey."

CHAPTER NINE

Nudger hadn't slept well. His mood, whenever he awoke in a sweat, was one of dread. His dreams were montages of swing dancers and sad music and darting shafts of light.

Was that in color? he asked himself, after the last and most violent dream.

He forgot the question when he was relieved to see light seeping in between the sharply angled slats of the venetian blind. Morning had arrived. Absolution. His guilt and dread dissipated. But a throbbing headache that was a residue of nightmare remained.

He climbed out of bed and staggered into the bathroom, where he ran cold water over a washcloth, folded it, and pressed it to his forehead.

Helped some.

He swallowed two Tylenol capsules and trudged back into the bedroom.

Exhausted as he was, his headache and jangled nerves made further sleep impossible. And there seemed to be some sort of grit beneath his eyelids that made opening and closing them painful.

He showered, dressed, and drank two glasses of cold orange juice for breakfast.

This was better.

He felt remotely human.

Then, as his headache subsided, he began to feel rather superior. Here he was, up almost with the sun, getting a jump on the day while lesser mortals snoozed on. What to do with all this energy and ambition?

He wanted to talk to Loren Almer to see if he knew about his late daughter's life insurance policy with First Security, with Brad Millman as beneficiary. Maybe he could catch Almer before he left for work.

Superior creature of the dawn though he might be, Nudger couldn't find Almer's phone number anywhere, so he had to obtain it from information.

When he punched out the number, he got no response. Not a busy signal or a ringing, only silence. As if the phone had been disconnected.

He replaced the receiver and glanced at the digital clock on the microwave oven. Seven-oh-five. Morning rush hour traffic hadn't started to back up yet, clogging the city's arteries like cholesterol in a meat addict's bloodstream. If he took the Inner Belt, he could probably drive to Almer's house in less than half an hour.

He popped two more Tylenol capsules into his mouth, washed them down with more orange juice, then went outside into the bright morning.

Industrious Nudger.

Nudger the early worm.

He'd exited from the Inner Belt and was driving east on Olive Street Road, five miles an hour over the speed limit, when he heard the siren and saw the flashing red and blue lights of a police car in his rearview mirror. Nudger's stomach did a flip and his foot found the brake pedal. The bitter taste of orange juice tainted the back of his throat as he slowed the Granada then pulled it to the side, watching in the mirror for the police car to park behind him.

Instead of stopping, the car flashed past him with a high-pitched scream of its siren that made his headache flare up again.

But he felt better despite his throbbing head. Even blessed. After all, he had been speeding, carried away by his mood and a static-marred Beatles song on the radio. The morning was warm enough for the car window to be cranked down, and the mysterious squealing from beneath the hood wasn't evident. Nudger had felt so good he hadn't noticed his speed.

He checked to make sure nothing was behind him, then steered the Granada back out into the street and accelerated, watching the speedometer now with a wary eye.

At the corner of Almer's street, he heard more sirens and had to stop so a bright yellow fire engine could swing wide and make the turn. The fire truck was followed by a police car. Then a bright yellow hook and ladder unit.

Then Nudger.

When he was halfway down the block, he saw a cluster of emergency vehicles with flashing lights. There were knots of onlookers on the sidewalk. A dark pall of smoke changed the morning to twilight on the block and carried the acrid, chemical smell of man-made materials burning.

How Nudger's mood could swing. The dread from his nightmares rushed back into his mind as he parked the Granada, climbed out, and walked toward the nearest group of onlookers held back by a uniformed cop.

The uniform looked annoyed and glared at Nudger as if he were another gawker come to further complicate matters.

Nudger stared at Loren Almer's house, which was burning as fiercely as if it were made of wax. Then at the ambulance parked nearby with its back doors hanging open.

The house was making a hearty crackling sound. Several fire hoses were trained on the flames, one of them blasting water through a window, another arcing to cascade more water through a gaping hole in the roof. Hoses were also trained on the roofs of the houses on either side of Almer's. The fate of Almer's house wasn't in doubt; it was going to be a total loss, and now the department's job was to contain the fire and keep it from spreading.

Smoke and cinders were stinging Nudger's eyes and making them water. As he wiped at them with his knuckles, he saw two white-uniformed paramedics roll a wheeled gurney into sight around the back of the ambulance with its gaping doors. They weren't being particularly gentle as they bounced the gurney down over the curb and wheeled it in a tight U-turn so they could shove it into the back of the ambulance.

Nudger's stomach twitched as he saw why there was no need to be gentle. A dark body bag, zipped all the way up and containing an obviously distorted human form, was strapped to the gurney.

"Poor Mr. Almer!" a woman onlooker said as the gurney's carriage and wheels folded up and it was pushed roughly into the back of the ambulance.

One of the paramedics slammed the doors and tested the handles to make sure the latches were set. Then he climbed in behind the ambulance's steering wheel while his partner got in on the passenger's side.

The driver turned the vehicle around in the driveway of a nearby house on the other side of the street, being careful to stay on the pavement and not make ruts in the lawn. Then the ambulance glided slowly past. Lights and siren were unnecessary, though for some reason the ambulance's headlights were glowing, as if it were the vanguard of a premature funeral procession. It turned the corner with slow and silent dignity and passed from sight.

"Poor Mr. Almer!" the woman said again.

"Poor us," said a man, "if those flames spread to the other houses."

Poor Nudger trudged back to his car, feeling sorry for the determined, grieving father who was now dead.

CHAPTER TEN

It didn't take the arson guys much time to figure this one out," Hammersmith said to Nudger, later that day in his office at the Third District station house. "The fire that burned down Almer's house and killed him was accidental."

Nudger stared out the window at the breeze skittering brown dried leaves over the surface of the parking lot. "How can they be so sure so soon?"

"Because it was so simple. The fire started with one of those cheap lamps that will only take lightbulbs of sixty watts or less. Like a lot of people, Almer ignored the warning sticker attached right there in plain sight on the socket. He had a hundred-watt bulb in the lamp. It melted the wiring, dropped sparks on some newspaper or a doily under the lamp, then the fire spread."

"Is Arson absolutely sure?"

"That the fire spread? Yeah, whole house burned down."

The day and his mood had changed and Nudger was in no frame of mind for Hammersmith's dark humor. He stared again out the window.

"Don't get petulant, Nudge. You know arson investigators can pinpoint the source of a fire. There isn't the slightest doubt about this one. Almer must have gone to bed and left the lamp on, and it did just what the manufacturer warns about if you don't follow instructions—it started a fire."

"He's the second person to die in that family in a little over a month."

"Maybe he wanted to die," Hammersmith said.

"What? We talking suicide here?"

"Only in a way. Almer was despondent over his daughter's death—she was all he had. It could be that he couldn't stand the grief, wasn't thinking straight, and had a subconscious desire to join her in death."

Nudger knew such a thing was possible, but it didn't seem to fit the facts here. "So he did himself in by going to bed and leaving the lamp on?"

"I didn't mean that, and you know it, Nudge. But suppose Almer woke up, smelled something burning, and could have stopped what was happening before it became a major fire. Only he didn't stop it; he accepted it. Sort of suicide by negligence and apathy."

"Paralyzed by grief, huh?" Nudger was skeptical.

"Exactly," Hammersmith said. "Sometimes people lose their will to live, and they die before they stop breathing. They kill themselves physically by not acting to prevent their death. Those things happen now and then, and the police or fire department never hears of them. And in this case maybe Almer just thought the hell with it and stayed in bed, maybe even let himself drop back to sleep hoping he'd never wake up." Hammersmith sank his chin into his collar, making his fleshy jowls wobble. "Could be, Nudge."

"Could," Nudger admitted.

"But as you know," Hammersmith said, "we here in law enforcement deal not so much with 'could be's' as with 'did happens.' " He picked up a pencil from his desk and began rotating its already sharp point in a little red plastic sharpener.

Nudger thought that might be a hint and stood up.

Hammersmith didn't urge him to stay. On the other hand, he hadn't threatened to light one of his noxious green cigars.

"I was at the fire because I was on my way to talk with Almer this morning," Nudger said, "to see if he knew about his daughter's six-figure life insurance policy, with her fiancé as the beneficiary. If he did know, I wonder what he thought about it."

"Doesn't matter now what he thought," Hammersmith said. He used the pencil to busy himself making notations on a sheet of lined paper on his desk. The pencil's point was so sharp now that it couldn't take the pressure and the lead broke. Hammersmith began sharpening it again. "You suppose Almer was insured?" he asked, without looking up.

"Could be," Nudger said.

Hammersmith began making notations again, this time being more gentle with the pencil.

"I think I'll drive over to the hospital and fill Lacy Tumulty in on what's happened, find out how she's doing," Nudger said.

"Good idea. Tell her 'lo."

Hammersmith didn't say anything else. Nudger got tired of listening to the pencil's sharp point scratch across paper and left the office.

As he started to push open the door from the booking area to outside, he decided to phone Lacy and see if she wanted him to bring anything. He used the pay phone near the door and called the hospital, then followed recorded instructions and punched in the extension number of Lacy's room.

Her "Hello" sounded hoarse and dispirited.

Nudger identified himself and said he was on his way over, could he bring her anything.

"Some Fuchsia Number Two," she said immediately.

Nudger had expected her to ask for a comb or magazine, something simple. "What's Fuchsia Number Two? A pencil? Makeup?"

"No."

"Art supplies? What are you doing, painting?"

"It isn't a color . . . or rather it's the identifying color of the incense."

Nudger was baffled. "You want me to bring you some incense?"

"Medicine. Listen, Nudger, write down this address." He dutifully wrote on the back of one of his business cards as she read off an address on Grand Avenue. "That's the office of Dr. Cushnion," she said. "He's my aromatherapist."

"Aromawhat?"

"He's a doctor, Nudger, sort of. Aromatherapy is a branch of medicine. Fuchsia Number Two permeates the room and alleviates pain when it's burned near a patient."

Nudger had actually heard of aromatherapy and didn't have much faith in it. He was slow to come around to such things. The CB radio had come and gone before he'd obtained one. He hadn't yet surfed the Internet. He might catch up with New Age sometime in his old age. "What about Dr. Ryker? He's in the branch of medicine that operated on your legs. Would he approve?"

"He already did. Just shrugged and said he didn't think it would do any harm. He knows about aromatherapy. Everyone knows about it but you, Nudger."

"Wouldn't you rather just have a *Cosmopolitan*?"

"Fuchsia Number Two, Nudger." She abruptly hung up. The infirm could be testy.

CHAPTER ELEVEN

Nudger knocked softly, then pushed the door all the way open and entered Lacy's hospital room.

She was propped up in bed, watching the local news on the TV that was angled out from the wall on an enameled steel support. She looked better despite the fact that both her legs were swathed in bandages from the knees down.

"Catching up on the outside world?" Nudger asked with a smile.

Lacy looked away from the TV and over at him. "Yeah, but it seems the same things happen every day. There's a fire or a police raid, then a car accident, then a reason to run the tape of a fire, police raid or car accident that happened some other time. Then it turns out there's a new medical study or wonder drug, or that a medical study's turned out to be wrong and a wonder drug doesn't work."

"You forgot sports and weather," Nudger said, placing the paper bag with Fuchsia Number Two, the aromatherapeutic incense Lacy had requested, on the table near the bed. He'd had no trouble getting the supposedly potent incense. The pleasant, middle-aged woman who was Dr. Cushnion's assistant and receptionist recognized Lacy's name and asked how she was doing. Nudger told her fine, trying not to breathe too deeply. There was a brass incense burner shaped like an elephant on the woman's desk, emitting wisps of dark smoke and a sweet, cloying odor reminiscent of incinerated garbage.

"Oh, right," Lacy said, "sports and weather, the lighter side of the news. The home team won or lost, some team's moving to a different city or not, some athlete got suspended, and there's a crucial game coming up. And it'll be partly sunny but might rain."

"You've been in here too long."

"That's surer than the weather." Lacy emitted a low, almost animal growl. "I'm going nuts in here, and television's driving me even crazier!"

"Why do you watch it?"

"Why do people pick at scabs?"

Nudger thought that was a fair enough explanation.

Lacy pulled what looked like a tiny, thin glass vase from the paper bag, and some pencil-thin sticks coated with a thick, rough-textured substance. The sticks were about a foot long and reminded Nudger of what he and the other kids in his neighborhood had called punk many years ago, slow-burning chemical sticks that kept a glowing ember for up to half an hour and were used to light firecrackers. "There are matches in that drawer," Lacy said.

Nudger opened the drawer and found a book of matches with a medical supplier's logo on it. Lacy had placed one of the incense sticks in the thin glass holder. She waited silently, and Nudger struck a match and held it to the tip of the Fuchsia Number Two medicinal incense. The end of the coated stick began to burn with very little smoke but a pleasant, scorched cinnamon scent.

Lacy tilted back her head and breathed in deeply. "Sometimes," she said wistfully, "I wish I still did drugs."

"You find enough other ways to get into trouble," Nudger told her.

"Not just me, Nudger. TV news is full of folks who find themselves in trouble. The fire on Channel Seven tonight was interesting. Loren Almer's house burned down."

"Not to mention Loren Almer himself."

"Really? The news said he was in serious condition."

"They don't always check their facts," Nudger said. "He's dead."

She looked dumbfounded for a moment. "Well, that is serious."

Nudger told her about his conversation with Hammersmith, about the fire and Almer's death, and what the arson investigators had determined.

"Sounds like accidental death, all right," she said, when he was finished.

"Is that what you think?"

"Arson investigators can read the ruins of a fire like witch doctors read bones. They can tell where and how a fire started."

"Do you think Almer's death so soon after his daughter's was coincidental?" Nudger continued to press.

Lacy curled her upper lip the way only she could, looking like a precocious ten-year-old. "I don't know. Maybe we'll never find out. I'm not going to think about Almer or his daughter anymore."

"Why not?"

"Figure it out. They're both dead, Nudger. Which means there's nobody left to pay our fee. Which means the investigation's over."

Nudger couldn't fault her logic.

"That's the way I do business, anyway," she said defensively, though he hadn't disagreed with her. "No fee, no services rendered. We aren't television detectives who don't have to eat between cases." She was certainly down on television.

He suddenly realized his eyelids felt heavy. "That stuff's making me sleepy," he said, nodding toward the smoldering incense.

"S'pose to," Lacy said, yawning. "Makes you sleepy while it dulls the pain."

"Does it really work?" he asked. Her yawn set him off and he yawned, opening his mouth so wide it hurt his jaw. "I mean, does it actually ease your pain?"

" 'Course it does. It was even on the TV news last night."

Nudger went to Loren Almer's memorial service a week later. There'd been no funeral. Almer had requested that he be cremated.

After the service, on the sidewalk outside the church, Nudger saw Brad Millman. He thought about going over and talking with Millman, then decided against it. Instead he watched while Millman got into a blue Ford Taurus with a young blonde woman and drove away.

At the end of the next week, Ollie Bostwick phoned Nudger and told him that Loren Almer's life had been insured for fifty thousand dollars. His daughter Betty was named as primary beneficiary, as he hadn't bothered to revise the policy at the time of his own death. Since Betty had preceded her father in death, the settlement check was sent to the secondary beneficiary, a cancer research institute in Arkansas. Almer's father and grandfather had died of cancer, and he'd been wary of the disease and sympathetic to its victims.

"So Millman doesn't benefit at all from Almer's death," Nudger said into the receiver.

"That's right. He would only have benefited if Almer had died before Betty." Bostwick paused. "A settlement check on Betty Almer's policy has been sent to Millman. I don't like it, Nudger, but the company has no choice."

"Does that mean you're suspending your investigation?"

"Sure. The claim's been paid, so now there's nothing to investigate."

Nudger was reminded of his conversation with Lacy two weeks ago; loose ends were being tied. It was the kind of closure that only death could bring.

A second after Nudger had hung up on Bostwick, the phone jangled and he snatched up the receiver and said hello.

"You must have been waiting for me to call, Nudger." Lacy's voice. She'd been out of the hospital for a while and was walking with the aid of crutches. "Want to meet someplace tonight for a birthday drink?"

"It's your birthday?" Nudger asked.

"Uh-huh. Yours, too, more or less. I'm a Sagittarius and

you're a Virgo, Nudger, which means there's a kind of astrological linkage."

"You're making that up."

"Nope. That's what my astrologer tells me. So we better stick together. You can have part of my birthday."

That sounded ominous to Nudger and he chose not to explore it. He didn't believe in astrology, but it made him nervous.

"You there, Nudger?"

"I'm still here. I've already had my birthday this year. With me it's an annual event, and one's enough."

"It'll be December soon, Nudger. Better not pass up this opportunity. Time for this year's birthdays is running out."

He'd forgotten it was mid-November, along with December, the time of his deepest loneliness. Thanksgiving and Christmas. Melancholy Nudger, lost among the sales and scams and decorated trees that could burst into flames as you slept. Most of the holidays he spent alone in his apartment with his artificial tree that opened like an umbrella and was fireproof. Christmas day with Claudia helped, but she was melancholy, too, during the holidays, so both of them had to be careful.

"You and Claudia still got it on?" Lacy asked, with the kind of intuition he'd come to expect of her.

"Still," Nudger confirmed.

"Does that mean you continue to think of me like you would your little sister?"

"More like my daughter," Nudger said. Feeling old, old. Almost December! "If I had a daughter, I'd like her to be like you, Lacy, only not so much so."

"Why, I think that might be the nicest thing anyone's

ever said to me, though I'll have to turn it over in my mind and figure out what you meant. One trouble with it is, it means you don't think of me erotically."

Nudger was silent, wondering if she talked to all men that way. Probably she did.

"So," she said, "what about that drink? Or are you embarrassed to be seen with a babe on crutches?"

"No," Nudger said hastily. He made a date to meet her the next night at Michael's Lounge, down on Manchester.

"Some interesting sexual positions are possible with the use of crutches," Lacy said.

Nudger hung up, wondering where the year had gone, imagining the prime of his life spiraling into the past. December! Crutches! Accidental deaths that would forever remain mysteries and roam the darkest reaches of his mind along with so much that was unresolved.

As usual, he wished Lacy hadn't called. He tried to cheer himself up.

Jingle Bells, he thought morosely.

CHAPTER TWELVE

Five months later, Nudger lay in Claudia's bed gazing out at the bright April morning. Sunlight illuminated the fresh maple leaf buds outside the bedroom window, making drops of rainwater from last night's shower glisten like sequins. The distant hum of traffic over on Grand Avenue was growing gradually louder as legions of St. Louisans made their way to work through exhaust fumes and gallantly blooming crocuses and tulips struggling to supplant the plastic flowers South St. Louisans were wont to display during winter gloom. It was a neighborhood where people understood the disconnection between mood and reality.

Nudger knew he should get up soon and drive to his office, where two days' worth of unopened bills awaited him—and a sealed letter in Eileen's tight, neurotic handwriting. He figured if it was anything he needed to know about, she would have phoned him. Messages in writing from Eileen he had come to view as legal documents, and since this one had arrived unregistered, he decided not to open it. That way he could face dealing with the rest of the mail, which meant he might now be able to muster the willpower to rise from the bed and meet the morning.

He was ruminating about how these acts of compromise had come to rule his life, when the newspaper next to him rattled. Claudia was propped up in bed, reading this morning's *Post*.

"This is interesting," she said.

"Is it about us and last night?" Nudger asked. The scent of sex was still evident in the bedroom.

She snorted. "I hope not. It's in the obituaries."

"Not us last night," Nudger said.

"Brad Millman."

It took a few seconds for the name to register in Nudger's mind. Recognition was followed by surprise. "Millman is dead?"

"Two days ago," Claudia said. "Car accident."

74

"What kind of car accident?"

"Doesn't say. This is the obituaries, not detailed news."

"But as you say, interesting." Nudger's stomach twitched, trying to tell him something. He found that he was energized by Millman's obituary, but he wasn't sure why. He did recognize this as one of those moments when his intuition might be ahead of his reasoning. He scooched around and then sat up on the edge of the mattress, making the bedsprings squeal. "When's the funeral?" he asked.

Newspaper rattled behind him. "Day after tomorrow. Visitation tonight and tomorrow at Holstetter's Funeral Home."

Nudger stood up and moved toward the bathroom. His feet and ankles felt stiff, which made him walk gingerly. Middle age, he told himself, just as Dr. Fell had told him recently. After half a dozen steps, the stiffness had pretty much gone away, though Nudger's toes continued to make crackling sounds.

Sounding like a string of firecrackers, he crossed the cool tile bathroom floor and turned on the hot and cold spigots in the tub, then waited for the tap water to get warm enough for his shower.

He stood under the hot needles of water for a long time, letting them massage and loosen the tightness of his back muscles and his shoulder, which hurt where he must have slept with his arm twisted beneath him last night.

Claudia was out of bed and slipping into her blue terry-cloth robe when he finally came out of the bathroom. It was Saturday, so she didn't have to teach.

"You want some waffles?" she asked, pulling the robe's

sash tight around her lean waist with such abruptness and force that it appeared for a second as if her body might be pinched in half.

Nudger's nervous stomach was still twitching after hearing of Brad Millman's death. It knew something his brain didn't, all right. "I'd better skip breakfast," he said. "Things to do at the office."

Claudia cocked her head and looked at him oddly. "That doesn't sound like you on a Saturday morning. In fact, you usually want to drive over to Uncle Bill's Pancake House and gorge yourself."

"Can't this morning," he said, putting on some of the fresh underwear he kept at Claudia's apartment. He adroitly kissed her cheek as she passed him on her way to the kitchen to make coffee. "But I want to take you out to dinner tonight."

"Date," she said, moving toward the door.

"Dress up a bit," he told her.

"Why? Are we going someplace nice?"

"Maybe. Either way, we have a stop to make first. Wear something dark if you have it."

Holstetter's Funeral Home was a hulking stone building set well back from Gravois Road. Its slate roof was lined with tiny dormers with fake windows as blank as the eyes of the dead, and what appeared to be an array of lightning rods that dated from the middle ages. It was five o'clock when Nudger steered the Granada onto the lone circular driveway that led to the entrance and tall portico. He drove past the portico, where a gleaming black Cadillac sat, and made a left where the driveway branched off into the parking lot.

After leaving the car next to a florist's van, he and Claudia crossed the blacktop lot to the baroque main entrance. Nudger held the heavy oak door open for Claudia and they entered the foyer. He was wearing his best sport jacket, the blue one that barely showed the wine stain, and taupe pants he'd just gotten back from the dry cleaners. Claudia had on her simple but elegant navy blue dress, cream-colored belt, matching high heels.

The inside of Holstetter's was quiet and furnished in somber colors and dark wood. A placard directed them to where Brad Millman was laid out in a simple bronze-colored casket with pallbearer handles that looked a lot like the handles on Nudger's dresser drawers. Colorful wreaths and funeral sprays were set up on either side of the casket. Only half a dozen mourners sat in upholstered chairs or small sofas arranged about the room.

With Claudia, Nudger crossed the plush gray carpet and stood for a moment viewing the deceased. Millman had died young and looked strangely vital and healthy. A clump of his dark hair stood out from the side of his head, as if he'd slept all night on it or hadn't combed it carefully, and might at any moment raise a hand and brush it back smoothly in place. This might all be a joke, Nudger thought inanely, uncomfortable as always in the company of the dead. This discomfort was one of the reasons his nervous stomach had eventually forced him from the police depart-ment—dead bodies unsettled him to the point of nausea and paralysis. Though this kind of situation, at a mortuary rather than a crime scene or the morgue, wasn't as bad, as there was no blood.

A tall blond man in a suit too light for mourning had moved to stand alongside them. "Were you friends of Brad?" he asked softly.

"I was," Nudger lied. "Though I hadn't seen him in a long time. I was shocked when I came across his obituary in the paper this morning."

"It was a car accident, wasn't it?" Claudia asked, perhaps deliberately distracting the blond man from asking when and how Nudger had known Millman.

"Yes, one of those unpredictable tragedies. Brad was driving along and missed a curve. His car struck a tree head-on, and he wasn't wearing his seat belt."

Nudger looked at the man, who seemed genuinely upset. He was about fifty and had watery blue eyes and high cheekbones, a thin slash of a mouth that arced down at the corners. His straight blond hair was combed sideways in front to conceal a receding hairline but hung lankly over his forehead, as it probably had most of his life. "His face . . . I mean, he looks all right," Nudger said. "Not as if he'd been thrown into a windshield."

"Yes, that's true." The blond man extended his hand, first to Claudia, then to Nudger. He said his name was Warren Tully, and that he was Millman's business partner in Mermaid Pools. Nudger said he and Claudia were Mr. and Mrs. Mumble. Tully wasn't listening anyway; he seemed ready to break into sobs.

"Brad's face and head . . ." Nudger persisted indelicately. "The impact . . ."

Tully appeared pained. "He didn't make contact with the windshield, they say. The impact crushed his sternum against the steering wheel, causing fatal internal injuries." Tully shook his head. "According to the accident report, he was only driving about forty. Speeding, but not by much. You wouldn't think this kind of thing could happen. A fender bender, some injury, maybe . . . but to be killed." Tully bit his lower lip hard and moved away.

"I'm sorry to have brought it up," Nudger said to his back, but Tully didn't turn around.

"You shouldn't have kept at him relentlessly about his friend's injuries," Claudia admonished Nudger. She was staring at him as if she wished he would exchange places with Millman in the casket.

"I guess you're right," Nudger said, "but remember, we're here to see what we can learn."

Claudia looked around at the array of flowers, then at the few mourners. She was still obviously miffed at Nudger for his tactlessness. "I don't think we learned anything you couldn't have found out some kinder and easier way."

What did she know? Nudger thought. She wasn't in his line of work. But he didn't give voice to his musings. "If you're uncomfortable here," he said, "why don't you wait out in the foyer. I won't be long."

"You won't be long doing what? I don't see what else there is to do here."

"I want to hang around, listen to what people are saying."

"Why?"

"To find out why," he said in exasperation.

She said nothing else. He watched her leave. Even in their mourning mode, the other men in the room watched her as she walked past them. She was the opposite of death.

When Nudger joined Claudia fifteen minutes later, she immediately rose from the comfortable-looking green chair she was sitting in and headed for the door.

Out in the parking lot, she said, "So what did you learn?"

He unlocked the Granada and waited until they were inside and he had the engine and air conditioner going before answering. "No one there is family. Only friends or business associates. There was mention of a sister in Omaha who was flying in for the funeral."

"Is that meaningful?" Claudia asked.

"It might be."

To assuage Claudia's obvious irritation, he drove to Bevo Mill, a wonderful old German restaurant located on Gravois beneath the vanes of a large windmill.

Her mood soon improved as they were shown to a table in the spacious and ornate main dining room with its oversized fireplace and German hunting lodge motif. High on the walls were mounted gigantic stag heads, trophies from long-ago hunts. One of the stags seemed to be staring at Nudger in amusement with its glass eyes, as if it were aware of where he'd just come from and knew about his delicate stomach.

The waitress came over to the table with their drinks, and they ordered from the rich and extensive menu. While she wrote in her notepad, Nudger stared over her right shoulder at the stag and it looked wisely back at him, as if about to wink.

He skipped the meat course.

"Funeral homes depress me," Claudia said, and sipped from her glass of water left by the waitress.

Nudger realized he shouldn't have taken her to view Millman's body. Holstetter's was a place of death, and Claudia and death had a longstanding love-hate relationship. Like Lacy Tumulty and her men. People on their treadmills in their cages. Such a world.

He was glad when the food arrived to brighten the mood.

CHAPTER THIRTEEN

The next morning, Nudger attended Millman's funeral at a South St. Louis cemetery. The grounds were well maintained, with ancient trees that had received obvious care. All around where Nudger stood were neat tombstones and plaques whose symmetry was occasionally broken by stone angels or Gothic memorials to the dead. On his left, Mary wept, while on his right, she sat with child while Gabriel trumpeted hope eternal. To the sparrows and jays that had defaced the stonework, it made no difference.

Nudger stood off to the side of a canopy erected over the kind of green artificial turf used in ballparks. Beneath the canopy, a brief service was read by a young minister in a dark suit that fit him much too tight through the shoulders. The only mourners were those who had been at the mortuary last night. Among Millman's pallbearers was his business partner, Warren Tully. Some of the others were probably furnished by the mortuary. There was no sign of the sister who was supposed to fly in from Omaha for the funeral. Maybe she'd missed flight connections. Or maybe she and her brother had missed more important connections long ago.

When the service was over, the mourners stood up from their metal folding chairs and drifted back toward their cars. Tully lingered and talked with the minister in the tight suit. He glanced over with his watery blue eyes and saw Nudger but gave no sign of recognition.

Trying not to tread on any of the ground-level brass grave markers, Nudger turned and walked back across the damp grass to where his car was parked at the tail end of the gleaming and sedate line of black mortuary limos.

In his office half an hour later, he dredged up Ollie Bostwick's business card and phoned the insurance investigator at First Security. It was Sunday, but Bostwick struck Nudger as more of a workaholic than a churchgoer.

Bostwick was there. He had no trouble remembering Nudger; in fact, he didn't seem at all surprised by the call.

"I guess this is about Brad Millman's death," he said.

It was Nudger who was surprised. "You knew about it?"

"Of course. In my line of work, you have to keep up on those things. I read the obituaries as faithfully as you might read 'Ziggy' on the comics page."

Nudger was surprised again. He did like Ziggy, unfortunately even identified with him. "I just came from Millman's funeral."

"Why?" Bostwick asked.

"Because it's been less than a year since the deaths of Betty and Loren Almer."

"Statistically speaking, that isn't so unusual."

"Gastronomically speaking, I'm not so sure about that."

"Gastronomically?"

"My nervous stomach tells me something is wrong here. It knows things before the rest of me does."

"Does it have a pretty good record for accuracy?"

"Almost infallible."

"Millman's death was a one-car accident, according to the news item, which I took the trouble to look up. Visibility was clear, the road was dry despite a recent rain, and he drove too fast into a turn. His car went off the road and hit a tree."

"Maybe someone tampered with his car's brakes."

"The police check those kinds of things, Nudger. And if Millman's life was insured, you can bet the insurance company will check, too, if they haven't already. One thing I do know: That's a dangerous stretch of road. He isn't the first driver to lose control and smash up there."

"He didn't leave much family, they tell me. Only a sister, but I don't think she made it to the funeral."

"If Millman left no will," Bostwick said, "she'll inherit after probate court drains the estate almost dry. If she's the beneficiary of a life insurance policy, I see no way the company can refuse to pay her, barring some dramatic development like mechanical tampering and a murder case. I can tell you, Nudger, that sort of thing happens more frequently in detective novels than in real life."

"In real life," Nudger said, "if Millman's car was tampered with, the sister would be the prime suspect."

"If she stood to profit by his death."

"Can you check and see if she's the beneficiary of Millman's insurance policy?"

A lot of time passed before Bostwick replied. Then he said, "You got a client in this case?"

"No." But Nudger was thinking about the two thousand dollars paid by Loren Almer. Almer hadn't received anything for the advance, and it couldn't be repaid. It wasn't right, taking an advance that size and not delivering, even if the client was dead. But Nudger wasn't about to mention to Bostwick that he had scruples. He had his professional reputation to protect. People hired private investigators for their pragmatism, not for their ideals. "All I'm asking is that you run a computer check and see if Millman had a life insurance policy with yours or some other company. Maybe find out if his sister is the big winner in his death. Insurance companies have files on everything about everybody, don't they?"

"Did you read that somewhere?"

"Everywhere."

"Well, it's the age of the computer. I can probably find out the first part, but the names of beneficiaries aren't so easily available. I'll work on it and call you back."

Nudger thanked him and was about to hang up.

"I can tell you Millman didn't have a policy with this company," Bostwick said. "I already checked, right after reading about his accident."

"Why would you do that, if statistically his death wasn't unusual?"

"You've got a nervous stomach, Nudger. Me, I've gotta

put up with a little voice that wakes me up in the middle of the night and nags at me. You know what it means to live with something like that?"

"I used to," Nudger said, "before my divorce. But I suppose your voice and my stomach amount to the same thing."

"That's right. I had to satisfy my curiosity, so I looked to make sure Millman's death was none of my business. For you I'll go further and see if he was insured someplace else. I don't like the idea of somebody beating the system and doing any insurance company out of six-figure sums."

"You and your company might be next, right?"

"It isn't that, Nudger, it's scruples. You might not understand it, but in this business we have scruples."

Nudger hung up the phone harder than was necessary.

He picked up the receiver again and called Hammersmith at the Third.

"I need some information on a traffic fatality," he said, after working through the usual voice mail labyrinth and finally reaching Hammersmith.

"City or county?"

"County. Probably Highway Patrol."

Hammersmith sighed loudly into the receiver. "I know you're a taxpayer, Nudge, but we're not a research service here."

"I'm asking a personal favor," Nudger said. "You have contacts who can give you the information."

"Why do you need this?"

"Has to do with Brad Millman."

"The name rings a bell, but not very loud."

Nudger refreshed Hammersmith's memory.

"You back into that mess?"

"I'm not sure. That's part of what I want to find out. Millman was killed in a one-car accident a few days ago. I need to know the details."

"You suspect hanky-panky?"

Nudger thought that was an odd way for a police lieutenant to describe possible homicide, but he was used to Hammersmith's off-center humor and approach to crime. "It could have been some sort of mischief," he said.

"Along what line?"

"Brake line, maybe."

Hammersmith was quiet for a while, no doubt thinking everything over, deciding if he shared Nudger's suspicions.

"Okay, I'll check on it," he said decisively.

"Tha—" Nudger managed to get out, before Hammersmith had hung up in his characteristic abrupt fashion. Apparently Hammersmith didn't require any thanks.

Nudger dropped the receiver into its cradle and sat back in his squeaking swivel chair. The office was becoming warm. For a moment he considered switching on the old window air conditioner for the first time this year, but he knew it might not work after the hard winter, the way it had been squealing like an injured sparrow toward the end of summer. He didn't want to cope with that possibility. He'd already spent a fortune for a new water pump for the Granada to stop it from squealing. He put the air conditioner out of his mind.

He thought again about what Bostwick had said about how he, Nudger, might not understand scruples. It irritated him anew. He understood scruples, all right. They were what complicated his life and made him miserable. Scruples and his stomach.

He realized he'd skipped breakfast this morning, and though he wasn't hungry, he'd better eat something to provide fuel for the only body he had to get him through the day and then the rest of his life.

Nudger decided to go downstairs to the doughnut shop and force down one of Danny's free Dunker Delites. Whatever else could be said about them, they were economical and they were filling. Awfully filling.

His stomach growled in protest at the mere thought of a Dunker Delite.

He ignored it. It might not like what was coming its way, but it deserved it.

CHAPTER FOURTEEN

Hammersmith had talked with the Missouri Highway Patrol and had the information Nudger needed.

In Hammersmith's office, Nudger sat down in the uncomfortable wooden chair angled to face the desk. On the desk were half a dozen of Hammersmith's horrible green cigars, still in cellophane but lined side by side and aimed at Nudger like a battery of Patriot missiles. Hammersmith peered over the cigars at Nudger as if gauging the range. Nudger knew this was going to be a brief visit.

"The Highway Patrol investigated the Millman accident

thoroughly," Hammersmith said. "They always do in one-car crashes where there were no witnesses. There's always the possibility of suicide."

"Or of someone else having been in the car," Nudger said.

Hammersmith gave him a look whose message was clear: Don't complicate my day.

"So what about the Millman accident?" Nudger asked, keeping the purpose of his visit in focus.

"Millman's death wasn't a suicide—not unless he lost his nerve and changed his mind at the last moment. There were skid marks where the car went off the road. Then it skidded over the ground and slammed into a tree. The pavement was dry but the grass was wet from a recent rain, so the vehicle didn't slow down much after it was off the road. Maybe even speeded up, like a baseball picks up speed skimming over artificial turf."

Nudger wasn't sure that could happen.

"Highway Patrol estimates the car was going about thirty miles an hour when it hit."

"That's not very fast," Nudger said.

"Fast enough, obviously. A tree is, for all practical purposes, an immovable object. It stopped the car cold and caved in the front end, shoved the engine back and pinned Millman with the steering wheel. Crushed his chest. He might have survived the crash, my source tells me, but he hit the tree just right."

Or just wrong, Nudger thought. "What about the possibility of mechanical tampering?"

"Investigators went over the car thoroughly after it was towed in. There was nothing wrong with it mechanically. The problem was that the brake pads were badly worn, and Millman had run the car through some oil or other slick substance that coated the brake disks and pads. The brakes slowed the car, but not enough to keep it from leaving the road."

"Oil on the brake pads," Nudger said. "That could have been deliberate."

"Sure. Somebody dumped some oil in a puddle they knew Millman would run through. It's a murder method old as time."

"What if the oil was put on the pads or brake disks while his car was parked?"

"He would have noticed the car had reduced stopping power almost immediately and driven more carefully, or had the brakes looked at in a service station."

"Was the steering checked?" Nudger asked. "If the power steering had been tampered with so—"

"The Highway Patrol knows cars, Nudge. There was nothing wrong with Millman's except it had plowed into a tree. His death was an accident. He was driving over the speed limit, missed a turn, and paid the price."

"I'm not so sure. My stomach says otherwise."

Hammersmith leaned back and lowered his head so that his jowls swelled, regarding Nudger the way a smooth, pink bullfrog might look at a fly. "You got a client?"

"In a way. Dead client."

"But you feel obligated to see this thing through, despite this client's obvious inability to pay any additional expenses you might incur. That's what's coming through to me here."

Nudger didn't say anything, only met Hammersmith's gaze over the row of noxious cigars.

"Hmm. I don't like you when you get stubborn, Nudge."

"It can be ugly," Nudger admitted.

"Just annoying, actually, and mostly ineffectual. You feeling stubborn?"

"Yes," Nudger said honestly.

"Well, I don't feel like being annoyed."

Hammersmith selected one of the green cigars and lifted it from the desk top.

"Did the Highway Patrol confirm that Millman was wearing his seat belt?" Nudger persisted. He knew his remaining time in the office was limited.

Hammersmith didn't answer. He unwrapped the cigar, dropped the crinkly cellophane into his wastebasket, and reached into a desk drawer. He withdrew a book of matches.

Oh-oh. This was not a drill. Nudger knew that one of the Patriot missiles was locked on to him. He felt like a doomed Scud.

Hammersmith tore a match from the book, but Nudger was long gone before ignition.

At his office, there was a message on Nudger's machine to call Ollie Bostwick at First Security. It was definitely hot in the office, and the place still smelled strongly of doughnuts from the day's baking downstairs. Before returning the call, Nudger took a chance and switched on the air conditioner.

It whined, pinged, gurgled, and began squealing in a manner that made the hair rise on the back of Nudger's neck. But when he rushed to turn off the laboring old unit, it suddenly stopped all its unnatural noises and settled down to a smooth, throaty hum. Pleasantly cool air began wafting from its plastic grill.

Nudger was pleased. Maybe his luck was changing. He sat down in his swivel chair, feeling the current of cool air on his back, and noticed the envelope from Eileen, still unopened, on the corner of the desk. Since his luck was running, he picked up the envelope and slit the flap with his letter opener, pulled the folded paper inside halfway out, and flipped it up so he could see the upper third:

Nudger, you bastard . . .

He crumpled the letter and envelope together and dropped them into the wastebasket. Eileen wasn't at all conciliatory. Most likely the letter had been written at the urging of loathsome Henry Mercato. Probably during pillow talk they'd decided it was time to try to wring more money out of Nudger with threats. Nudger saw no reason to read an unpleasant letter like that.

He forgot about the letter and used the eraser end of a tooth-marked yellow pencil to punch out Bostwick's phone number.

"Anything yet on Millman?" he asked, when Bostwick had picked up.

"What's wrong? You sound irritated."

"Nothing to do with you," Nudger said. "My ex-wife."

"Oh. In the course of my work I see a lot of ex-wives. Husbands leave and forget to change the beneficiary on their life insurance policies. Then they die and—"

"I'm not insured!" Nudger snapped.

"Okay, so calm down."

"Millman," Nudger reminded him.

"I made a few phone calls to some contacts," Bostwick said. "They tell me Millman's death was definitely an accident. He simply drove off the road and hit a tree. Not murder, fate."

"I know. The tree had been there for decades, waiting for him."

"Maybe that's how it works," Bostwick said seriously. "If you toil long enough in my business, you stop laughing at fate, karma, the role of genetics in human behavior."

"My contacts tell me there was an oily substance on the brake pads." Nudger was determined to move the conversation from the abstract to the practical, to something that might be used to help build a murder case.

"On the pads, disks, and to some degree on the tires," Bostwick said, "indicating only that Millman had driven through some kind of minor oil slick recently. It rained a few hours before the accident, and the highway was still puddled. Also, it hadn't rained for a while before that day. When rain falls for the first time after a dry spell, some of the oil that's soaked into the concrete rises and floats on top, and cars drive through it. The people who examined Millman's car know their stuff, Nudger, and they say the oily substance was a contributing factor, but not nearly enough to cause the accident. Also, there were skid marks, beginning a few feet from where Millman's car left the pavement, and continuing over the ground all the way to the tree. The grass was wet, so the brakes didn't help him much during the final twenty feet before the crash."

"You sound convinced he died accidentally."

"As you should be."

"I can't be convinced," Nudger said, "no matter how hard I try."

"Your stomach telling you there's something wrong?"

" 'Fraid so."

"Well, how's this? The medical examiner said the collision wouldn't have been violent enough to be fatal if the car hadn't crumpled just so and forced the wheel back at an angle so its edge crushed Millman's chest. In other words, it was something of a fluke that he was killed in the accident. Does that sound like a murder attempt to you?"

Nudger decided not to answer.

"Does it?" Bostwick asked again.

"I thought the question was rhetorical. What about the computer check of any life insurance policies in Millman's name?"

"He didn't have a personal life insurance policy, only a standard business policy with National Triad on his life or disability."

"Business policy?" Nudger asked.

"Mermaid Pools is the beneficiary. A lot of businesses carry that kind of policy to protect them from loss if an executive's services are suddenly lost."

"What will the policy pay?"

"With the double-indemnity clause for accidental death, a million."

"Sounds like a lot."

"Most such policies are larger," Bostwick said.

"So Millman's partner, Warren Tully, gets a million dollars?"

"No. Mermaid Pools gets a million."

"But now Tully owns all of Mermaid Pools."

Bostwick laughed. "If you think that guy is a murder suspect, good luck. You can find hundreds like him around the country every year."

"I guess it is pretty thin," Nudger admitted.

"I wouldn't skate on it," Bostwick said. "And if Millman had any relatives, they'll probably inherit his half of the business."

"There's a sister," Nudger said glumly.

"So there you are," Bostwick said. "You gonna give up on this now?"

"Sure."

"That sounds like a lie."

"It was. I hope your little voice nags you tonight."

Nudger hung up.

He sat in the cool flow of air, not noticing the scent of grease and burned sugar anymore from downstairs. He knew that was probably more because he'd gotten used to it than that the air conditioner had displaced it. He also knew he would probably smell like doughnuts the rest of the day.

What he didn't know was what to do next.

His was a state of mind conducive to miscalculation and mistakes.

He called Lacy Tumulty.

CHAPTER FIFTEEN

They agreed to meet again at Michael's on Manchester, down the street from Nudger's office. Nudger arrived early and managed to get a table. He sat sipping a Budweiser while he waited for Lacy.

It was supper time, and the restaurant area of Michael's was crowded with diners. The bar was crowded, too, mostly with people waiting to be seated. The TV in the bar was tuned to the Cardinals pregame show in Cincinnati. Standing near hitters warming up in the batting cage, an announcer was interviewing a young Cincinnati Reds player Nudger didn't recognize. The announcer congratulated him on the game he'd played last night. The player said he'd been lucky and it was a team effort and the Reds could win it all this year if their pitching held up and being in the major leagues was a dream come true. Nudger wondered how many dreams came true.

Lacy came in and looked around. Nudger raised an arm and she saw him and started across the restaurant toward him. She was walking somewhat jerkily with a cane, but her movements were strong and decisive. Her dark hair was still in its shaggy cut and needed a trim, but then it always looked as if it needed a trim. She'd lost weight but somehow gained curves, and though she wasn't dressed suggestively—wearing a loose-fitting white blouse and jeans—the eyes of several male diners followed her as she made her way to the table. Even with the cane, every move she made, every look she gave, seemed to carry a good-natured sexual challenge.

She sat down across from Nudger at the table, hooked her walnut cane over the back of an empty chair, and smiled with her wide, mobile mouth. She had on very red lipstick, and violet eye shadow that made her brown eyes appear blue at a glance. Her perfume or shampoo gave off a scented soap smell, as if she'd just stepped out of the shower.

"How are the legs?" Nudger asked.

"You'd love to have them wrapped around you, Nudger."

"My God, Lacy!"

"I'll be walking okay without the cane pretty soon," she said in a softer tone, and three women seated at the next table turned their attention back to their food. "It takes a long time to come back from Achilles tendon injuries. Till then, I manage to get by picking up stakeout work, research, that kind of thing, from other agencies. I'm learning to make maximum use of my computer."

A waitress came over and Lacy ordered a beer and a Greek salad. Nudger ordered the same.

"Your hearing seems okay now," he said when the waitress had left.

Lacy nodded. "It's back a hundred percent. I can hear that geek ballplayer being interviewed. He sounds like all the rest of them."

"They're team players," Nudger said. "Not like us. The day of the rugged individual and independent operator is fading. We're dinosaurs."

"Speak for yourself, Nudger. When you're extinct and in some tar pit, I'll be in cyberspace."

He didn't doubt it.

When their drinks had arrived, Lacy said, "I don't know why you're still digging around in the Almer case. We got our money."

"For doing practically nothing."

"I don't feel guilty about getting my half, so I don't see why you should feel that way about yours."

"It isn't guilt," Nudger said, "it's obligation."

"I think it's stubbornness."

"That, too," Nudger said. He was unlucky at love and cards, and demonstrably unskilled at business. What was he if not dogged? He took a sip of cold beer. "You still seeing the cop?"

"Cop?"

"At the Third District. Hammersmith mentioned last year you were involved with one of the uniforms, a guy named Dan Kerner, exchanging presents and . . . whatever."

"Oh, yeah, him. No, I got what I needed from him so I let him down easy and split."

Nudger decided not to pursue that subject. He wondered how it would be to have a daughter like Lacy, and decided it was a good thing he and Eileen had never had children. He probably wouldn't have made a very good father. Anyway, if there had been children, they'd be living now with Eileen and Henry Mercato, maybe calling Mercato "Dad." Nudger grimaced and took another pull of beer.

When the food came they ate their salads slowly and deliberately while he told Lacy about his conversations with Hammersmith and Bostwick.

He was pleased when she skipped trying to argue that Millman's death was an accident. Instead she said, "Tully would be the prime suspect, if Mermaid Pools stood to make half a million. Unless . . ." She stopped buttering a roll. "Did Millman have any heirs?"

"Maybe. I heard about a sister who was supposed to come in for the funeral, but she didn't show."

"Maybe Millman cut her out of his will."

"If he had a will."

"It's still early for one to be a matter of public record, but I can check on it."

Nudger was a little surprised by how easy it had been to steer her into agreeing to help. "Then you're interested in pursuing this with me?"

"Sure. If you're buying dinner."

"I'm buying," Nudger said.

"She cocked her head terrier-fashion and smiled at him. There was lettuce on one of her front teeth. "You still clicking with that whazzername . . . Claudine?"

"Claudia," Nudger said. He knew Lacy hadn't really forgotten Claudia's name. "We're still clicking."

"That's a shame."

"Depends on the point of view."

"It's my point of view. Since I'm me, my point of view is always mine."

Nudger slid his half-eaten salad away and stared across the table at her. "Why are you doing this, Lacy?"

"I want your hot love, Nudger. You're a very sexy man despite the bald spot and the developing potbelly."

Nudger made a mental note to check on his bald spot. "I'm not talking about that," he said.

"We don't have to. I'm even willing to overlook the doughnut scent."

"Or that," he said.

Lacy looked puzzled. "About what, then?"

"Working with me on the Almer case, Millman's death."

She took a big bite of roll. "Money," she said after a few chews.

"We already got our money."

"You said Millman's life was insured for a million dollars with National Triad, right?"

Nudger nodded.

"If we were to uncover evidence that Millman was murdered, it would void the double-indemnity clause and cut the million-dollar settlement in half. What percentage of that saved half-million do you think National Triad would pay for the information?"

Nudger hadn't considered that approach. To save half a million dollars, an insurance company would pay . . . well, he didn't know, but it would be plenty.

"I'd guess maybe even half," Lacy said, while he was still thinking about it.

"There's one problem," he told her. "We can't conceal evidence of a murder, so National Triad would know we'd have to turn the information over to the police. They'd just wait for that to happen, and for murder charges to be brought. That way they wouldn't have to pay us, or pay out any of the policy settlement."

"But we don't tell them we already have the evidence," Lacy said, looking at him as if he'd gone insane. "You better let me deal with National Triad, Nudger."

"I don't want to be involved in extortion, Lacy."

"You won't be. I know how to approach them in the right way."

Nudger tilted back his head and finished his beer. He placed his glass down hard on the table. "Getting involved with you is . . ."

"What?"

"Dangerous."

"You asked for me, so you got me. Now I feel the same sense of obligation you do, only my motive's a little different. There's nothing immoral about the desire to make a profit. You might not like it, but it's the same as your scruples. We're both working toward the same result."

Scruples again! "Greed and scruples aren't the same thing," Nudger told her.

"I scrupulously take every opportunity to make money," she said with a grin. "But if it will help you sleep, you can return your half of the money to National Triad."

Nudger decided to put off that decision. He motioned the waitress over for the check.

"Where do we go from here?" Lacy asked.

Nudger wasn't sure. "Got any suggestions?"

"My place. Bedroom."

"Forget that, Lacy!"

"Okay, here's another suggestion." She reached into her purse and pulled out a handful of papers. "From the Almer file," she explained. "Millman's address is written down in here someplace. Let's go pay him a visit."

"He's dead," Nudger reminded her.

"Well, he doesn't have to be home."

"Dangerous . . ." Nudger said again, looking at her and shaking his head, knowing he was going with her to Millman's, because if he didn't, she'd go alone.

She smiled while he paid for her dinner.

CHAPTER SIXTEEN

Millman had lived in the Beau Moderne Apartments, a complex of white brick two-story buildings not far from South County Shopping Mall. The architecture was vaguely Gallic, with mansard roofs, blue wooden trim and shutters, and beside each building entrance gold inlaid tile forming a fleur-de-lis. Nudger figured it worked kind of like in restaurants: all that French made the rent higher than it should have been.

Nudger and Lacy parked their cars on the street and made their way along a curving walk, past a clubhouse and fenced-in swimming pool, toward Millman's building. The pool hadn't yet opened for the summer, so there was no one around. Through a clubhouse window, Nudger caught a glimpse of some men playing billiards. The night was pleasant, and two buildings away, a cluster of people sat in the gathering dark, drinking and talking on one of the patios. One of the women kept laughing at something a man was saying. She had a high, musical laugh. They must have been barbecuing, because Nudger could smell the tangy scent of seared meat and sauce. It made him a little nauseated, so soon after supper.

"You don't have to walk slow," Lacy said. "I can keep up."

Her cane had a rubber tip and made no sound on the sidewalk. Nudger had forgotten she was using it.

"I'm walking my usual speed," he said.

Nudger was pleased to find that Millman's address belonged to a town house with a separate entrance. He and Lacy wouldn't have to try to figure out the lock and get the door open while standing in a hall or foyer, hoping they wouldn't be interrupted by a neighbor coming or going.

They stood in front of the door. Millman's was an end unit, and there was shrubbery nearby, so Nudger was pretty sure nobody could see them.

"Did you bring your lock picks?" Lacy asked.

"I don't have any lock picks. If I owned some, I wouldn't know how to use them. What about you?"

"I usually just kick doors open."

"Well, we can't do that here. It calls for something more subtle."

"Why? It'll look like a break-in, but nobody'll know who was here. You kick it in, Nudger. I would, but my legs . . ."

"It would make too much noise," Nudger said.

The only visible lock was set in the doorknob. A cool spring breeze kicked up and ruffled his hair as he got his expired, honed Visa card from his wallet and attempted to slip what looked like the usual cheap apartment hardware that builders were using these days.

But the door was tight. Even the thinly honed plastic

card wouldn't slide between it and the doorjamb to depress the latch lock.

"Let's try this," Lacy said. She drew from her purse a long screwdriver with a red plastic handle.

"How is it you just happen to have that with you?" Nudger asked.

"I always carry it. The end is sharpened. It's as good as a stiletto but its not legally a concealed weapon like a knife or gun. And it has other uses."

She forced the sharpened end of the screwdriver blade into the thin space at the door's edge, then leaned hard against it. When it didn't penetrate, she beat on it with the heel of her hand. No result.

"You try it," she said.

Nudger used all his strength to cram the end of the screwdriver into the crack near the latch, but he could force it in only a fraction of an inch.

"Here, watch out!" Lacy said in frustration.

Before Nudger could stop her, she used the crook of her cane to hammer the screwdriver deeper. It made a lot of noise, and he was terrified someone was going to look out a window or open a door and see them. He couldn't hear the people talking and laughing on the patio anymore.

"Your turn again," Lacy said, stepping back and leaning on her cane.

Quickly he leaned his weight against the screwdriver, forcing it sideways.

The door popped open.

"That was nosier than if I'd kicked it," he said.

"That's what I told you in the beginning."

"Hello! Is anyone down there?" A woman's voice, from the dark balcony above.

Nudger's heart stopped, started, leaped into his throat and expanded.

"Hi! I'm Brad's sister," Lacy called up without hesitation.

"Oh," the woman said after a pause. "I'm sorry about poor Mr. Millman . . ."

"Thank you. We all are." Lacy opened the door all the way and limped inside.

Nudger followed, almost tripping over her cane and knocking them both down as she groped for a light switch.

There was no overhead fixture, but large lamps on tables at either end of a long green sofa came on.

They were in a living room furnished modern, with stainless steel and black leather sling chairs, thick glass wall shelves that held golfing trophies and a few books and knickknacks, and an angular coffee table with a gray marble top. On the wall behind the sofa was a large abstract painting made up of formless black, red, and gray objects that here and there overlapped. What appeared to be startled, bloodshot eyes stared out from the spaces between the unidentifiable objects. Nudger didn't know art, but he knew what he didn't like.

Lacy closed the door behind her and grinned. "Let's root around and see what we can find," she said with mischievous enthusiasm.

"Put things back the way you found them," Nudger cautioned her.

"Sure, sure."

Nudger wondered if tonight was real, if he was actually doing this with Lacy Tumulty. He hadn't seen her for a while and had forgotten how she could be, he decided. That explained his lack of judgment. Now here he was involved in breaking and entering in the apartment of a dead man. Was this smart? Was it even sane?

"You going to help me search?" Lacy asked, pausing as she rummaged through a drawer in one of the tables by the sofa.

Nudger got busy. The sooner to get out of there.

In Millman's bedroom was a folding screen behind which was a desk with a computer and printer on it. Nudger went to find Lacy.

She was in the kitchen, looking to see if Millman had hidden anything in the refrigerator.

"You said you've been using a computer," he said. "C'mon into the bedroom and see if you can learn anything from Millman's."

"Wow!" she said, as soon as she entered the bedroom. "Look at that round bed!" She leaned over and pressed on the mattress with her palm. "A water bed," she observed, as the padded surface undulated. She glanced up at the ceiling. "No mirror," she said. She winked at Nudger. "My offer still stands."

"Business!" Nudger said. He was reasonably sure she was serious. "We're here on business."

Within five minutes she had the computer's monitor glowing and was into the programs on the hard disk. Her fingers were quick and decisive on the keyboard. She seems to know what she's doing, cyberphobic Nudger thought enviously. He moved around her and began searching the desk drawers.

In a bottom drawer he found half a dozen diskettes and laid them on the desk.

"Good," Lacy said, glancing down at them. "We'll take them with us and I'll use my computer to see what's on them." And back she went to cyberspace.

In the desk's top drawer Nudger found a small black vinyl book full of phone numbers. He leafed through it slowly. Most of the numbers looked like those of business associates. One number, under H, was scrawled in blue ink after the crude drawing of a small heart.

"Who exactly are you?" a woman's voice asked.

Nudger spun around and saw a tall, redheaded woman standing in the bedroom doorway. Her simple yellow dress clung to a full, muscular figure. She had tiny green eyes and would have been attractive but for her lantern jaw. She looked as if she could bite cold steel in half with that jaw. She looked as if she wanted to bite Nudger.

He began stammering, trying to find words that he might string together to make a plausible lie. He was sure by her voice that this wasn't the woman who'd called down to them from the balcony.

"Who exactly are *you?*" Lacy asked with calm indignation, turning away from the computer.

"I'm Irma Millman," the woman said. "Brad's sister."

CHAPTER SEVENTEEN

Recovering from his shock, Nudger knew this wasn't the sort of situation Lacy usually handled with proper tact. A courtroom loomed in his future. Before she could say anything more, Nudger said, "We're involved in investigating your brother's death, Miss Millman."

The redheaded woman looked at him dubiously with her narrow green eyes. "You're police?"

"We're private," Nudger said. He introduced himself, then said, "This is my associate, Lacy Tumulty." He shot Lacy a threatening glance so she'd be quiet. To his horror, she seemed amused.

"Who hired you?" Irma Millman asked.

"A man named Loren Almer, the father of Betty Almer, your brother's late fiancée." Nudger didn't mention that his client was dead.

No reaction. Apparently Irma didn't know about Almer's death, which struck Nudger as odd. But he was relieved.

"Does Almer think Betty's and Brad's deaths are somehow related?" she asked.

"He hired us to find out," Nudger said, bending truth and time, but speaking more or less accurately. "They, uh, were expecting you for the funeral," he added.

"I came down with a case of food poisoning and missed my flight from Omaha." Irma stepped all the way into the room and walked over to where Lacy was seated at the computer. She moved ponderously, as if she were twice as heavy as she appeared. Nudger guessed that she was very tired. "I take it this is part of your investigation," she said, nodding toward the glowing computer monitor.

"Yes. It's routine, in the era of the computer," Lacy said. "Sometimes a victim's hard drive contains names and addresses, maybe E-mail that can be retrieved that might tell us something."

"Victim?" Irma asked, not too weary to seize on the operative word. "You *do* mean accident victim?"

"Well, yes and no," Lacy said.

"Hold on here. You think Brad was murdered?"

"We're merely touching bases to make sure he wasn't," Nudger said.

"And has the computer told you anything?"

"Not yet," Lacy said. She was enjoying verbally fencing with Irma Millman now, manipulating the woman. "We have to know what to ask it."

Irma's gaze flicked to the half-dozen disks Nudger had laid on the desk.

"I'm sorry you missed your brother's funeral," Nudger said, "but I'm glad you showed up here tonight. Do you happen to know the name of Brad's attorney?"

She shook her head no. "To tell you the truth, Brad and I grew apart some time ago. For the past ten years, we haven't had much contact with each other beyond exchanging Christmas cards." Irma looked uncomfortable. "He had some kind of falling out with our parents. I never knew what it was really about, and Brad never told me. But I was forced to choose sides, and I chose Mom and Dad's. Brad never forgave me, even when we were the only ones left."

"Then there are no other relatives?"

"That's right. I'm twelve years older than Brad. He was born when Mom and Dad were in their forties. Dad's been dead six years, and Mom passed away four years ago. There's no one now other than Brad and . . . other than me." She looked suddenly forlorn, as if struck by the reality of her solitary role in life.

She bent gracefully and removed her shoes, then seemed to luxuriate in the feel of the carpet on her toes and the soles of her stockinged feet. Her toenails were enameled bright pink beneath the nylon.

After a deep breath, she sighed long and loud. "I've had a rough day getting here. If you wouldn't mind giving me a chance to rest for a while, before I look around here and see what needs to be done . . ."

Nudger saw Lacy's right hand move toward the stack of computer disks, then hesitate and draw back. Irma was watching her. The muscles along Irma's nutcracker jaw flexed, unflexed, flexed, unflexed. Lacy switched off the computer and stood up.

"Have you talked with Warren Tully yet?" Nudger asked.

Irma looked puzzled. "No. Who is he?"

"He was Brad's business partner. He might know about any financial or personal matters concerning your brother."

"Thanks. I will talk to him. Brad's company built swimming pools, is that right?"

"Yes. It's Mermaid Pools. Their number's in the yellow pages."

Irma stood staring at them, obviously waiting for them to leave.

"What did you think of your prospective sister-in-law?" Lacy asked.

Irma blinked at her. "Betty Almer? I never met her. I doubt if she and Brad were going to invite me to the wedding. He obviously wanted to cut all ties with the past, and she probably knew that."

Nudger edged toward the door, and to his relief Lacy followed with her cane. Irma glanced at the cane but said nothing. She paused and then trailed them through the living room to the outside door. Nudger could hear her breathing behind them, as if she were out of breath or might have an asthmatic condition.

As he stood aside to let Lacy leave first, he saw that the lock itself looked okay, and there were only a few deep nicks in the doorjamb to indicate there had been a forced entry. The odds were good that Irma wouldn't notice. He was glad now that he hadn't followed Lacy's advice and kicked open the door, leaving a splintered door frame and probably a broken latch or lock.

"I don't trust her," Lacy said, when they were outside in the night.

"It's her jaw," Nudger said. "She can't help how she looks."

Lacy glanced over at him with an expression of disgust. "I thought you were a professional. It has nothing to do with how the woman looks. It's what she said about exchanging Christmas cards with her brother."

"Family is family," Nudger said. "Even brothers and sisters on the outs with each other get sentimental about Christmas and exchange cards."

"One of the things I found on Millman's computer hard drive was his Christmas card list. Irma's name wasn't on it."

Nudger shrugged. "That doesn't stack up as evidence. Maybe he knew her address by heart."

"That doesn't seem likely. If I had a sister I hardly ever saw, I'd have her address written down on my Christmas card list."

Nudger wondered if the sister would send Lacy a card, but he kept the thought to himself as he opened his car door.

Lacy opened the door of her car, a friend's Ford Taurus she'd borrowed for the night, parked behind Nudger's humble Granada. "You've never sent me a Christmas card," she said.

"I don't send them to anyone," Nudger lied. "And I don't recall ever receiving a card from you."

"They're against my religion," Lacy said.

"I wasn't aware that you had a religion."

"I fluctuate."

"And I've never noticed you getting dewy-eyed during the holidays," Nudger said, lowering himself into the Granada.

"I've been known to drink too much and sing 'Danny Boy' on St. Patrick's Day." She leaned on her car door and aimed her cane at him as if it were a gun. "I have my soft side."

"So does a swamp," Nudger said under his breath, shutting the car door and twisting the ignition key. "It's called quicksand."

Lacy limped over to his car before he could drive away, so he cranked down the window.

"I think we better talk with Warren Tully before Irma does," she said, leaning on her cane with both hands folded over its crook.

Nudger knew she was right. "Tomorrow morning," he told her, putting the transmission lever in drive. "I'll call you about nine."

She leaned down to peer in through the window as he steered away from the curb.

"Think about that burglar fantasy," she advised.

CHAPTER EIGHTEEN

It was almost 10:30 P.M., but Nudger decided to stop by his office on the way home and call the phone number with the heart drawn after it that he'd seen in Brad Millman's address book.

He parked on Manchester and jogged across the street toward the office, noticing that the lights were on in the back of Danny's Donuts on the ground floor. Danny would be manning the oven and the deep fryer, preparing doughnuts for tomorrow's brave souls who would chance a Dunker Delite and a cup of his acidic coffee to start their day.

Nudger went through the street door next to the doughnut shop entrance and made his way up the narrow wooden stairway as quietly as possible. He didn't want Danny to hear him and offer him food or coffee that he'd have to turn down in the interest of a longer life. Though a cup of decaffeinated coffee sounded good, he knew that with the shop closed, the burner that kept the single glass pot of the stuff hot would be turned off.

When he reached the landing, he unlocked his office door then stepped carefully, trying to keep the ancient hardwood floor from squeaking and being heard below as he crossed it to his desk and sat down. His swivel chair eeeked, and he sat as still as possible while he punched out the heart number on the desk phone. The exchange was for an area in North County, beyond the airport.

A phone on the other end of the connection began to ring. Nudger wondered who might answer. A motel or lodge where someone and Brad had met and enjoyed each other? A secret lover? Nudger the romantic, making his job seem more glamorous than it was.

The phone was picked up and a voice, obviously a male though raspy and high-pitched, said hello.

Nudger decided to forge ahead full speed. "I'm calling for Brad Millman," he said.

"Who?"

Nudger repeated the name.

"I never heard of—Oh, wait a minute. You mean the fella with the swimming pool company?"

"That's right."

"Well, he's not here. And why would he be? I mean, I only met the guy once and he left me his card."

"Why did he leave you his card?"

The voice on the phone waited a few beats before re-plying. "Who is this?"

"We're investigating Brad Millman's death," Nudger said. Let the man on the line assume he was the police.

"His *death*, did you say?"

"Yes, he was killed in an auto accident last week."

"Well . . . that's too bad." There wasn't much sadness in the voice, only politeness.

"We found your phone number in an address book with a heart drawn beside it."

The man laughed. "People do that all the time when I tell them my number and they're writing it down. It's be-cause of my name."

"Your name?"

"Yeah. Wayne Hart. H-a-r-t. People jotting down my name and number sometimes just draw a heart instead of bothering to write my name. That way they can remember who the number belongs to, and still be too lazy to write. That must be what Millman did when I talked to him the first time over the phone."

"What was the conversation about?" Nudger asked.

"A swimming pool. Millman drove out to my place and gave me an estimate on a pool. I thought it was a little high, and anyway, I wanna go with an all concrete pool and—"

"Is that the only contact you had with Millman?"

"Sure. I'm sorry to hear about him dying. He was a healthy-looking young guy who figured to have a lot of years left to live. You say it was an accident?"

"Yes. Car accident."

"That's sure too bad."

"Thanks for talking to me, Mr. Hart."

"Sure," Hart said, as Nudger hung up.

So much for late-night detective work. Nudger wished it could be like in the movies, where every clue led to a dramatic development on the road to a satisfying solution.

A creaking sound made him sit up straight.

Someone was on the landing.

The door opened slowly, and Danny stuck his head into the office. His droopy, basset-hound features looked melancholy even though he was smiling.

"I thought I heard you up here, Nudge." He opened the door wider and stepped all the way inside. "Brought you something." In his right hand was a cup of the dreaded coffee, not from the decaffeinated pot but from the bowels of the giant steel urn. In his left was an equally ominous Dunker Delite wrapped in waxed paper.

Nudger wanted no part of what was in Danny's hands, but hurting Danny's feelings was like kicking the lame. "I just came from eating a late supper," he explained, "or I'd take you up on the offer."

"Just the coffee, then," Danny said, setting the foam cup on the corner of Nudger's desk.

"Thanks," Nudger said, before he could stop himself.

"I came up for another reason," Danny said. "You had a prospective client come by this afternoon." Danny juggled the Dunker Delite in his left hand and switched it to his right, as if it might still be hot from its submergence in grease. Because of the proximity of the office and doughnut shop, and because Nudger couldn't afford to hire anyone, Danny served as his ersatz receptionist. A sign taped to Nudger's office door directed clients downstairs when he was away. "Big fella, he was," Danny went on, "said he wanted to use you."

Nudger wasn't sure he liked the man's choice of words. "Use me for what?"

"That he didn't say. I told him you probably wouldn't be back today and asked his name, but he clammed up. Probably a juicy divorce case. Or maybe he's wanted by the police."

"Sounds like my kind of client," Nudger said. "Did he say he'd be back?"

"Said you could count on it."

"Well, I need something to count, business being what it is." Nudger pried the plastic lid off the coffee cup and pretended to take a sip.

"I gave him one of your cards. One of the old ones with the big staring eye printed in the corner. He kinda smiled when he took it, like it made him reassured."

Nudger stood up from the desk. "I'm done here, Danny. I better get home if I'm gonna catch the rest of Jay Leno."

"Don't forget your coffee, Nudge. It'll help keep you awake for the show. I always watch Dave on the portable down in the kitchen."

Nudger dutifully picked up the foam coffee cup and carried it to the door. Danny followed and waited while Nudger locked the office, then went with him down the stairs.

When Danny said good-night and opened the doughnut shop door, the sweet sugar scent from the kitchen wafted out. It wasn't an unpleasant smell from this distance, and Nudger was glad, since the scent of the doughnuts permeated the building and his clothes and even him. He only wished it was a scent that didn't travel so well. If Danny ever marketed it as a perfume, he could call it Cling.

He waved to Danny as he crossed Manchester to his car, careful to hold the coffee cup steady so the searing liquid wouldn't slosh over the rim and take the flesh off his hand.

He drove several blocks before tossing the coffee out the car window. Though he wanted to avoid Danny's acidic brew, the smell of it remained in the car and whetted Nudger's craving for a cup of decaffeinated coffee, very real coffee compared to Danny's.

As soon as he got inside his apartment on Sutton, he went to the kitchen and found a can with a few scoopfuls of caffeine-free ground beans. He got Mr. Coffee going, then went into the living room, sat on the sofa, removed his shoes, then used the remote to switch on Leno.

Jay was interviewing a petite brunette actress who looked familiar to Nudger, but he couldn't remember her name. She was talking about her latest movie, the story of a gang of female train robbers in the old west. Nudger wondered if it was historically accurate.

He wasn't much interested in the movie, so he leaned back for a moment and closed his eyes, paying more attention to the coffee perking in the kitchen than to what Jay and the actress were saying. Then he stretched his legs straight out and crossed them at the ankles.

So comfortable . . .

Possibly he dozed off, but he wasn't sure. He sat with the back of his head resting against the soft sofa, still with his eyes closed, listening to Jay's next guest:

". . . see that you quit blundering around where you don't belong."

The guy sure had terrible breath.

Huh?

Nudger opened his eyes and saw a huge face looming over him.

It wasn't a handsome face. The features were thick, with a low forehead and greasy black unkempt hair. Either the man's head grew to a point or his hair made it appear that way. His oversized ears were almost perfect pink crescents and stuck straight out. One was larger than the other, making him look like a Mr. Potato Head with mismatched parts.

Something about the face rang a bell in the back of Nudger's mind, but in his surprise and fear, he couldn't grasp where he might have seen the man before.

Then the man drew back a gigantic fist and rang Nudger's bell.

Nudger found himself lying on the floor alongside the sofa. The left side of his jaw was numb. He managed to get to his hands and knees before a boat-sized brown shoe came his way. He rolled away from the kick, noticing that the shoe was unlaced and the foot in the white sock appeared swollen. As he struggled to his feet he saw that both the man's shoes were laced only halfway and left untied, as if he had chronic foot problems and sought comfort.

"You're not going anyplace but down again," the pointy-headed goon rumbled. Nudger thought he sounded confident.

The giant leaped forward and took another swat at Nudger but landed only a grazing blow that set Nudger's left shoulder afire and sent him reeling backward. He kept his momentum and ran for the kitchen and the back door. But just inside the kitchen he was tackled hard from behind and hit the tile floor with a thunk, hurting both his elbows. The big man was amazingly fast as well as powerful.

"No back doors for you, my friend." The voice rolled like thunder, and for the first time Nudger noticed a slight accent. "No escape at all."

He had a firm grip on Nudger's ankle, which felt as if it were clamped in the jaws of a shark. Nudger glanced up and wondered if he'd be able to snatch a knife from the drawer by the sink. Or at least grab onto some hard object he could throw at his assailant. He wished now he hadn't refused Danny's Dunker Delite.

"You're staying on the floor with the rest of the crumbs," the big man said.

But Nudger raised his free leg and slammed his foot into the hand clutching his ankle. The goon grunted, surprised, and released the ankle.

Nudger scooted away and leaned his back against a table leg. He was gasping for breath, but his attacker seemed fresh. He grinned down at Nudger, revealing teeth that appeared to have been filed to sharp points. That terrified Nudger, who had recently seen a TV National Geographic special about cannibals who had such teeth.

Then the grinning goon reached inside his shirt and withdrew a huge knife with a scimitarlike blade that ended in a sharp point. Nudger recognized it as the bowie knife he'd seen in dozens of western movies.

The leering giant, who looked like no one Nudger had ever seen on TV or in the movies, growled, "Going now to cut the backs of your heels so you won't be getting around so good for a long time, causing trouble and all like the bad boy you are."

Nudger realized then why the man seemed familiar. He fit the description of the thug who'd severed Lacy Tumulty's Achilles tendons.

Nudger panicked.

Energized by terror, he scrambled to his feet.

That seemed to amuse the big man. He flipped the knife into the air and deftly caught it by the handle. Then he grinned wider and moved toward Nudger.

Nudger backed away, his eyes darting to the door to the back stairs. It was locked at the doorknob and with a chain lock. There was no way he could get it unlocked before the man with the knife would be on him.

In his panic, he tried it anyway.

He fairly flew to the door, and he was fumbling with the chain lock when a gigantic hand grabbed his neck and yanked him backward, flinging him across the kitchen and up against the counter by the sink. There was a sharp pain in the back of Nudger's hand and he yanked it away. The hand had come in contact with the glass pot on the Mr. Coffee burner.

"Operation time," the grinning thug said. He hefted the knife in his right hand and came toward Nudger.

Fear and instinct made Nudger act. Without conscious thought, he grabbed the handle of the coffeepot and flung the hot liquid in his attacker's leering face.

The man growled like a bear and backed away, dropping the knife. Both hands flew to his face.

Then he roared with pain and rage and hurled himself in the direction of Nudger.

But Nudger was already running from the kitchen. He didn't look back as he crossed the living room to the front door. Didn't look back as he got the door open and half fell, half ran down the steps to the street door and burst outside. Not checking for traffic, he dashed across Sutton Avenue to where his car was parked.

Then he looked back.

There was no sign of the pointy-headed, pointy-toothed giant.

Nudger dug his key ring from his pocket and climbed into the car.

The starter ground, but the engine wouldn't turn over.

His heart hammering, Nudger heard himself whine as he groveled in the glove compartment for the long screwdriver that had become standard equipment in lieu of carburetor repair.

Finally his fingers closed on the screwdriver's plastic handle, and within seconds he was out of the car and had the hood raised. He removed the air cleaner and set it on the curb, then poked the screwdriver down the throat of the carburetor to hold the butterfly valve wide open. As he scrambled back into the car to try to start it again, he saw the enraged giant stumble out of the apartment building, a towel pressed to his face.

Nudger twisted the ignition key and the engine caught and then roared steadily, attracting the man's attention.

"Oh, God!" Nudger heard himself say. With the engine snarling full throttle, he slammed the transmission into drive.

Somehow everything held together. The engine didn't explode and the transmission didn't drop to the pavement.

The old Granada leaped forward with a screech of tires and blasted down the street.

Nudger could see only the flat surface of the raised hood until he poked his head out the window and craned his neck. The speeding car swayed and swerved down Sutton as he tried to see where he was going and keep his grip on the steering wheel that was slippery with perspiration.

There was a violent lurch and the steering wheel spun and hurt Nudger's thumb. The right wheel had jumped the curb. Steel screamed as the car scraped a metal utility pole.

For a few seconds Nudger was buffeted around in his seat. Then he fought with the steering wheel and won, and the Granada was back in the street. He stamped hard on the brake pedal, but the car barely slowed. He could smell brake pad burning. Yelling almost as loud as the engine was roaring, he gripped the shift lever and yanked it into neutral.

The Granada rolled to a stop, its engine still screaming.

Nudger felt as if he'd driven terror-filled miles, but he was only a block away from his apartment.

He hopped out of the car, yanked the screwdriver from the carburetor, and slammed down the hood.

The engine idled quietly, hissing as it breathed without the air cleaner.

"Shuddup down there!" a voice yelled. A man in a sleeveless white undershirt was leaning from a second-story window, registering his complaint about having his sleep disturbed by noise.

Nudger ignored him and stared down the dark street. He saw no sign of the large man with the large knife.

"Get outa here!" the man in the window yelled. "I'll

come down there and teach you to wake up me and my wife in the middle of the night!"

Trembling, Nudger climbed back in the car and drove away fast.

Glancing up and back, he saw the man in the undershirt puff out his chest, then slam the window shut so he could return to bed and wife a hero.

Society needs heroes, Nudger thought, knowing he could do little to fill the void. He despised the kind of fear he felt now, that lived in him like a parasite and occasionally erupted into terror.

He tried not to think about it as he drove.

CHAPTER NINETEEN

His heart still hammering, Nudger pulled the Granada into the parking lot of the White Castle at the corner of Manchester and Big Bend. Most of White Castle's business was drive-through, but there was space for customers to eat the square little bargain-priced hamburgers inside. Nudger occasionally had lunch there, or stopped at the almost identical White Castle on Gravois to take a carry-out order to Claudia's apartment. Near one corner of the lot was a public phone.

Nudger parked the Granada near the phone and got out. He waited while a man in a green jumpsuit with his name stenciled over its breast pocket finished talking. Though he was anxious enough to leap straight up and spin in a circle, he casually leaned on the Granada's front fender to let the guy know he was waiting to make a call, but not being pushy. His left shoulder hurt, his hand stung where he'd burned it on the coffeepot, and he didn't feel like any more confrontation tonight.

When the phone was free, Nudger fed it a quarter and called Lacy Tumulty, hoping she was home. It was almost one A.M., which was about the time Lacy often started to prowl for fun.

On the sixth ring, she answered in a sleep-thickened voice. Maybe the cane had slowed down her social life, Nudger thought, as he identified himself.

"Brad Pitt, did you say?" Lacy asked.

"Nudger. Don't play with me, Lacy. I've just had a run-in with the goon who cut your tendons. He tried to cut mine."

"Big guy, pointy head, jug ears?"

"Him or somebody else who looks like him and happens to slice people's Achilles tendons."

"How'd you stop him from cutting yours?" She sounded awake and alert now, curious as a just-roused cat.

"I threw hot coffee in his face. He's even uglier now."

"Great! Good for you, Nudger!"

"Last I saw of him, he was staggering around outside my apartment holding a towel to his burns."

"Did you burn him good?"

"Hard to say. I was busy running for the door and didn't take time to assess the damage. He wanted to take me out of action to stop me from probing Brad Millman's death."

124

"Did he say that?"

"Good as. You're investigating the Millman accident, just like me, Lacy. The reason I called is, maybe I was only his first stop. Maybe the goon might be on his way to your place now."

"I'm sitting here on the edge of the bed thinking about that. It's possible, Nudger." Her voice quavered. She wasn't so tough. This wasn't a burglary fantasy. "The whole damned thing was harder than you can imagine. I don't want it to happen to me again. Don't know if I can go through it another time."

"Get out," Nudger said. "Go somewhere else."

"Where?"

"A motel for now. You can let me know where you are later. Call my office tomorrow, but don't leave a message on the machine giving your location."

"Do you have a gun, Nudger?"

"You know I don't. I hate them." He didn't mention that he was also afraid of guns.

"I want a gun."

"Don't you have one?"

"Not anymore. I got short of money and sold it."

"Sold it to who?"

"Don't ask me that, Nudger."

His stomach was churning; he absently felt in his pocket for his roll of antacid tablets. "Time's ticking away. You'd better hang up and get out of there."

"I'm packing even as I talk." He heard some banging around that sounded like drawers being shoved shut. "I hope you burned the skin right off that bastard's face. I hope—"

"Get away from there before he shows up. He left my apartment almost ten minutes ago."

"We should both have guns, Nudger."

The receiver clicked in his ear as she hung up.

Nudger found the antacid tablets, pried two of them off the roll, and chewed and swallowed them. They weren't thoroughly chewed and scratched his throat going down, almost choking him.

When he thought he could talk okay, he phoned the Maplewood police, then got back in his car.

They took his statement and examined his apartment door. There were only a few scratches near the lock where it had been skillfully slipped. The goon who'd broken in possessed at least one delicate skill despite being crude.

"Better get yourself a deadbolt," the larger of the two Maplewood uniforms advised him. He was a young man going to fat, with a shave so close that it had left his fleshy face red and raw.

Nudger knew he was right, but deadbolt locks weren't cheap, and he'd have to hire somebody to install one.

When they were finished examining the scene, the two uniforms told Nudger to come to Maplewood Police Headquarters the next afternoon and look over some mug shots in the hope of identifying his assailant.

"Even though you changed his looks with the hot coffee," the smaller cop said, "it could still help us locate him."

"Guy in your line of work should have a deadbolt on both doors," the large cop said. "Some good brass chain locks, too."

I know, I know, Nudger thought, but he only nodded,

wondering if the large cop had an interest in a nearby hardware store.

When they were gone, he looked around the apartment, then at the door whose lock had done little to thwart his attacker. Even though it was 2:00 A.M., the goon might return, and he'd enter more effortlessly than the first time. Nudger had been struck twice by lightning before. It was impossible for him to go into hiding, but he knew he wouldn't be able to sleep in the apartment tonight.

He weighed the notion of sharing Claudia's bed. It would be safe there. And he could make sure he wasn't followed to her apartment. At this hour, any car tailing his would be easy to spot, and he could make use of the many one-way South St. Louis side streets to drive a circuitous, wrong-way route that would guarantee no one was behind him.

But the goon knew things about him, and one of them might be his involvement with Claudia. He might *already* know where she lived and go there searching for Nudger.

And find Claudia alone!

Nudger's stomach kicked.

He left the apartment immediately, setting the ineffectual lock out of habit. Taking the stairs to the street door two at a time, he thought life was like a cruel board game with no safe moves and no respite.

But there was no acceptable choice other than to keep playing.

He retrieved the Granada's air cleaner from where it sat on the curb, fastened it back on the carburetor with a few quick turns of its wing nut, then drove fast to Claudia's apartment.

CHAPTER TWENTY

The intercoms in Claudia's building hadn't worked for years. Nudger stood in the vestibule and leaned on the doorbell button for about ten seconds, trying to wake her so she could answer his knock by the time he climbed the wooden steps to the second floor. As he trudged up the stairs, his left shoulder was throbbing, and the burn on his hand felt as if it were being stung by bees.

He approached her apartment door and drew back his fist to knock.

"Who's there?" came her wary voice from the other side of the door. So the doorbell had roused her as he'd hoped.

Nudger wondered for a second why she couldn't identify him through the peephole, then remembered that the convex glass had long ago been broken.

"Me," Nudger said.

"Nudger?"

"Yes, me."

She opened the door about four inches on its chain. He was glad to see her being so cautious.

"It is you," she said, as if he'd asked her a question. "It's also two-thirty in the morning. Why is it you at two-thirty A.M.?"

"I was worried about you."

She stared at him with one dubious brown eye that was

partly concealed behind an errant lock of dark hair. She would disagree with him, but he always found her at her most beautiful immediately after waking.

"What are you gawking at?" she asked.

"You. I love to look at you when—"

"You mentioned being worried," she said, cutting him short, letting him know this wasn't acceptable behavior, turning up on her doorstep at this hour.

"Let me in," Nudger said, "and I'll explain to you why there's good reason to be worried."

She did. He did.

"You need to leave here," he said, when he was finished telling her about his near-death experience with the giant assailant.

"Why?"

"Because the oversized goon, or whoever hired him, probably knows about us, where you live, that I might be found here."

"And here you are," Claudia said.

"But not for long. Neither should you be here for long. If he comes here looking for me and finds us—or worse still, you alone—it could be . . ."

"What?"

"You know what. Dangerous. Tragic."

She took a deep breath and closed her eyes, as if drawing into herself to consider everything Nudger had said. She seemed so vulnerable when she did that. Nudger couldn't help noticing how her small but firm breasts strained the material of her robe that was tied tightly at her narrow waist with a sash. Her neck was lean and graceful, and the line of her jaw—

"No," she said, interrupting his errant thoughts.

"Huh?"

"I can't leave. I live here. And if I took up temporary residence somewhere else, couldn't whoever is after you find out about it and simply come there?"

"Possibly," Nudger admitted, "but it would be more difficult for him."

"You don't know for sure he's even coming here."

"That's true," Nudger admitted.

"I stay."

He'd been afraid of this. "You're being stubborn."

"Why is it stubborn when I dig in my heels, and courageous when you dig in yours?"

"I rarely do dig in mine," he pointed out.

She didn't differ with him, which for some reason rather annoyed him. "If you're not going to leave, what then?"

"We can discuss that in the morning."

"Now would be better," he said, sort of digging in his heels.

She sighed. "Let me put something on that burn on your hand first to keep it from hurting."

He wasn't stubborn about that.

She went to the bathroom medicine cabinet and returned a few minutes later with a tube of some kind of lotion that contained an ingredient from an aloe plant. The stinging in Nudger's hand abated almost as soon as she applied it.

They talked in the kitchen while Claudia prepared instant coffee. With her back to Nudger, she ran tap water into two identical chipped cups with a yellow flower design on them. The pipes in the old building banged and clanked, probably waking the tenant downstairs.

Claudia leaned back against the sink and crossed her arms while waiting for the first cup of water to heat in the increasingly inefficient microwave oven that would have taken forever to heat two cups simultaneously. Nudger had bought the microwave at Three Nice Guys Appliance Warehouse's Going-out-of-Business Sale and given it to her for her birthday. That had been over a year ago. The Three Nice Guys, ostensibly brothers who advertised heavily on local cable TV, were still in the process of going out of business, a more lengthy and complex matter than Nudger had assumed.

"You mentioned that you called the police," Claudia said.

Nudger nodded. "The Maplewood police." Claudia's apartment was in St. Louis proper, a different jurisdiction.

"Are they going to protect you in some way?"

"More or less," Nudger said.

He knew it was less; no police department could possibly supply round-the-clock personal bodyguards for every crime victim. But there was no reason to tell that to Claudia.

"Call the city police," she suggested. "Your friend Hammersmith. Get some protection here."

He was going to do that, if she was determined to stay in the apartment. Hammersmith would do what he could to help, which would certainly be better than nothing. But Nudger thought he still might be able to talk her out of staying.

"You aren't going to talk me into changing my mind," she said, with her uncanny knack of seemingly reading his mind.

He knew she was right. He got up from where he was sitting at the enameled oak table and went into the living room, where he used the phone to call Jack Hammersmith's house.

As he was standing listening to Hammersmith's phone ring and ring, he heard the defective microwave chime in the kitchen, signifying that time had finally run out and the first cup of water was heated. Nudger didn't like thinki g about time running out.

Finally Hammersmith picked up his phone and mumbled a thick hello.

Nudger identified himself, then said, "Did I wake you up, Jack?"

Hammersmith hung up.

Nudger called back.

Hammersmith, having made his point, picked up on the second ring.

"I've had some trouble," Nudger told him.

"So now you're looking for more, phoning me at three in the morning?"

Instead of answering, Nudger told him about the attack in his apartment.

"You think this guy was trying to kill you?" Hammersmith asked.

"No. He was going to cripple me by severing my Achilles tendons."

"Then technically your life isn't in danger."

"Dammit, Jack!"

"Only joking, Nudge. I got a right, considering the time of night—or morning—it is. You gonna stay with Claudia tonight?"

"That's my plan."

"I'll make a call. Man and woman power being in short supply, I'm not sure what I can manage, but I'll try to get a uniform stationed outside Claudia's building until dawn, then have frequent patrols run past the place. 'Bout all I can do, if that much."

"I appreciate it, Jack."

"Is Claudia going to teach tomorrow?"

"No. She's on spring break for a while."

"I wish cops would get spring breaks. But that would mean criminals would have to take them, too. And—"

"Jack."

"Okay, Nudge. The guy who worked on you, is this the same geek who carved up that crazy Lacy Tumulty?"

"It has to be," Nudger said. "He fit the description, and he threatened the same kind of operation. In fact, that's what he called it, an operation."

"Did you phone Tumulty?"

"Yeah. She took the warning a lot more seriously than Claudia. She's hiding out at a motel. I don't know where yet, but she's supposed to call and tell me. Claudia's stubborn as hell," he added.

"The frail often are," Hammersmith said. "They have to be. You're stubborn, Nudge."

"I'm not frail," Nudger said.

"No, you're even about twenty pounds overweight. I was thinking about your delicate stomach."

Nudger was rankled by the idea of the grossly fat

Hammersmith calling him overweight. "Listen, Jack, I'm not—"

"What?"

"Twenty pounds overweight. Ten, maybe."

"Okay. But you *are* stubborn," Hammersmith said.

Nudger wasn't going to dig in his heels. "Sometimes. That I admit."

"The stubborn are often frail," Hammersmith said, and hung up.

Aggravated as he was by the lieutenant's usual abrupt termination of a phone call, Nudger was sure Hammersmith was at that moment calling the local district station house so he could use his rank and influence to provide at least a modicum of protection for Claudia.

The microwave oven chimed again. It made a sound like cheap glasswear being plinked.

"Your water's hot, Nudger!" Claudia called from the kitchen.

My usual environment, Nudger thought, and went to drink coffee with the woman he loved.

CHAPTER TWENTY-ONE

As soon as he woke up next to Claudia in the morning, Nudger was afraid. His mind focused in on the apprehension he'd felt even as he'd slept. They should have gotten out of her apartment last night when the getting was good.

Then he calmed down, soothed by the regular sound of Claudia's sleep-breathing, barely audible over the low hum of the window air conditioner. He glanced over at her in the sunwashed bedroom and saw that she was lying on her back, covered only by a thin blue sheet that followed the graceful contours of her slender body. A bright pattern of sunlight reflected by the dresser mirror lay across her hips. Her dark hair was fanned wide on her pillow and her eyes were closed lightly. A strand of hair, touched by sunlight, was caught in the corner of her mouth. He watched her breasts rise and fall as she breathed.

Maybe she was right, he decided, and he'd overreacted. Of course, it was easy to overreact after being attacked by a giant cretin with a knife the size of a sword.

"Are you staring at me, Nudger?"

"Yes." He continued to stare.

Claudia daintily spat out the hair in the corner of her mouth and rolled over to face away from him. He lay on his side and scooched across the mattress to lie against her warm body spoon fashion. As he moved, the burn on his hand slid over the sheet but didn't hurt much; the ingredient from the aloe plant was still doing its job. His shoulder still ached, but it was better.

He listened to Claudia breathe for a while, until she said, "You're obviously not as afraid as you were last night."

"Obviously?"

"You're standing firm this morning."

"Oh. Well, I was in an excitable state last night."

"Like this morning?"

"Only something like this morning." He kissed the back of her neck.

She twisted her body around, smiling at him, then moved so she was facing him. Her hands twined around his neck and she pressed herself against him. She kissed him on the lips, then nibbled on his earlobe. Her breathing was not at all as it had been a few minutes before. It was faster now, more ragged. He could feel the pressure of her breasts moving softly against his chest with each breath.

"Wait a minute," Nudger said.

"Okay," she breathed. "They're in the top dresser drawer."

Nudger kissed the tip of her nose, then climbed out of bed.

Instead of going to the dresser, he left the bedroom. He tiptoed cautiously into the living room, then went over to make sure all the locks were fastened on the door. Then he padded barefoot into the kitchen and did the same with the door that led to the rear landing and stairwell. Everything seemed to be in order. He tested a few windows on the way back to the bedroom to make sure they were fastened.

When he reentered the bedroom, Claudia had her head propped up on her pillow and was staring at him. He ignored her and went to the top dresser drawer.

"Did you check under the bed?" she asked.

For only an instant, he considered it.

Then he got into the bed instead.

After breakfast, Claudia told him she was going to meet a teacher friend at the Art Museum to see an exhibit of Dorothea Lange depression-era photographs. Nudger tried briefly to talk her out of it, then knew it was hopeless. He told himself the goon who'd gotten after him last night wasn't the sort likely to haunt museums, so if Claudia was going anywhere, the photo exhibition was a good choice. Still, walking her to her car and watching her drive away plunged Nudger into a depression of his own.

He was cheered somewhat when, walking to his own car, he noticed a police cruiser parked down the block on the other side of the street. Through the reflections on its windshield, Nudger could make out the forms of two uniforms in the front seat who were watching the apartment. He wished they'd followed Claudia, but he realized that wasn't their assignment. Hammersmith had been as good as his word, but no one could provide anyone absolute protection for very long.

Nudger climbed into the Granada to drive to his office. He could talk to Danny before going upstairs, and be reasonably sure no one was lying in wait for him.

As he drove past the parked patrol car, he nodded to the uniform behind the steering wheel, who nodded back poker-faced. The uniform next to him, a young guy with a blond buzz cut, was actually eating a doughnut. Nudger didn't think he should do that, right in plain view of the public. But right now, he'd be the last to complain.

After parking the Granada directly across Manchester from his office and Danny's Donuts, Nudger sat and surveyed the street and sidewalk. He was reassured by the activity on Manchester, lots of traffic, and ordinary-sized, normal-looking people walking around. A couple of young women dressed in long, loose-fitting skirts leaned forward in unison, poised over the curb, waiting for a break in traffic, then fled like elegant gazelles across the street and entered the office building where Nudger went to the dentist when he absolutely had no other choice.

After a bus had fussed and fumed its way past, he got out of the car and crossed Manchester, noticing that the pavement was already heating up in the morning sun.

It didn't look as if anyone other than Danny was in the doughnut shop. Danny's breakfast trade, such as it was, would have left by now and be sitting over desks or standing at workstations, stomachs growling.

Before opening the shop's door, Nudger peeked through the glass and saw that indeed Danny was alone, standing behind the counter and polishing the huge, many-valved coffee urn.

When he entered the shop, Danny heard him and turned around, and the smile on his basset-hound face rearranged itself into a creased frown. "You don't look so good, Nudge. Have a bad night?"

"One of the worst," Nudger said, and told Danny about the attack of the giant goon.

"Hey, that sounds like the guy I told you about, the one that came around looking for you. Pointy-headed, big galoot. Had kinda pointy teeth, too, now I think about it."

"Have you seen him around this morning?" Nudger asked.

"Nope. And I sure would be able to recall him. You had breakfast, Nudge?"

"Yeah, thanks. At Claudia's." The cloyingly sweet smell of doughnuts was making Nudger's stomach twitch. He glanced up at the grease-spotted ceiling. "Anybody come looking for me this morning?"

"Nobody," Danny said. "I'd have heard if anyone went up those creaky old stairs."

Nudger moved back toward the door. "Thanks, Danny."

"Phone mighta rung a couple of times, though," Danny said. "Your machine might have some messages."

"If anybody does start upstairs," Nudger said, "give me a phone call and let me know."

"You can count on it, Nudge."

Nudger knew that he could. He smiled at Danny and went out into the warm morning, then entered the slightly cooler stairwell and climbed the steps. The stairs sure did creak a lot, and loudly, something he'd always been glad of. His office had drawbacks, but it was difficult to sneak up on.

The messy, somewhat depressing lair of the office was waiting for him as always, the desk and file cabinets and battered Smith-Corona electric typewriter posed like objects in a still life, awaiting his presence and touch to grant them life and meaning. He switched on the window-unit air conditioner, waited a few seconds to make sure the metallic clanking of the fan would fade as usual, then sat down in his squealing swivel chair behind his desk.

There were three messages on his impossibly complicated answering machine. Nudger had mastered only a few of its myriad features. Staying within the narrow parameters of his understanding, he used the PLAY and ERASE buttons. PLAY was first, he was sure.

Beep: "Mr. Nudger, my name's Lois Brown." Long pause. "I . . . well, not to sound melodramatic, but I'm sure I'm in danger. Several things make me think so. Close calls. Someone seems to have been in my house recently when I wasn't home. I get late-night phone calls, and the party just hangs up when I say hello. Explainable events, maybe, but so many of them. And there's another reason I think someone's trying to kill me. It's not something we could discuss on the phone. If you'd call me back we might set up an appointment so we could talk in private. I think you'd be interested in what I have to say." She recited a phone number, which Nudger duly jotted down on his past-due electric bill, then she hung up.

Beep: "This is Henry Mercato, Mr. Nudger. Eileen has informed me that you're several months behind on your alimony payments. According to Missouri law . . ."

Nudger ceased to listen.

Beep: Pause. Buzz.

Whoever had called stayed on the line a few seconds, then hung up without leaving a message.

Nudger replaced the receiver and pressed the ERASE button.

When the machine was finished clicking and whirring, he picked up the receiver again and punched out the Lois Brown number.

The phone on the other end of the line rang ten times before Nudger hung up.

He was disappointed. He hadn't been able to talk to Lois Brown, and there had been no message from Lacy Tumulty.

Carefully, he raised the plastic lid of the answering machine, where instructions that reminded him of a legal document were printed on a sheet of paper stuck to the lid with adhesive. With a blunt pencil, he copied the instructions for "remote message retrieval" on a blank envelope, then copied Lois Brown's phone number on the flap and stuck the envelope in his shirt pocket. Trying not to look at the instructions printed in Spanish and German, he closed the machine's lid. All seemed well. The little green light signifying that the machine was ready to record was still glowing, and the absence of digital numerals indicated that his earlier messages had indeed been erased. Nudger felt smug about having tamed technology, even to such a small degree.

He stood up from his desk, decided to leave the air conditioner running on low, then left the office and trudged downstairs and made a tight loop on the sidewalk to enter the doughnut shop.

Danny was still alone, standing hunched over and leaning with both hands on the stainless steel counter. He looked up from the *Riverfront Times* he had spread out before him. The *Riverfront Times* was a small and lively giveaway newspaper with much influence. Every year it included a ballot for its readers to vote for the best of this or that in the St. Louis area. Last year, Danny's chief rival, Munch-a-bunch Doughnuts, located farther west on Manchester, had won Best Doughnut Shop and proudly displayed the victor's plaque just inside its door. Though Danny's Donuts hadn't been mentioned in the voting tabulations even as a runner-up, Danny had become convinced that he could win a similar plaque for this year. Nudger hadn't the heart to try to dissuade him, and promised to vote for Danny's Donuts, though in truth when he yearned for a good doughnut he sneaked away to Munch-a-bunch.

"It's still too early for that annual Best of St. Louis ballot," Danny said, somber eyes again downcast on the paper.

"It comes out toward the end of the year, I think," Nudger said logically.

"I'm watchin' for it, though," Danny said. "I'm gonna vote for that Bill McClellan for best columnist." McClellan had recently written a piece about how doughnuts were much-maligned by dietitions and actually worked better than melatonin as sleep inducers. Danny hadn't realized the column was written tongue in cheek. Nudger figured there was no reason to set him straight; McClellan, who often stood up for the little guy like Nudger, deserved the plaque anyway.

"Any sign of our overgrown friend?" Nudger asked.

Still staring at the paper—an article about obtuseness in the state legislature—Danny shook his head no.

"I'm leaving for a while," Nudger told him. "Maybe I'll phone you later and find out what's going on."

"You're really scared of this guy, aren't you, Nudge?"

"He'd win the *Riverfront Times* plaque for Best Thug."

"Sounds like he would at that. Where you going?"

"Art Museum. Only you don't know that."

Danny looked at him oddly for several seconds.

"In case anyone asks," Nudger said.

Danny's expression remained blank. Then he grinned and nodded. "Oh, yeah, I getcha. I don't know where you are."

When Nudger left, Danny was absorbed again in the article about obtuseness in the legislature. Danny voted in every election without fail.

It made Nudger wonder.

CHAPTER TWENTY-TWO

As Nudger climbed the concrete steps to the Art Museum's main entrance, he had to admit that one reason he'd come here was to make sure Claudia wasn't with Biff Archway. Archway, the soccer coach and sex education teacher at the all-female high school where Claudia taught English, was tenacious in his attempts to win Claudia. Handsome, muscular, accomplished, Archway was the sort of man women fell for like dominoes. Nudger hated Biff Archway.

Nudger left the marbled, sculpture-strewn main hall of the museum and began roaming its spacious rooms and corridors displaying paintings. He lingered in a gallery of impressionists' works, staring with yearning at a colorful, dreamy world he wished existed, then walked quickly past a Picasso that more accurately reflected his world. Eventually he left the paintings and became lost among displays of furniture from various historical periods. In a roped-off, Art Deco model office of the thirties was a wooden desk that looked disturbingly like his own, and the typewriter was an easily recognizable ancestor of his Smith-Corona. Soon, he thought with some alarm, he would be a man of the past century. He swallowed.

Near an Edwardian bedroom with a fantastic fringed canopy bed, he became more determined to find Claudia. He asked a security guard directions to the Dorothea Lange photograph exhibit.

Five minutes later he was within sight of Claudia. He was relieved to see that she wasn't with Archway, but with a woman he'd met last year, another teacher at Stowe High School, a middle-aged, kindly looking gray-haired woman whose name Nudger thought was Nancy.

Relieved, he stayed well away from the two women so neither would notice him. When they wandered from one room to the next, he remained in the previous room, but in a position where he could see them if they left by the far exit, which led them either to another display of Lange photographs or was the end of the exhibit.

Lange's stark black-and-white depression-era photos fascinated Nudger. Some of them were in fact galvanizing. So engrossed did he become in a shot of a farmer driving a tractor in an endless field of parallel plowed furrows, that Claudia and Nancy somehow moved on without him noticing.

In a mild panic, he quickly but cautiously left the exhibit and made his way from one set of exhibitions to the next. He was furious with himself. This was basic detective work, tailing two unsuspecting people indoors in a public place, and he had muffed it.

At last, in the vast main hall of the museum, he saw Nancy's coiffed gray hair. Claudia was next to her. They were moving with several other people toward the exit.

He followed and saw them get into Claudia's car where it was parked in front of the museum, near Art Hill. Nudger hurried around to the tree-shaded parking lot behind the museum and climbed into the Granada, but by the time he wound his way back to the front of the building, Claudia's little blue Chevy was nowhere in sight.

Again he was lucky. Driving glumly along winding roads in an attempt to find his way out of Forest Park, where the Art Museum was located, he happened to see Claudia's car ahead of him as it rounded a corner.

He fell in behind it, with three cars between the Chevy and his own, and followed Claudia as she drove from the park and exited on Hampton. He stayed well back of her as she traveled along Hampton to Oakland and turned left, then made a left on Kingshighway and a right turn on Forest Park Boulevard. She turned left on Euclid and was soon in the Central West End, St. Louis's small version of Greenwich Village.

Nudger watched as Claudia parked on Euclid, then she and Nancy entered Duff's, a mainstay restaurant in the area. He loved the food there and for a moment pondered following them inside. Duff's was large and comfortably dim, and seemed to have almost as many rooms as the Art Museum, so maybe he could remain unnoticed.

Then he decided against it. This was stupid and ineffectual, tailing Claudia. He couldn't do it constantly, any more than could the police. And he wasn't carrying a gun. Hadn't owned one since his police department days. So his options were limited even in the unlikely event the giant goon would confront Claudia and Nancy in broad daylight in a public place.

He told himself he wouldn't be leaving Claudia in any imminent danger. After all, she *was* with someone.

Who wasn't Biff Archway.

But wouldn't she be safer with Archway, the martial arts expert and prime physical specimen who was more macho than a truck commercial?

Yes and no.

Fighting off guilt for being selfish about Claudia, Nudger decided to trust in her safety with Nancy and return to his office.

On the drive there, hunger overcame him and he stopped at the Parkmoor Restaurant on Clayton and Big Bend. There they served something called the Premium Frank, which was one of his favorites. That and a vanilla milk shake would make a fast and delicious lunch.

Before ordering, he used the public phones near the cashier to check for messages on his answering machine via its remote retrieval system. He got the crumpled envelope he'd written on in his office, carefully followed the instructions he'd copied, and was amazed when they worked and there was a series of high-pitched beeps. Then an electronic scream signaled that he had no messages.

His ear still pulsating from the noise, Nudger hung up. He almost smiled with satisfaction. He knew for sure there hadn't been any important phone calls in his absence. He'd managed to cajole the answering machine into obeying his remote commands. A small victory in his battle with technology, but a win nonetheless. And in looking after Claudia, he hadn't totally lost touch with his office and missed another call from Lois Brown, who was in danger. Or thought she was. And even if she was, which woman might be in the most danger—Lois Brown or Claudia?

He enjoyed his Premium Frank with cheese and bacon and relish and without guilt.

When he entered his office an hour later, he saw the glowing digital numerals on the machine. Two messages. Nudger wondered if one was from Lois Brown.

He sat behind his desk in the cool breeze from the still-laboring air conditioner and punched the PLAY button.

Beep: Buzz. Click.

Message number one was a hang up.

Beep: "This is Lacy, Nudger. I'm okay. I'm antsy. I'll see ya."

Nudge pressed the ERASE button and sat back in his *eeek*ing swivel chair. He watched the cool rush of air from the plastic grill behind him ruffle the hair on his forearm. It made the burn on the back of hand feel better. "Antsy," he said to himself. He didn't like to think of Lacy as antsy, which he knew from experience was her way of saying she had cabin fever. She'd been afraid the last time he'd talked to her, but she wasn't the type to stay afraid for long. She had the reckless gene. Nudger didn't. He had the worry gene, though. Maybe two of them.

There was a loud knock on the office door, and his heart leapt.

Then he realized the giant thug with the bowie knife would hardly knock, and Danny surely would have seen or heard him enter the building and phoned upstairs.

Unless . . .

Nudger slid open a top desk drawer and laid his hand inside it. He could bluff by pretending he had a gun.

He called for whoever was out there to enter.

The door opened a few inches, then all the way.

Danny stepped into the office and looked somberly at Nudger.

Nudger removed his hand and pushed the drawer shut.

"Scruffy little woman came into the shop 'bout an hour ago," Danny said. "No biggern' a minute. She told me to give you this."

He handed Nudger a folded yellow Post-it.

Avoiding handling the adhesive strip at the top, he unfolded the square sheet of paper and read: "*Hostelo Grandioso motel, Ext. 299.*"

"I couldn't help seeing it when she folded it and gave it to me," Danny said. "It's in some kinda foreign language, ain't it?"

"It would like to think so," Nudger said.

"She didn't leave no name, Nudge."

"I know her, Danny. Her name's Lacy. We're in the same business. More or less."

Danny's brow unwrinkled for a second. "No kidding? Heck, she's too little a mutt to be working a job like that. She know marital arts or something?"

"That's *martial* arts, Danny. And she knows some or thinks she does. She's tougher than she looks, but not nearly as tough as she thinks."

"She got in and outa the shop in a hurry, like she didn't want to be seen there. Didn't even go upstairs to see if you were in your office."

"She knew better. And she knows I trust you." Nudger doubted if Danny had unfolded the Post-it to read carefully what Lacy had written. "Thanks, Danny. I'll get in touch with her."

"Try and talk her into doing something less dangerous for a living, why doncha?"

"I've tried. She thrives on danger. She infects other people with it. The goon who tried to work me over last night beat her up and cut her with a knife last year."

Danny appeared shocked. "Why, that bastard! That's like picking on a kid!"

"He wasn't interested in her lunch money," Nudger said, somewhat surprised by Danny's protective instinct. "And Lacy's no kid."

"She reminds me of a kid I knew once. You tell her she can rely on me if she needs any help."

Nudger nodded. He didn't tell Danny he might as well be offering protection to a wolverine. Small and cute could be deceptive.

When Danny had left, Nudger dragged the phone book from a bottom desk drawer and looked up the Hostelo Grandioso. Its address was on Spanish Moss Drive, which he thought was a street that ran off Natural Bridge up north near the airport. He pulled the phone-answering machine closer to him, then lifted the receiver and pecked out the Hostelo Grandioso's number.

A man's voice answered with the name of the motel, and Nudger asked for extension 299.

The phone rang five times before Lacy picked it up and said hello in a tentative voice.

"Nudger," Nudger said.

"Say something else."

"Something else," Nudger said.

"Okay. I had to be sure it's really you, Nudger. The stupid humor proves it."

"Are you still antsy?"

"Yeah. I'm going crazy sitting around here. The only time I've been out was to deliver the note to that guy in the doughnut shop. I didn't want to phone again. Your line might be tapped. And I remembered you telling me about the doughnut shop guy."

He doubted that she was right about his phone being tapped.

"That was Danny," Nudger said. "You can trust him. You even awoke some kind of protective paternal instinct in him."

"Yeah, I can do that when I try. Any news on the pointy-headed goon?"

"Not yet. I'm going to look at some photographs today at Maplewood Police Headquarters."

"I looked at mug shots after my heels were cut, and I couldn't make an identification."

"Well, if I can't make an ID in Maplewood, I'll drive down to the Third District and see Jack Hammersmith, look at some more photographs. The goon must have some kind of history with the law."

"Hammersmith that fat guy? A lieutenant?"

"The same. You can trust him just like you can Danny, only he won't feel so paternal." Nudger glanced out the window at the pigeons on the ledge across the street. "Don't tell him you have a gun, though. He'll ask about license and registration, training, those kinds of trivialities."

"Guys like that are a pain. Sticklers about the law."

"He is a cop," Nudger reminded her.

"You call me from time to time, you hear, Nudger. It might be the smart thing for me to stay cooped up like this, but just the thought of it is driving me bonkers. I've gotta know what's going on out there in the world."

"Watch CNN."

"Hah! This place has a television set that still gets Milton Berle."

"I'll keep you informed. Didn't I phone and warn you last night?"

"Yeah. Now inform me what you're going to do next. After you hang up."

"I'm going to phone a woman named Lois Brown. She left a message on my answering machine saying she was in danger, and that I'd be interested in knowing why. Does her name strike a chord with you?"

"Never heard of her. But after you get in touch with her, call me here and let me know what she had to say."

Nudger promised that he would, then hung up.

It bothered him, to have Lacy ticking away like a bomb in a motel room. She was right; she wasn't made for that kind of seclusion. A full day and night in the Hostelo Grandioso hadn't even passed and she was already going mad. Somewhere along the line there would be an explosion.

He called Lois Brown's number again and got no answer. Then he decided to drive down the street to the Maplewood Police Department and see if he could try to make an identification on the violent goon.

A cop named Kamerer who wore too much deodorant or cologne ushered Nudger into a small bright room, where he looked at countless photographs, then at some video stills. No one unlucky enough even to resemble his assailant appeared before him.

It was four o'clock by the time Nudger left Maplewood police headquarters and returned to his office. He had a headache. His shoulder was sore again. The burn on the back of his hand itched. His eyes were so tired that opaque dots were swimming before them like exotic fish.

He tried Lois Brown's phone number again, and again got no answer.

Then he called Claudia and got no answer.

Story of his life: no answer.

His swivel chair *eeeked* at him as he leaned back and laced his fingers behind his head. Events seemed to be whirling all around him, but just beyond his knowledge or understanding. He stared at the four badly painted walls of his office and understood precisely how Lacy Tumulty must feel, trapped in her tiny motel room, her internal fuse burning like the one in *Mission Impossible*.

It was worrisome.

CHAPTER TWENTY-THREE

Still in a worried state, Nudger chomped a few antacid tablets, drove too fast to Claudia's and rang her doorbell, then knocked on her door.

She hadn't returned home yet from her outing with Nancy. Or else she'd touched down and then gone elsewhere.

Or . . .

He let himself in with his key.

"Claudia?" She might be in the shower and hadn't heard his knock. Or asleep.

"Claudia?"

No answer.

It was warm and there was no sound of any of the window air conditioners running, only the low hum of the refrigerator from the kitchen, the soft cooing of pigeons perched on an outside sill. Down in the street, two men were talking loudly, each laughing at whatever the other was saying, but their voices were too faint for Nudger to understand.

He walked through the apartment and found it empty. Breakfast dishes were still stacked in the sink.

So Claudia hadn't been home. Nudger breathed easier knowing she hadn't been here and was, for the moment, safe.

He used the bathroom to relieve his bladder. During the past few years apprehension made him have to do that more often. Getting older. Prostate problems on the way. Male pattern baldness. Thickening waistline with potbelly. The entire panoply of male degeneration. He didn't want to think about any of that now.

Back in the living room, he thought about sitting around and waiting for Claudia, but he didn't want to lose his sanity. Instead, he went to the phone and called Hammersmith's number at the Third District.

Hammersmith wasn't there, but he'd left word that Nudger might be in to look at mug shots, and that respect should be shown. That was exactly how Merriweather, the old desk sergeant who'd been stationed in the Fourth with Hammersmith and Nudger years ago, said it. "Captain Springer isn't to know," he bluntly added.

Nudger thought that went without saying but appreciated Merriweather saying it anyway. Springer was an ambitious and not exactly scrupulous political climber in the department. He was also Nudger's sworn enemy, and, to an extent, Hammersmith's, for no apparent reason other than that Hammersmith remained Nudger's friend. To Springer every ex-cop was like his ex-wife—not to be trusted after the split. Guilt by disassociation.

Hours spent at the Third reaped no reward. Incredibly, Nudger's giant attacker seemed to have no police record. When Nudger was about to leave, a police sketch artist named Chalmers sat down across from him and offered to draw a composite from Nudger's description.

"Is this your idea?" Nudger asked.

Chalmers, an earnest, blond young man with no chin, shook his head. "The lieutenant said you'd probably be by and might need the help."

Thoughtful Hammersmith again.

Nudger gave Chalmers a precise feature-by-feature description of the pointy-headed goon while the sketch went through a series of transformations. "Like so? Like so?" Chalmers would ask as he sketched. "More this" or "less that," Nudger would answer, increasingly fascinated as the sketch developed. "More, more, less, less . . ."

"That him?" Chalmers finally asked, when Nudger had run out of instructions.

"More or less."

Chalmers showed Nudger the sketch of Lacy's assailant he'd made last year from her description. Now Nudger understood why Hammersmith had wanted Chalmers to work with him.

Nudger looked from sketch to sketch. Neither subject was attractive, but they were unquestionably similar. Lacy's goon was definitely the uglier.

"I'll try to sketch something in between," Chalmers told Nudger.

When Nudger returned to Claudia's apartment, the first thing he noticed even before using his key to enter was the pungent scent of garlic-laden spaghetti sauce simmering on the stove. When he opened the door he found that the window unit in the dining room was humming and the apartment was cool. Claudia was home.

There she was in the kitchen, standing at the stove and stirring with a wooden spoon. The dishes in the sink had been transferred to the dishwasher. She was barefoot and had changed to faded Levi's and a baggy white T-shirt with a St. Louis Cardinals birds-on-bat logo on its chest. Nudger remembered buying the shirt for her a few years ago at the ballpark after a Cardinals victory over the Cubs. The shirt had faded. So had the Cardinals.

She glanced over at him and smiled. "I'm still alive."

"I was worried," Nudger said.

"I know. There was indication you were here. I figured you'd be back, so I started supper. Spaghetti okay?"

"Better than okay." He thought she was a champion spaghetti maker. And apparently she had some talent as a detective. "Indication I was here?" he asked. He didn't recall having moved anything, or leaving anything behind, when he was in the apartment earlier.

"The toilet seat was up."

"Oh."

She stirred, smiling faintly as if the gentle motion soothed her. Maybe it wasn't politically correct, but Nudger loved seeing a beautiful woman happily busy in a kitchen.

"There was a police car parked down the street when I drove past," she said.

"Good."

Nudger set the table, then found half a bottle of the wine he'd brought with him last time they'd had spaghetti. He hooked a finger through the jug's loop handle, removed the wine from the refrigerator, then unscrewed the cap to let it breathe.

"I think I'll just drink water," Claudia said.

He put some ice in a glass and ran tap water over it, then got down another water tumbler for his wine.

Nudger tossed the salad while she dumped hot spaghetti into a colander to drain before placing it in a bowl.

They ate slowly, enjoying the food while they told each other about their day. Nudger was going to suggest driving to Ted Drewes frozen custard stand for dessert, but when they were finished eating he felt too full even to talk about leaving the apartment in a quest for more food. He had to mentally prod himself even to rise from his chair and help Claudia clear the table.

Maybe, since she hadn't had any of the wine, he'd drunk too much. Or maybe the wine was particularly potent. It was a pugnacious vintage with an agreeable price, a brand unfamiliar to him, from a country he'd never heard of and couldn't pronounce. But it was red so he was sure it went with spaghetti. Whatever the reason, sated by pasta, bread, and wine, Nudger sat with Claudia on the sofa and soon fell asleep.

He dreamed about being back in Dewey school in the fourth or fifth grade, sitting sleepily at his desk and worrying because he hadn't done his homework and might be called on by the teacher to recite some fact he didn't know. If it was the fourth grade, and his teacher was that nice Miss Hogan, he'd be okay. She got exasperated with Nudger often, but she obviously saw in him something she liked. On the other hand, Miss—

The bell sounded loudly, signaling the end of the school day. There had been no reason to worry.

The dismissal bell rang again.

He opened his eyes and found himself alone on the sofa.

Claudia had answered the phone.

"For you," she said to Nudger. "A woman."

She brought the phone to him on its long cord. He still had to scoot to the end of the sofa to take it from her.

"Fell asleep," he told her, trying to clear his mind of lingering guilt over not doing his homework.

She stood watching, not moving far away, possibly because it was a woman who'd called.

Nudger said hello.

"That you, Nudger?" Lacy's voice. He hadn't given her Claudia's number, but she could have found it in the directory.

"I think so."

"Your voice is funny. You been sleeping? Or did I interrupt you and Claudia in flagrante delicto, doing the wild thing?"

"The former," he said, glancing at Claudia.

"In flagrante delicto?"

"Sleeping."

"Either way, you apparently weren't watching the news. You should have been."

Nudger looked at his watch: ten thirty-two. "Why?"

"On Channel Four, they mentioned toward the end of the broadcast that a woman named Lois Brown had been killed, electrocuted by her clothes dryer."

Now he was awake as if electrically charged himself. "You're sure?"

"I called, didn't I?"

"What else did they say about it?"

"Only that tomorrow night they were going to start a series about deadly appliances in the home."

"It could have been another Lois Brown," Nudger said, doubting it even as he spoke.

"Could have been," Lacy agreed without conviction.

Nudger sat silently digesting the news for a minute.

"Still there, Nudger?"

"Yes. And you'd better stay where you are. And make sure you're locked in."

"I've got a gun now, Nudger. You should have one, too. I can arrange it for you."

"No."

"Okay, it's your . . . It's up to you."

"Make sure you're locked in," he repeated. Ineffectual advice, he knew, imagining the pointy-headed goon casually smashing through a flimsy motel door, or possibly chopping through it with the axe-sized knife he carried.

"I want to talk to you some more about this tomorrow, Nudger."

He agreed that they'd talk, then hung up.

"Something wrong?" Claudia asked, setting the phone back on its table then sitting down beside Nudger on the sofa.

He told her what was wrong.

"Maybe it *was* another Lois Brown," she said. "It's a common enough name."

She sounded more hopeful than Lacy had, but still unconvincing. Nudger raised his eyebrows at her. She raised an eyebrow back.

"Let's sleep on it," she suggested. She reached out an elegant hand and stroked his cheek. "We'll think about Lois Brown tomorrow."

The late Lois Brown, he thought. He wondered if he should buy a gun, then reminded himself there was good reason not to have a gun in the apartment. He had met Claudia after she'd attempted suicide. And not that long ago, she had again demonstrated suicidal impulses. Bringing a gun into their lives might be like inviting the serpent into the garden.

"We'll sleep," he said, with what he intended as a reassuring smile but knew was a sad mask. "Maybe tomorrow she'll be alive again."

After checking the locks on all the doors and windows, he finished the wine and they went to bed.

CHAPTER TWENTY-FOUR

Nudger awoke a little after eight o'clock the next morning. He was pleased to notice that the burn on the back of his hand was no longer sensitive, and the dull ache in his shoulder had subsided. But when he started to sit up, his head seemed to explode.

The wine from the unknown country.

He dropped his head back down onto his pillow hard enough to make the bed jiggle, which caused Claudia to moan softly and roll over to face away from him. Which wound the sheet around her lithe body so that Nudger was uncovered, nude and cold. The thermostat on the old window-unit air conditioner malfunctioned most of the time and didn't know the day hadn't yet heated up. St. Louis weather! Possibly tomorrow it would snow. Possibly today. This was a city of meteorological whimsy. If you didn't like the weather here, Nudger thought, go to San Diego.

Moving carefully, so as not to rouse Claudia or the pain in his head, Nudger eased his body out of bed. He picked up his pants from where they were folded on a chair, ignoring the dime that fell soundlessly from a pocket onto the carpet. Then he found his Jockey shorts tangled in the sheet, remembered last night with a flush of pleasure, and left the bedroom.

In the comfortably warmer bathroom, he splashed cold water onto his face, rinsed out his mouth, and smoothed back his mussed hair with his fingers. Good enough until he showered and shaved later. He studied himself in the mirror, middle-aged guy but looking older this morning, brown hair thinning on top, faintly puzzled blue eyes. Not really fat, but his abdominal muscles had disappeared when he wasn't looking.

"Age sneaking up on you," he said softly to his reflection, then put on the Jockey shorts and pants. More and more frequently he found himself contemplating the passing of his years. He wondered if that was healthy. Most people did that as they grew older, he assured himself, looking again for his missing abs.

He ducked back into the bedroom, found his wrinkled shirt from yesterday, and slipped it on before going downstairs to the vestibule and picking up one of the morning newspapers the deliveryman had left there.

Back up in the apartment, he got Mr. Coffee chugging, then sat down on the sofa and enjoyed the aroma while he looked at the paper.

Lois Brown's death wasn't big news, but it was on page four of the front section, half a column captioned "Woman Electrocuted."

Thinking the paper made it seem as if she'd been executed for some crime, Nudger read on. Lois Brown, who the article said had been forty-one years old, was found by a neighbor, lying dead in a puddle of water in the basement of her St. Louis Hills home. Faulty wiring in her electric clothes dryer was the cause, according to police. She'd been standing in water leaked by the washer, which was next to the dryer, and that intensified the current running through her body and proved fatal.

"Here, Nudger."

He looked up from the paper to see Claudia standing over him holding two cups of coffee. He accepted one of the cups and handed her the front page of the paper folded to the Lois Brown story.

Still standing, she read and sipped simultaneously.

"Accidental death," she said, giving him back the paper.

"Some coincidence," Nudger said. He took a swallow of coffee, burned his tongue, and yanked the cup away from his lips abruptly enough to slosh some onto his shirt. "She leaves a message on my phone saying she's afraid, and she's dead by nightfall."

"Put that way," Claudia said, "it does strain credulity." She sat down in a chair across from him, adjusting her robe so it covered her knees. "You should notify the police about the message."

"I'll do it after breakfast," Nudger said. "Let's get dressed and go to Uncle Bill's and dine with abandon." Already he'd forgotten his thickening image in the bathroom mirror.

"I wish I could, but there's no time. You should have awakened me earlier."

"No time? Are you going somewhere this morning?"

"Work."

"But it's spring break. You're supposed to be off work for the next two weeks."

"I'm aware of that, Nudger. But my bills go on. Another teacher, Nancy Rollins, has arranged for me to do part-time work where's she's employed."

Nudger almost blurted out something about Claudia and Nancy Rollins going to the museum together yesterday but caught himself. He would have been forced to equivocate. And when he bent the truth, it often took the shape of a boomerang.

"It's telephone work," Claudia said. "I'll be inside, with other people, and quite safe."

"Selling things by phone?" Nudger asked.

"Not exactly. It's a suicide prevention line."

Nudger sloshed more coffee out of his cup and stared at her.

"I can help people, Nudger. I know what to say because

I know what was said to me. I was there and can empathize."

"But will it affect you, talking to potential suicides?"

"Not in the way you might think. Maybe I'll tell them the gorilla joke."

He simply looked at her.

"You told me a gorilla joke when I was on the phone with you. It was you who talked me out of attempting suicide, Nudger."

But only for a while, he thought, but didn't say. What had really saved her was that she'd tried to hang herself with some of his ties knotted together, and they were of cheap polyester-blend material that stretched and allowed her toes to touch the floor.

"Are you sure you want to do this?" he asked.

"Of course." She bent down and placed her coffee cup on the floor. "Toss me some of the newspaper, Nudger." Subject changed. He knew better than to continue discussing it.

He found the comic-strip pages and tossed them to her.

She smiled sadly, shook her head at him, and began to read.

After a breakfast of bacon and eggs in Claudia's kitchen, Nudger walked with her to her little blue Chevy and watched her drive away. Then he returned to the apartment and called Hammersmith.

"Lois Brown," Nudger said, when Hammersmith answered the phone.

"This some kind of knock-knock joke?" Hammersmith asked.

"She's the woman who was electrocuted by her clothes dryer yesterday afternoon."

"Ah!" Hammersmith said. "Well, she can't come to the phone, then. And if she'd used static guard—"

"She was on my answering machine yesterday morning, saying she was in danger and I'd be interested in knowing why. I tried several times to call her back but never got through to her. Am I getting through to you?"

"Sure. I know which Lois Brown you're talking about. You're telling me her death was a homicide?"

"No. I don't know that."

"But there is that call she made to you," Hammersmith said thoughtfully. "Did she actually say her life was in danger?"

"No, she just said *she* was in danger. But that seems to amount to much the same thing."

"Maybe. Why do you think she figured you'd be interested?"

"Betty and Loren Almer, Brad Millman."

"Other accidental death victims, eh, Nudge?"

"Right. And don't forget what was done to Lacy Tumulty, and almost done to me, by the pointy-headed thug."

"We got a good composite drawing now, Nudge. It shouldn't be hard to get an ID on the guy, considering he looks like he was just discovered in an iceberg from ten thousand years ago. He's distinctive."

"Don't brush this off, Jack."

"Well, Nudge, there isn't any doubt about those being accidental deaths."

"Never say any, as the politicians say."

"That's not exactly what they say, even when they're

telling the truth. But I get the idea. You know me, Nudge, I got an open mind."

Nudger knew it was true and didn't disagree with Hammersmith.

"You ever talk to Lacy Tumulty like you said you were going to?" Hammersmith asked.

"Last night, on the phone. She's restless, and she's got a gun."

"Great. That all you got to tell me?"

"More or less."

Hammersmith hung up in his usual abrupt fashion.

Nudger didn't mind. He appreciated Hammersmith not asking him where Lacy was hiding.

He depressed the phone's cradle button, then called the Hostelo Grandioso and asked for Lacy's extension.

"Nudger?" she said, when she answered the phone.

"How'd you know?"

"Nobody else has the number. No best friends or cop friends or deliverymen or even relatives. I'm taking this seriously, Nudger. I want you to know that so you understand it isn't lack of fear that makes me want to get out of here before I crawl up the walls. It's . . . well, it's just my nature. Birds gotta fly."

"And sharks gotta swim."

"And we gotta talk, and work something out."

"Can't help—Never mind. You stay put. I'll drive over there soon as I can. It's that old motel that looks like a ruined Mexican village up by the airport, right?"

"Yeah. I should have chosen other surroundings."

"I don't know, they never found Pancho Villa, and an entire army was searching for him."

"What are you, Nudger, some kinda history buff?"

"I watch the History Channel a lot on cable."

"Well, it's a reassuring thought to know old Pancho couldn't be found." But she didn't sound reassured at all as she hung up.

Nudger left the apartment, locking the door carefully behind him.

He hadn't mentioned to Lacy that Pancho Villa had eventually been assassinated. Like her, the wily Mexican revolutionary could be cautious only up to a point. Rebel blood was like that.

CHAPTER TWENTY-FIVE

Nudger drove beneath a Spanish arch of cracked and dirty gray stucco to enter the parking lot of Hostelo Grandioso. It was a motel that probably dated back to the forties, with separate stucco cottages, each with a faded red-tiled roof, sagging gutters, and crooked, weathered red shutters. The office was a similar cottage only with a red neon sign out front featuring a man in chaps and a sombrero twirling a rope that spelled out the name of the motel. Nudger drove past the office, listening to the Granada's tires crunch on the gravel lot.

Four of the cottages had vehicles parked in front of them, two pickup trucks, a gray Honda Civic, and an elderly pink Cadillac convertible with fins and a patched and ragged black top. There was no vehicle parked directly in front of the cottage whose number matched Lacy's phone extension. Nudger was glad to see she was being careful.

He parked the Granada beneath a massive tree on the opposite edge of the lot, then walked over to the cottage. Ivy was growing up the cracked stucco on either side of the door, a contrast of vital green growth against gray ruin. Above the door was a rusted Spanish fixture with the glass broken to reveal a dirty yellow bug light. Nudger used a steel knocker in the form of a bull's head to rap on the door.

The rapping sound was sharp and clear in the morning air, but there was no sound or answer from inside.

He knocked again. "Lacy, it's Nudger."

After almost a minute, the door opened a crack and an eye peered out from interior gloom. "Ah, Nudger." Lacy held the door open wide.

She closed and locked it as soon as he'd entered.

"Wanted to make sure who it was," she explained. She was wearing faded jeans with one knee worn through, what looked like a man's pinstriped blue dress shirt, and brown sandals. In her right hand was a small blue-steel revolver.

"Are you good with that?" Nudger asked, nodding toward the gun.

"Better believe it. I shot the eye out of a gnat once, though I was aiming at its nose."

It was warm in the dim cottage, and it smelled like the sort of place where mushrooms might flourish. The venetian blinds were lowered and their slats angled to create a constricting pattern of shadow bars across the low ceiling. Nudger's flesh crawled.

"How do you like my new home?" Lacy asked.

"It's like bad film noir. How can you stand it in here?"

"I can't. Not for very long, anyway." She walked over and pulled a cord that tilted the venetian blind slats to alter the direction of the light. Some of it fell at her feet and he could see the scars on her heels above the backless sandals. He fully understood then how frightened she was, and why. "But it's not the kind of place people who know me would figure I'd be, so I do feel safer here and I'm gonna stick it out. At least for short stretches."

Nudger watched her as gravel crunched and the dark shape of a pickup truck passed beyond the angled slats. He and Lacy stood still until the sound had faded.

Lacy moved closer to the blinds and craned her neck to glance out the window, like a thousand desperate heroines in a thousand old movies, then placed the gun on a table next to a rough ceramic Spanish lamp with a cocked shade. Nudger guessed that a part of her was enjoying this, but only a small part, and not enjoying it much. "We making any progress in the outside world?" she asked.

He told her about his conversation with Hammersmith.

"I don't buy the coincidence of all those folks meeting untimely accidental deaths," she said, when he was finished.

"Neither does Hammersmith personally, but officially he has no choice. If the Medical Examiner finds no evidence of murder, there's no crime for the police to investigate."

"Then we investigate," Lacy said. Her hair was disheveled and she was wearing no makeup; he thought she looked like a pugnacious leprechaun. He admired her fire if not her wisdom. "And I mean you and me as a team, Nudger. Unless you want a madwoman on your hands."

He figured he already had that, but he didn't want the situation to worsen. "All right." He looked over at the revolver on the table. "I guess I don't have to warn you about staying on your guard."

"No, you don't. But whatever the danger, we need to find out more about Lois Brown. Maybe we can come up with some evidence that the police will have no choice but to take seriously."

"We'll look near and far," Nudger said. "I'll take near."

He knew she understood what he meant. "That's chivalrous of you, Nudger, near being more dangerous. But okay, I'll do the safe and monotonous research, and you see what you can find inside the victim's house."

Nudger's stomach did some aerobatics. "Breaking and entering, you mean?"

"Sure. If necessary."

Nudger gazed up at the cracked ceiling and thought about that.

"I've got the gun," Lacy said. "You want me to do the B and E part?"

"No, it'll be better if I do," Nudger said, knowing that she might shoot someone, or herself. Knowing also that she was right, that whatever the danger, special circumstances made risk-taking necessary. He hated those kinds of circumstances and always did what he could to avoid them. But now they had him, and here he was agreeing to take a risk by breaking the law to get evidence against law violators while protecting the well-being of a reckless young woman who carried a gun illegally. Was chivalry the same as stupidity?

"Between us," Lacy said, "we should come up with

something. I've got a computer in my apartment, and I'm plugged into the Net."

"You shouldn't go back to your place."

"I'll be there only briefly to pick up the computer along with some more clothes. It's a laptop and I can take it wherever I want to work." She stared intently at him from behind her shaggy bangs. "We *need* a computer, Nudger. This is the information age, and there's only one efficient way to take part in it."

She made him feel like a technophobe in spats. He remembered the disturbingly familiar Art Deco office display in the museum. The typewriter that was an easily recognizable ancestor to his own. He could easily imagine himself seated at the desk in the museum display, using the typewriter to compose letters explaining why his unpaid bills would certainly soon be settled. It was disturbing.

"I'll drive behind you," he said, "and make sure you get in and out of your place all right without being followed."

Lacy grinned. "My white knight. Sir Lancelot. I always thought that was a sexy name for a knight." Now that she was about to escape the dreary little cottage, her mood had shifted to high. She had him in an even earlier era, out of spats and into chain mail.

He glanced at the old console TV squatting in a corner. "Have you been watching *Camelot?*"

"No, but it's one of my favorites." She untucked her blouse from her jeans and clipped a little leather holster to her belt, then slid the revolver into it. With her shirt hanging out, the gun wasn't very noticeable.

"Which car is yours?" he asked, peering outside between the blind slats.

"The Caddy convertible parked two cottages down. See it?"

"How can I not? It's just perfect for hiding out."

"I got a good deal on it," she said defensively. "It rides smooth and it's fast."

"And large. And pink."

She put her hand on the doorknob, then turned around. "If you find out anything and want to call and leave a message here for me, I'm registered under another name."

"Julia Roberts?"

She shook her head no. "Guinevere Arthur."

"Surely you joust."

"Nope." Before opening the door, she gave him a mock adoring gaze and said, "Thanks for looking after me, Nudger. It makes my libido sing, to know that chivalry isn't dead."

He wished she'd get off that knight and damsel-in-distress notion.

"That's how I want to stay," he said, "not dead."

CHAPTER TWENTY-SIX

Oh, did his stomach hurt!

As he drove behind Lacy, Nudger reached into his pocket and found his roll of antacid tablets. Apprehension always did this to him, gave him an aching stomach and heartburn.

And he had plenty of apprehension about trying to get into Lois Brown's house to search for meaning in her death. Maybe he shouldn't have been so nervous about this; after all, the house wasn't a crime scene. But he knew that if there was no other way to gain entry, he'd have to make it a crime scene and hope for the best. Logically, he knew he could probably get in and out without arousing attention or suspicion. But his digestive tract was more intuitive than logical. It knew he was scared and wouldn't let him forget it. He was gastrointestinally cursed.

Two antacid tablets had been chewed and swallowed by the time he pulled the Granada to the curb and watched Lacy park her obsolete, finned fantasy of a car in front of an apartment building that didn't look much better than her cottage at the Hostelo Grandioso. She had to parallel park, and her maneuvering of the ponderous pink car reminded Nudger of a ship being docked.

She didn't look at him as she got out of the Caddy and limped into the apartment building. She was getting around without her cane now. Viewed from a distance, her slight limp was more noticeable than when he'd walked beside her.

Watching Lacy's limp made the pointy-headed giant spring to mind. Nudger's stomach did a flip, causing him to swallow a metallic taste that had gathered at the base of his tongue. He leaned forward to peer through the windshield at the block of similar brick apartment buildings, then he checked behind him in his rear-view mirror. Nothing unusual. No sign of the oversized assailant with the bowie knife he wielded like a scalpel. Nudger felt a little better. His stomach growled, telling him not to be a fool or let himself relax; the hard part of the day lay ahead.

Ten minutes later, Lacy emerged from the building rolling one of those black carry-ons like airline attendants used, and carrying a brown attaché case that probably contained her laptop computer.

This time she glanced at Nudger but didn't change expression as she opened her car's cavernous trunk and placed the suitcase and attaché case inside.

It took her almost as long to cajole the long Cadillac out of its space as it had to park it. Then the huge car emitted a cloud of oily black smoke and set off with aged pomposity down the humble street.

Nudger drove behind it for a few blocks, then figured there was no point in following Lacy all the way back to the Hostelo Grandioso. Instead he stopped at a National Supermarket and used a pay phone just inside the door to call Hammersmith and ask some more questions about Lois Brown's death.

Among Hammersmith's answers was the dead woman's address.

Lois Brown's house was in the middle of a block of attractive homes in St. Louis Hills, one of the better areas of the city proper. It was constructed of brown brick and had a large attached garage that had obviously been built recently. Though the house's roof was shingled, its peaks and edges were lined with dark brown tile. The roof was steeply pitched and there were plenty of dormers. Set in the bricks around the door were pale stones. There was more fancy stonework above the windows, which were equipped with yellow shutters, awnings, and narrow wooden flower boxes sporting bright red geraniums. The architecture was remotely Gothic, like so much of South St. Louis. If Hansel and Gretel had seized title to the witch's house and built onto it, it would have resembled Lois Brown's house.

St. Louis was pretending it was already summer today. The temperature was in the mid-eighties and climbing, and there wasn't much activity on the block. Everyone with good sense who wasn't terrified and about to commit a crime stayed inside in the air-conditioning.

Nudger, who was terrified and perhaps about to commit a crime, parked the car across the street from the house's driveway, which was bordered by flowers in planters atop low stone walls. His gaze caught movement and he noticed a frail, gray-haired man in the yard next door to the Brown house. He was wearing a perspiration-stained green shirt, unbuttoned and hanging loose, knee-length white shorts, and white tennis shoes, and was using a bright orange electric hedge trimmer to clip and shape bushes on the property line between the two houses. As Nudger opened the car door and climbed out, he could hear the spasmodic whir and rattle of the clippers as the man worked and perspired and improved on nature.

The old guy trimming the foliage only glanced over at him and smiled as Nudger walked up the driveway toward the gingerbread porch. He was pleased to find that once on the porch, he was out of the man's sight. In fact, because of the angle of the driveway, he was barely visible from the street. He'd have the time and privacy to work on the door and get inside. Maybe use his expired, honed Visa card to slip the lock. He pushed the doorbell button to make doubly sure no one was home before getting down to the business of breaking and entering.

He was about to try the knob to confirm the door was locked, when the door opened.

"Hello," said a teenage girl, smiling out at him.

"I, uh, hi," Nudger said.

She stood with her wide, slightly cockeyed smile, waiting for him to state his business. He guessed her age as about sixteen. Her eyes were huge and green and her red hair was pulled back and tied in long braids with green ribbons. She was wearing flower-print shorts, low-heeled white shoes, and a crisp white shirt with the name SALLY embroidered on its pocket flap. Nudger noticed that while she wasn't at all overweight, her knees were dimpled. The detective in him.

"I'm here about Lois Brown," he said.

"Oh. She was my aunt." The girl's smile disappeared, but she didn't look particularly sad. "I'm Sally Brown. My mom's here to take care of arrangements and stuff. That's where she is now. Can I help you?"

"Your mother is Lois Brown's sister?"

"That's right. There are some other relatives, but they won't be here till tomorrow. Did you know my Aunt Lo?"

"No," Nudger said. "I'm a detective, here to look things over." Fairly vague, he thought. Let the trusting, naive youngster assume he was with the police.

"Are you with the police?" she asked.

"No, I'm not that kind of investigator."

"But you said you were a detective."

"And I am."

"So how come you're here? My aunt wasn't murdered or anything, was she?"

"Probably not," Nudger said.

Sally's green eyes shone. "*Probably not?* Then you think she *might* have been murdered?"

"*Might* is a strong word," Nudger said.

"Huh? No it isn't."

"I guess not, at that. But my visit is simply routine, to examine the premises, to insure that death really was accidental."

"Then you're with the insurance company."

"Well—"

"So come on in. Aunt Lo maybe was murdered. That's so cool. You can talk to me about it. We weren't close. I only met her half a dozen times. But she was my mom's sister, so here I am. I won't have a cow and start to cry if we discuss Aunt Lo. I'll give you a statement."

"I only want to look around," Nudger said, stepping past her into a foyer with a tiled floor. On one wall was a fancy walnut coatrack and an umbrella stand. On another what appeared to be an original oil painting of a prim-looking woman with stiffly permed hair. She was seated on a bench with her hands folded in her lap.

"That's Aunt Lo," Sally said, noticing the direction of Nudger's gaze. "She had that done about six months ago by some portrait painter down in the Central West End. Not very good, if you ask me."

Nudger moved out of the foyer into a living room furnished somewhere between Early American and contemporary Las Vegas, a visual explosion of eclectic taste. An overstuffed plaid sofa squatted next to a delicate white leather sling chair. On the pale blue carpet was a multicolored woven oval rug. Everything looked new and expensive.

"Examine anything you want," Sally said. She sounded slightly miffed that he didn't want to interrogate her. "I'll be out by the pool."

"Maybe I'll have a few questions afterward," Nudger said.

She looked pleased.

He watched her as she sashayed through the living room and disappeared down a hall. A few seconds later he heard the sound of a sliding door opening and closing.

Nudger walked through the dim, cool house and found the doors leading to a patio behind the house, and beyond them a swimming pool with glittering blue water reflecting the sun. He saw Sally reclining in a lounge chair, wearing tinted glasses now and reading a paperback book.

He felt considerably better about being in Lois Brown's house, even though things hadn't gone as planned. He wasn't exactly alone, and he'd been seen. On the other hand, he hadn't entered the house illegally. And teenage girls being what they were, Sally might not think to mention to her mother or anyone else that he'd been here.

This just might work out okay, Nudger decided, assuming the mother didn't return while he was still in the house. His stomach growled and kicked at the thought.

Wasting no time, he found the basement door and went downstairs.

The basement was large and very cool. Beneath a glass-

177

brick window, a gleaming white washer and clothes dryer sat side by side. A drainhose ran from behind the washer to a standpipe affixed to a floor drain a few feet away.

Nudger examined the washer and dryer but could find nothing unusual about them. The floor around them was dry now, the concrete painted a glossy gray. The dryer was unplugged, but behind and above it was a 220-volt socket. The oversized three-pronged plug dangled nearby, the thick cord tucked behind a pipe. The basement was spacious, and the nearest object to the washer and dryer was a black steel shelf with an array of junk and household items on it: a very old wind-up alarm clock, a kitchen mixer with its steel blades resting in its bowl, some glass vases, a paintbrush and sponge, a bottle of bleach, another of stain remover, an opened box of detergent.

Nudger stood where Lois Brown must have stood in front of the dryer and looked around. Everything seemed domestic, normal, and benign. Not like a crime scene. But then, not like an accidental-death site, either.

He trudged upstairs, out of the almost cold basement, and found a study with a small cherry wood desk standing against a wall near the window. Nudger quickly went through the desk's drawers but found nothing unusual. There was a statement from an investment company revealing that Lois Brown had owned slightly over a hundred thousand dollars worth of common stock at the time of her death. Considering the value of the house, that didn't seem excessive.

Nudger left the study and found the master bedroom. It wasn't as spacious or grand as he'd anticipated. In fact, though the house was definitely upper middle class, and was in a fairly expensive neighborhood, it wasn't very large.

The bedroom was cohesively furnished and smacked of a professional decorator. One who hadn't yet made it to the living room. It was done in restful grays and blues and had gray lacquered furniture, including a gleaming gray headboard trimmed in brass. Nudger went to the closet and slid open the door. Lois Brown had possessed good but subdued taste in clothes and favored blue skirts and dresses. Also hanging in the closet was a plastic shoe rack. He looked at the array of high heels, slip-ons, and sandals. On the floor was a worn pair of very expensive jogging shoes. There were stacks of shoe boxes on the closet shelf. Nudger lifted the lids of a few of them and found—shoes. She'd liked shoes, had Lois Brown.

He closed the closet door and began examining the contents of the dresser drawers. The smaller top drawers contained jewelry and cosmetics. In the lower drawers Nudger found pantyhose, coiled belts, lingerie, and folded slacks and shorts, some dark blue sweatpants and tops. In the bottom drawer were folded sweaters, and on one side a milk-glass jar with a lid. Carver looked inside the jar and found that it was full of pennies. Beneath the sweaters he found an anatomically correct rubber vibrator and a tube of K-Y lubricant. Feeling ashamed of himself, he was about to drop the sweaters back in place when he saw a small, yellow slip of paper beneath the K-Y tube. He pulled it out and unfolded it. It was a charge card receipt from a restaurant in the amount of thirty dollars and change. Its date was faded and illegible and it was signed by Lois Brown. Written on the back of it in pencil was "Close calls." Nudger slid it back beneath the tube of lubricant, replaced the sweaters, then closed the drawer.

His knees popped in unison as he stood up straight, another reminder of mortality. He realized he'd been so engrossed in what he was doing that he'd forgotten to be afraid.

Now he remembered.

His stomach remembered. And moved slightly.

It would be smart to make this visit as brief as possible, said his stomach.

He left the bedroom and found his way to the sliding glass doors to the pool. Then he went out into the hot sun and approached Sally Brown.

She sensed his approach and slowly lowered her sunglasses and gazed questioningly but wisely at him over their rims, the way she'd seen it done in movies and on TV. Nudger appreciated her flair for drama.

"Find what you were looking for?" She asked the question with wry amusement, as if it were her line in a movie. Nudger figured he must be playing the nosy, not-very-bright detective blundering along the wrong trail.

"I wasn't looking for anything in particular," said Nudger the shamus. "I'm curious, though. What did your Aunt Lo do?"

"Do?"

"I mean, her occupation."

"Oh, *do*," She removed the sunglasses entirely and rested them on her flat stomach with her paperback. It was a romance novel, Nudger noted. On the cover was a shirtless guy with long, wavy black hair, leaning down to scoop a

180

woman up onto his horse with him. The woman had thick blonde hair that cascaded down over her torn dress. If this thing worked out for them and they married and had children, Nudger thought, their kids would never go bald.

"Aunt Lo was a bookkeeper for a man who sold cars," Sally said. "She worked for him forever, at least ten years, and when he died a year ago, he left her part interest in his business. She sold it, and I guess that's all the money she needed."

"Is that when she bought this house?"

"Yes, right after poor Mr. McClary died."

"McClary of McClary Motors?"

"That's right."

Nudger remembered the large used-car lot on Kingshighway. It was called something else now. "How old was Mr. McClary when he died?"

"Oh, an old man." Sally gazed out at the glittering blue water of the swimming pool. "At least forty-five, maybe even older."

Nudger listened to the breeze-stirred water lapping softly at the sides of the pool, like time itself.

"Mr. McClary slipped on the ice and hit his head. He died the next day." Sally smiled brightly, looking up at Nudger from the fire of her youth. "That kinda thing can happen to old people anytime, I guess."

Nudger glanced at the diving board. "I can still do an almost perfect swan dive," he said, before he even thought about speaking.

Sally smiled broadly, obviously humoring him. "I just bet you can."

He thanked her for talking to him, then turned to go.

181

"Wait a minute," she said behind him. When he stopped and turned around, she'd replaced the tinted glasses on the bridge of her nose and was gazing over their rims at him again. "Tell me the truth, okay? Did somebody murder my Aunt Lo?"

"It doesn't look that way," Nudger said.

"But they might have, right? Or you wouldn't have even come around here."

"The world is full of *mights*," Nudger told her. "This one isn't very likely. Your Aunt Lo just got unlucky while she was drying her clothes."

Sally looked disappointed, but she managed another smile for him.

By the time he'd gone out through the gate and glanced back at her, she was lost again in her paperback novel, hooked on romance.

Nudger hoped it was for life.

CHAPTER TWENTY-SEVEN

That little mutt of a woman was by here a while ago," Danny said, when Nudger checked in at the doughnut shop after returning from Lois Brown's house. "She said you should meet her tonight in Spain." Danny appeared puzzled. "You leaving the country, Nudge?"

"Sometimes it seems that way," Nudger said, sliding

onto one of the counter stools. He looked at the Dunker Delites resting on their greasy white doilies in the glass display case and was shocked to find himself hungry. He'd skipped lunch and it was—he glanced at the clock above the coffee urn—almost three o'clock. Maybe he'd drive down the street to Shag's or McDonald's for a cheeseburger and milk shake.

Danny must have noticed him staring with obvious hunger at the doughnut case. A Dunker Delite thumped down on the counter before him.

"On the house," Danny said. "Left over from the lunch crowd."

Nudger couldn't remember any kind of crowd ever in Danny's, and he did not want a Dunker Delite. But there the thing lay like a defective brown bomb that had landed intact. And Danny, with his back to Nudger, was already coaxing a cup of sludge-like coffee from the complex steel urn with its many valves and serpentine coils.

"I just came from a big lunch," Nudger said, shaking his head as if in denial of his own lie.

"So? Why not a snack?" Danny turned and smiled at him, placing the foam cup of coffee next to the Dunker Delite. Here was a one-two punch that could level Evander Holyfield.

"I'm absolutely stuffed," Nudger said, patting his stomach. Danny's face fell—farther. "But it sure does look good," Nudger added, "so if you don't mind, I'll take it upstairs with me. I'll drink the coffee now, then have the Dunker Delite later as a treat."

Danny smiled. "Sure, good idea." He bent down and

got a small white paper sack and plunked the Dunker Delite into it. Nudger accepted the sack from him, surprised by its weight. "Need a lid for that coffee, Nudge?"

"Naw, I'm gonna drink it right away." Nudger swiveled around and slid off his stool. He carried the steaming coffee in one hand, the greasy little white paper sack in the other, and made for the door. "Remember to give me a call if you see or hear anybody headed toward my office."

"Will do, Nudge."

Managing to open the door with the hand holding the sack, Nudger pushed outside then turned and opened the door to the stairwell. He was careful not to trip over his mail, lying on the floor just inside the street door and bound with a dirty rubber band. A colorful supermarket flier was folded over it, advertising a sale of pork steaks to herald the coming barbecue season, so he couldn't see if anything important had arrived. Partly out of uninterest, partly because his hands were full, he ignored the mail for the time being.

Once inside the office, he went to the half bath and poured the coffee into the washbasin drain slowly so Danny wouldn't hear it gurgle down the pipes. He didn't know quite what to do with the Dunker Delite, so he carried it with him to his desk and laid it on top of his stack of overdue bills, where it sat like a petrified feces paperweight.

Nudger wasn't so hungry anymore.

He saw that there was a message on his answering machine and pressed the PLAY button.

Beep: "Nudger?" Eileen's voice. "Nudger, you odious son of a—"

He pressed ERASE. Eileen had never called him odious before. He decided it must be a Henry Mercato word.

Twisting his body, he adjusted the air conditioner to high, then leaned far back in his *eeeking* swivel chair, thinking about his conversation with Sally Brown. He wondered if he should have asked Sally about the concealed note reading "Close calls." Probably not, he decided; Lois Brown and Sally hadn't known each other well despite being family, and would hardly have exchanged confidences. Of course, Nudger was assuming the note was placed beneath the sweaters in the drawer to conceal it, considering what else was concealed there, and that Lois Brown had written it. Also assuming that it hadn't been in the drawer for years and was now irrelevant. He knew that was a considerable amount of assumption, and probably the note would lead nowhere. "Close calls" could be anything from a book title to a reminder that someone named Close had phoned.

Such a pessimist was Nudger.

"Shouldn't be that way," he told himself. "Every day is the first day of . . . well, something."

He stood up and clomped back down the stifling stairwell and picked up his mail, then returned to the office and sat down again behind his desk. He'd noticed that even over the creaking of the steps, he could hear the grinding sounds his knees made as he descended and climbed the stairs. No pain yet, but surely this meant something ominous for his mobility and medical future.

After working off the rubberband and throwing away the pork steak sale flier, he examined the half-dozen envelopes that were left, studying them hopefully. He was owed money. Not as much as *he* owed, but he *was* owed, and it was always possible that a check had arrived. And there was always the prospect of Publishers' Clearinghouse Sweepstakes. Always.

But the mail was comprised only of two advertisements, three bills or past-due reminders, and a letter addressed to him in Eileen's handwriting. He threw away the advertisements, but not before yielding to curiosity and opening them. One was an offer of term life insurance. The other urged Nudger to purchase steaks through the mail. (It struck him how small the world was, that the steak-by-mail offer should appear in his mail along with the pork steak sale flier. What might it mean?) He resisted both offers, then stared at the Eileen letter for a few seconds before dropping it unopened into the wastebasket on top of the first two envelopes. The woman was a plague.

Then his eye fell on a pink envelope in the wastebasket. It must have been stuck inside the folds of the supermarket flier.

He reached down and plucked it from the trash, immediately recognizing the return address of a client whose husband he'd followed and reported on last month. Inside the envelope was a check for the five hundred dollars he was owed, along with a note thanking him for his services and expressing how relieved his client was that she now knew for sure her retired husband really was playing golf five days a week. He actually went to one of the nearby courses even when it was cold and snow was falling. She had read his passion correctly, but it was for the dogleg and the putt and not for another woman.

Nudger was cheered.

He decided to write checks for some of his overdue bills, then drive to Citizen's Bank and deposit the client's check in his account before mailing them. He dug his checkbook from the top desk drawer, removed the Dunker Delite from on top of the stack of bills, and set to work. He pondered for a while which bills to pay first, then settled on the greasiest ones rather than those longest overdue.

At six o'clock, he wrapped the Dunker Delite in the supermarket flyer than placed it in the bottom of the wastebasket beneath crumpled papers and envelopes. From the wastebasket, he retrieved the postal service's dirty rubberband and bound his stack of bills, noticing that grease was already seeping through the envelopes. Then he switched off the air conditioner and left the office.

He would use the bank drive-through to deposit his check, and immediately afterward mail the paid bills at the post office on Marshall Avenue. Then he'd have some supper, maybe at Shoney's. It was angel-hair pasta special night, he was pretty sure. After narrowly avoiding a Dunker Delite, his stomach would welcome angel-hair pasta.

After supper, he would wait until nightfall and then drive to Spain.

Lacy's cottage at Hostelo Grandioso was dark, but the ostentatious Cadillac was parked near the back of the lot, no more conspicuous than a calliope.

Nudger parked the Granada near the Caddy, then climbed out and looked around. The lot was dimly illuminated by Spanish, curlicued-iron overhead lights that were placed too far apart. Near the driveway and office was a faint red glow from the neon caballero spinning his lariat.

As he approached Lacy's cottage, he heard its laboring air conditioner. Then he heard her voice.

"C'mon in, Nudger."

Lacy was standing in the dark with the door open about six inches.

"I heard you drive up," she said, "then I looked out the window and saw you blundering around out there."

Nudger didn't know how he might have blundered, but he said nothing as he stepped past Lacy and into the cottage.

The only illumination came from the old TV. On the flickering screen, O. J. Simpson, noticeably older since his trials, was talking soundlessly, his eyes wide and sincere, his expression one of wronged innocence.

"Why don't you have a light on?" Nudger asked.

"I don't need one to watch television." She walked over and switched on a lamp that had a bullfighter silhouetted on its shade. She still had on her faded jeans from this morning, but now she was wearing only a bra and was barefoot.

"Thanks for getting dressed up for me," Nudger said.

She shot him a wicked grin. "Lots of men would rather see me in this than a ball gown." She turned off the TV and made sure the drapes were closed all the way. "I'm only trying to stay cool, so don't get any ideas." But she winked as she said it. She sat down in the room's only chair, a red vinyl creation with heavy dark wooden arms that looked as if they'd been attacked by worms. Spain was everywhere. Nudger sat on the edge of the bed. Briefly, its springs sounded like a mariachi band as his weight settled.

Lacy smiled at him and hooked her right thumb beneath her bra strap above the cup, sort of the way old men did when they were about to snap a suspender. "I'll tell you mine if you tell me yours."

Nudger found himself staring not at her meager breasts,

but at the slight roll of fat above the waistband of her jeans, surprising on such a slight woman. He averted his gaze and related what had happened at Lois Brown's house.

"Are you sure there was nothing suspicious about that washer and dryer?" she asked.

He shrugged. "Not that I could see. But I'm not an electrician."

"You haven't accomplished diddly," Lacy said.

"It felt like at least diddly."

"I'm ahead of you, Nudger. I've been researching, checking back issues of newspapers, talking to contacts. I found out about McClary leaving part interest in his business to faithful and probably loving Lois Brown. She sold it almost immediately for three hundred thousand dollars."

"How did McClary die?" Nudger asked.

"The kid Sally told you right. He went outside his front door to get his newspaper from his lawn one morning after an ice storm, and his feet went out from under him. Struck the back of his head on the porch step and died almost instantly."

"Did any surviving McClarys object to Lois Brown inheriting that much money?" Nudger asked.

"He didn't leave much family. His wife had died of cancer two years before his death. Some distant relatives in Oklahoma got their share of the wealth. Faithful, fucking Lois got the rest."

"Ease up," Nudger said. "You don't know anything about their relationship." He wasn't sure why he was defending Lois Brown and McClary, except that they were both dead and couldn't defend themselves.

Lacy snorted. "Live in the real world, Nudger."

"What about the 'Close calls' note? That mean anything in your world?"

"It might." She stood up and walked over to her laptop computer where it sat on the tiny Spanish desk. The chair she'd been sitting in went with the desk, so she remained standing as she switched on the computer and began working its keyboard. "It might mean a lot of things," she said, not looking at him, "or it might mean the Close Calls shops that are located in several shopping malls around town. They sell telephones and audio equipment and such, but their specialty is cellular phones."

Nudger didn't see any likely connection, but the possibility shouldn't be ignored. "Can't we check that out without using a computer?"

"I use Nexis-Lexis," she said. "Know about Nexis-Lexis?"

"Isn't one of them a car?"

"Not in this case. They're an on-line service lawyers use regularly for research. They put a hell of a lot of paralegals out of work. I can log on and and easily gain access to state public records." Her fingers moved expertly across the key board. "I tell you Nudger, I don't see how you can do detective work these days without knowing at least something about computers."

"I know something about them," he said defensively. "More than you might think."

"Sure," she said, concentrating on Nexis. Or possibly Lexis.

Nudger sat watching her with envy and regret. He knew he'd have to start using a computer in his work soon, maybe get that software program he'd seen advertised, the one with every listed phone number in the country, perfect for skip tracing. Maybe he should even get a cellular phone, call people from restaurant tables and traffic signals. Maybe everybody in the software program. He shuddered, causing the bedsprings to whine musically.

"Close Calls is listed as a private company," Lacy said. "I was hoping it was public, so we could get some heavy information. Incorporated five years ago right here in Missouri, owner and CEO a man named Wayne Hart." She lifted her bare shoulders in a shrug, then switched off the computer. "That's it."

"Wayne *Hart*, you said?"

"Right."

Nudger stood up from the bed and walked over to her. She looked up at him. "Something, Nudger?"

"Does that computer have a redial button?"

CHAPTER TWENTY-EIGHT

Nudger sat on a bench near a fountain, sipping a café au lait from Merry-Go-Grounds, which was located only a few stores away from Close Calls in the West Gallery Mall.

Even considering it was a weekday morning, the mall wasn't crowded. He observed several walkers stride vigorously past, silver-thatched and somber-faced and wearing expensive hiking shoes. And a few packs of roaming teenagers, giggling, shoving, and yammering at each other, passed Nudger's bench. But when it came to actual shoppers, folks in the mall to make purchases, he didn't see many. And he'd been only one of three customers in Merry-Go-Grounds. Maybe the experts who claimed the day of the mall was past were correct. Specialty shops you could drive to, park in front of, and walk in and out of within a few minutes might be the fad of the future.

But it seemed to Nudger that malls were more than anything clumps of small specialty shops, even if they were anchored by major department stores and usually connected by a roof. He looked around at Pretty Plus Sizes, Cards Are Us, Just Luggage, and Glamour Puss Cat Accessories, and decided that shopping malls were far from dead.

He dropped his empty paper cup into a trash receptacle, then stood up from the bench. After waiting for a woman staring into a window to move on, because he thought that from the back she resembled Eileen, he strolled along the mall with the sparse flow of pedestrian traffic, listening to the pleasant trickling sound of the fountain fade.

At the sunglasses kiosk, he turned right and walked past a jewelry store, a Quicker Image gift shop, and found himself standing before Close Calls.

The doorway was wide, opening onto a red-carpeted area with podiums or ornate tables on which various phone products were displayed. Nudger stuck his hands in his pockets and wandered in, taking a cursory look at a cellular phone in the shape of a cartoon character he didn't recognize, some sort of rodent with a sword, and a shield that apparently flipped down to form the phone's mouthpiece. There was an answering machine much like his own, only several generations later. Pagers that looked like colorful bars of soap were on sale. A low table held a symmetrical display of cordless phones.

Ordinary desk and wall phones were relegated to the back of the store. Also in the back of the store was a wide counter with a cash register and charge card machines.

Behind the counter was a kid with scraggly black hair and a fuzzy mustache. On the wall behind him was a display of plastic-wrapped phone accessories. He seemed to sense Nudger looking at him, so he put down whatever he'd been reading and walked around from behind the counter.

"Let me know if there's any—" he began.

"I'm only browsing," Nudger said, cutting him off. On the kid's stained white shirt was a name tag that said he was DEREK. Nudger would have guessed Derek.

"Our sale on pagers is in its very last day," Derek said earnestly.

"Do I look like I need a pager?" Nudger asked.

Derek grinned. "No, but you look important, like maybe you need a cellular phone." So saying, he rested his hand on a sleek gray model that was only two dollars if you signed up for the service at time of purchase.

"Don't those things give you brain cancer?" Nudger asked.

Derek didn't blink; he'd heard the question before. "If they do," he said, "it wouldn't be for a long time anyway. Years, I've heard them say. And the real experts say there's nothing to that brain-cancer scare. Hey, our phones are less dangerous than smoking cigarettes." He moved nearer to Nudger with a smooth little shuffle, like a boxer sensing the advantage and moving in to land a blow. "If you're super-stitious about the brain-cancer thing, why don't you buy a pager, then you can call people back on a conventional phone."

"You the manager?" Nudger asked.

"No, he's away right now. But I can page him." Derek winked. Nudger was beginning to dislike him. "Really, I can probably help you with whatever it is you need," Derek said.

Nudger thought maybe he could. "I'm a freelance writer doing a piece on shopping malls," he said.

Derek didn't seem any more excited at meeting a real writer than if he'd discovered a hangnail.

"How's your business been here the last six months or so?" Nudger asked, forging on like a genuine writer.

Derek looked sad and rubbed his peach-fuzz mustache. "The whole mall's been falling off. Nobody can figure out why business is so bad. Socks and Clocks, just a few doors down, closed up last month. They say a calendar shop is going to move into their space."

"That might work," Nudger said.

"It's kind of seasonal," Derek said with a gloomy air of confidentiality.

Nudger looked around. "The owner have any plans for this store?"

Derek shrugged. "Far as I know, he doesn't plan on clos-ing it down."

"You know much about the owner?"

"Just what I've heard. He owns all four of the Close

Calls shops, and they say next year he might open one in Crossrivers Mall in North County."

"So the cellular phone business is doing okay?"

"Nope," Derek told Nudger. "But compared to some of these other places, we're in really good shape. What I hear is that Close Calls makes a solid profit per unit every year on fewer units than our competitors. Not that we aren't realistically priced or competitively flexible per product according to the new industry paradigm."

"I never thought you were," Nudger said, recognizing that Derek was speaking company rote that even he probably didn't comprehend. "Or weren't."

Derek blinked. "And we're not just cellular phones, as you can see." He waved a long, skinny arm in an inclusive gesture. "We sell all types of phones as well as answering machines, caller ID devices, pagers, and various accessories."

Nudger pulled his little spiral notebook from his pocket, unclipped his pen, and pretended to be taking notes. "Your name is . . . ?"

"Derek Wilson. I'm assistant manager."

"And the owner's name—no, I guess you wouldn't know that."

"It's Hart," Derek said. "Wayne Hart. I've never met him personally, but everybody working for Close Calls knows who he is. He's plenty rich. Lives in a big house, like an estate, up near the river. I went up there once for a company picnic."

"I thought you said you never met him."

"He wasn't at the picnic. He's the kind of chief executive that keeps his distance. Some chain-of-command thing. I don't believe in that sorta crap myself."

"Me either," Nudger said, and drew a reasonable likeness of a cat in his notepad. He hadn't gotten the ears quite right.

"Not that Mr. Hart's not a nice guy," Derek said. "It's just that he's busy. Most any place doing business in a shopping mall is in a fight to survive, so nobody begrudges Mr. Hart working to keep us all employed."

"Guess not," Nudger said, pressing down hard with the pen and rearranging the cat's ears. Still not right.

"Each quarter we do a little less in gross unit sales," Derek said. "We're hoping the new miniature pagers will boost sales next month."

"I'd like to talk with Mr. Hart," Nudger said. "I don't suppose you'd have a phone number for him among all these communication devices."

"Oh, gosh no. Nobody here calls Mr. Hart. He calls us, and not very often."

Nudger made the cat's ears come to sharper points. That did it. "This big house where Mr. Hart lives, is it right on the river?"

"Yeah. He's got himself a neat boat, like a cabin cruiser, and his own dock right there in his own back yard."

"One of those ritzy places off Rogers Road?"

"Nope. His is off Peterson Road. But it's plenty ritzy. Heck, he could fish from his own dock, only he's so busy he probably can't take the time to fish. Isn't that something? Man's got everything he wants and can't enjoy it."

"Life," Nudger said, closing and pocketing his notebook.

"Life," Derek agreed sagely.

CHAPTER TWENTY-NINE

Peterson Road ran parallel to the bank not far south of where the Mississippi was joined by the Missouri River. It seemed a peaceful and deserted country lane. The sun-touched plane of the river was barely visible through the trees on Nudger's left, and only gates to driveways and wooded lots suggested there might be houses along the road.

But houses there were. And expensive ones. Every now and then Nudger glimpsed a wide brick facade, or a vast stretch of slate, gabled roof among the treetops. He'd learned which of the houses belonged to Wayne Hart from the proprietor of a quick-stop market and gas station where Peterson Road began.

Slowing for a squirrel crossing the road, Nudger almost missed the black wrought-iron gate with the numerals 333 welded in the center of its elaborate design. It was on Nudger's left, the river side of the road. He braked the Granada and pulled to the road's gravel shoulder about a hundred feet beyond the gate. He finished the Yoo-Hoo chocolate drink he'd bought at the convenience store and tossed the empty bottle onto the car's floor on the passenger side of the transmission hump. In doing so, he noticed a small paper bag on the floor, then bent over and opened it to see what was inside. He recoiled as he found himself looking at a week-old Dunker Delite he'd accepted from Danny out of compassion, but not eaten. He'd meant to throw the dreadful thing away long ago.

He straightened up and looked around. Maybe he'd throw it away here, along with the empty Yoo-Hoo bottle.

But Nudger decided against that. He wasn't a litterbug. A sap for pun and jingle, the government's long ago "Every Litter Bit Hurts" campaign still echoed in his conscience and stayed his hand whenever he impulsively started to throw something from a car window.

A pickup truck sped past going the opposite direction fast enough for its wake of wind to rock the parked Granada. The sound and motion brought Nudger's mind back to what he really didn't want to think about. Should he sneak onto the Hart estate, or should he play aboveboard and simply press the intercom button on the box near the gate and ask to see Wayne Hart?

Neither prospect appealed to him. He was not by nature a risktaker. Yet the more dangerous alternative, he decided, might be to make his presence known and alert Hart that he was being investigated. That might be like telling a bear you were entering his den.

So like it or not, it was time to trespass, to sneak and see. This was a part of his job that Nudger and his stomach barely tolerated.

He drove the Granada another hundred feet down the road and parked in the shade of a big maple tree wearing the fresh green leaves of spring. It was noticeably cooler there, and a dense stand of white birch saplings made it difficult to see the car from the road.

Nudger got out and walked over to what should be

Hart's property line and found concealed in the woods a ten-foot high chain-link fence topped with razor wire. Terrific! He hated razor wire; just get near the stuff and you needed stitches.

Walking casually, as if he might be somebody's gardener—wishing he *were* somebody's gardener—he made his way along the fence line back to the wrought-iron gate. Now he noticed a small sign down low on the gate that said GUARDED BY ARMOR ALARM. When he looked up, he could see the taut chain-link stretching away out of sight into the foliage on the other side of the gate.

He returned to his car. So Hart lived surrounded by security. Nudger knew what he had to do, even though he didn't want to do it. It would require waiting till dark. He cringed. There was a lot of talk about cover of darkness, as if the dark were a security blanket for cowards, but he couldn't remember the night ever being his friend.

At least he had plenty of time to get what he needed. He started the car and pulled back onto Peterson Road.

As it turned out, he didn't have to rent a boat. Lacy had a friend who owned a canoe.

"We have to paddle at the same time, Nudger!" she whispered to him that night, as they pulled away from the bank half a mile upstream from Wayne Hart's estate.

The night was sultry and dark and the river sounded immense and powerful. Nudger wished they didn't have to go so far in the flimsy aluminum canoe, but Lacy assured him it would be safe. He was dressed in a black T-shirt, Levi's, and dark blue jogging shoes. Lacy had on black slacks, a dark green blouse, and a black beret.

"We look like a couple of wartime commandos," Lacy said with a grin.

Nudger thought they looked like a couple of French hoodlums. It was the beret.

"Dammit, Nudger, you're making us go in a circle!"

"You sit up front," Nudger said, lifting his paddle from the dark water and starting to stand up. "That way I can see when you paddle."

"My God, Nudger, sit *down!*"

He sat. Obviously he was ignorant of canoe etiquette.

"You know where we're going," Lacy said, "so it's better if you're up front. You motion with your head when we're going to change directions, and I'll key off you. Paddle three times, then switch sides. If we start paddling together on opposite sides, we should be in synchronization and go in a straight line."

"The current's got us anyway," he said with some trepidation, "moving us downstream."

"But the canoe's crosswise to the current, Nudger. That isn't right. It increases our chances of capsizing."

That made sense and alarmed Nudger. He dipped his paddle back in the water. "On three," he said.

He and Lacy finally began paddling in unison. Once he'd worked up the rhythm, the strain felt good in his back and arms, and steering the canoe became easier.

As soon as they moved well out into the river, the current did most of the work and they used the paddles mainly for steering. Nudger's eyes had adjusted some to the dark. The lights of large houses began gliding past on the right; starboard, he thought smugly. Some of them had wide lawns and lighted docks. They passed a cabin cruiser tied up at one of the docks, then there was a stretch of black shore and another dock with a big boat moored close to it.

"That has to be it," Nudger said, recognizing the bend in the shore as the same as the bend in Peterson Road near the Hart estate.

Lacy inserted her paddle in the water and used it as a rudder, veering them toward the bank. "I'll steer, Nudger. Stop paddling and let the river take us there until we get in close."

As they neared the bank, he saw a glint of moonlight off razor wire and was sure they had the right estate. Beyond the dock, which was dark, glowed rows of windows in a large house whose shape could only be imagined against the black sky. Off to one side of the house, a blue-green swimming pool lay like a glimmering jewel set in the dark hillside.

Lacy guided the canoe in close to the dock, behind the boat. It was a white boat with a dark blue or black stripe along the waterline, and a white-and-blue cabin. Some sort of navigational equipment jutted from the cabin roof and looked as if it should revolve when the boat was underway. An aluminum ladder led from its stern down to a transom, providing a platform for swimmers or sunbathers. BLUE DESTINY was lettered boldly across the stern. Nudger thought it would be ridiculously easy to board the boat. From inside the hull came a steady humming sound.

"That noise is only the generator," Lacy said, noticing how he'd leaned to the side and tilted his head toward the hull.

Nudger wondered how she'd learned so much about boats, ships, whatever.

"I used to date a navy man who had a boat," she said. Reading his mind now as well as his body language. He watched her tie the canoe to the dock with a frayed-looking rope, deftly creating a complicated knot with a few flicks of her wrist. "C'mon, Nudger," she said, climbing out of the canoe. She seemed to have taken charge of the mission.

He followed her up onto the dock, almost slipping and falling into the lapping dark water. The canoe bumped against the rubber tires lashed to the dock as buffers, making a dull metallic sound that wouldn't carry far.

"Let's hope there's no one home," Nudger said. What he wanted was to get into Wayne Hart's house, then search for some connection between Hart and the deaths of Brad Millman and Lois Brown.

"We'll know soon," Lacy said, staying low as she went up rough wooden steps made from railroad ties, then started up the dark slope of lawn toward the house.

Nudger followed her. He was suddenly aware that crickets had been chirping, and now were silent. The smell of freshly mown grass mingled with the smell of the river. His stomach moved.

"What if there are dogs?" he asked. "We should have brought some meat to throw to them."

Lacy didn't answer, staring straight ahead at the lights of the house.

"You didn't think about dogs, did you?" Nudger persisted. "If you had, you would have brought something."

"I brought you," she snarled back at him.

The plong! of a diving board and the sound of a splash made them both freeze in the night.

Nudger looked beyond Lacy at a young girl or small woman in a one-piece black swimming suit pulling herself up out of the pool. She leaned forward and shook water from her long blonde hair. "The pool," he whispered to Lacy.

"I see."

They moved closer cautiously and saw by the reflected light from the pool that the swimmer was very young, maybe prepubescent. She wasn't alone. Sprawled in a lounge chair was a fat man with thick graying hair. His eyes were closed and his bare chest was rising and falling slowly in sleep. His right hand held an empty glass. He wasn't wearing swimming trunks.

"Look at that ape!" Lacy said. "With that kid running around!"

"I doubt if it's his daughter," Nudger said.

Lacy hissed. "Why, that bastard!"

"Maybe she's older than she looks."

"Idiot!" Lacy snapped.

"We don't know her age." Nudger had seen forty-year-old women who could look like teenagers from a distance. "And there's nothing we can do about it now anyway. And he hasn't actually done anything to her. Maybe he's a nudist or something. Maybe she actually is his daughter. Let's concentrate on the house."

"You're kidding yourself, Nudger."

Reluctantly, they moved to the left, toward what appeared to be illuminated French doors that led inside from a stone patio. There were chairs on the patio, and a table with an umbrella sprouting from it. Next to the patio was a statue of what appeared to be a woman astride a horse.

As they drew closer to the house, Nudger saw that it was a vast affair with a many-gabled tile roof and ivy growing up two walls of an alcove. There were canvas awnings over the windows, their white trim dancing gently in the breeze. A curved walk lined with flowers led away from the patio to a garden and greenhouse. What Nudger had at first assumed was a smaller, guest house, about a hundred yards to the side of the main house, now appeared to be a three-car garage, perhaps with living quarters above it.

"Too bright there," Nudger said, pointing toward the French doors. He and Lacy moved toward a dark window surrounded by shrubbery. "Remember the Armor Alarm company," he said softly.

"The window's not wired," Lacy said. "See if it's locked."

Nudger tried the window and couldn't raise it.

Lacy picked up a stone and smashed the glass up near the latch.

"Watch the noise!" Nudger whispered.

"Noise isn't something you can watch, Nudger. Anyway, they can't hear anything from the pool."

"Maybe there's somebody else in the house."

"Servants?" Lacy asked, as if she'd just thought of the possibility.

Nudger nodded. Quietly, he unlocked the window without cutting his hand on a glass shard, then raised the lower section. It went up quietly and without resistance.

He climbed inside first, then helped Lacy in.

They were standing on soft carpet in a room illuminated by moonlight sifting in through the window.

Nudger watched Lacy cross the room toward the door. She closed it softly, then worked the wall switch.

The room sprang alive with light.

"Hey!" Nudger said.

"They can't see the window from the pool," Lacy assured him.

Hoping she was right, he looked around. They were in a large den with darkly paneled walls and royal blue carpet. Over a stone mantle a stuffed swordfish mounted on wood was posed in an eternal leap. What appeared to be a genuine sea anchor was leaning against the wall nearby. The furniture was teak and oak and cream-colored leather and shouted money. In front of a long leather sofa was a marble-topped table with magazines fanned out on it. On the other three walls were rows of paintings, most of them of young women or girls posed nude but not erotically.

"These are genuine oils," Lacy said, moving close and staring at a painting of a pale young woman stepping gingerly out of a large brass bathtub. On a hook nearby hung a white tutu and ballet shoes.

"This is a genuine Degas, Nudger! Worth a fortune."

"I had no idea you knew about art," he said.

"I was once involved in an . . . er, art scam case."

"Legally involved?"

She gazed around her, ignoring his question. "All this stuff is worth a fortune."

"Hart's rich, Lacy," he reminded her. "He's a collector."

What really interested Nudger was a large polished

wood desk in a corner. He moved toward it, leaving Lacy to admire Hart's art collection.

When he was five feet away from the desk an alarm began to screech.

"Pressure plate!" Lacy said. "You must have stepped on a damned pressure plate!"

Dogs began to bark. They sounded like big dogs.

Nudger was already moving toward the window.

He didn't remember actually diving through the open window, but there he was, lying on the lawn, one foot in a bush whose branches were scratching his ankle above his sock.

He saw Lacy scramble out through the window. She almost landed directly on him, stepping on his arm as they both struggled to their feet.

Then they were both running down the slope of lawn toward the dock. Nudger glanced back and saw that all the lights were glowing in the house. And there were outside lights. He could see several figures moving around near the stone patio.

"Stay low! They haven't seen us!" Lacy whispered.

Cover of darkness! Cover of darkness! Nudger kept repeating to himself as they half ran, half rolled down the sloping lawn toward the steps to the dock.

When they were almost there, Nudger allowed himself to believe they might make it.

Then he heard a snarl and something clamped around the heel of his shoe.

He twisted around and saw a large black Doberman pinscher glaring at him, its long white teeth sunk into his shoe, somehow missing flesh and bone.

There was a soft pop and hiss. The dog released its grip and began wheezing, spinning in a circle.

"Pepper spray," Lacy said, holding up a small aerosol can. The nightmare dog continued to whirl like a puppy chasing its tail.

They clattered into the canoe. Nudger couldn't believe no one would hear them.

Lacy unhitched the rope from the dock and picked up a paddle.

This time they worked in perfect unison from their first strokes, moving out into the river and the night, feeling the current take them.

Lights winked on around the dock, inside the boat. Flashlight beams probed out above the black water, but none of them were strong enough to pierce the darkness for any distance.

A motor turned over then steadied out to a deep hum.

"They're coming after us with the boat!" Lacy said.

"Paddle toward shore!" Nudger told her, his eyes fixed on a dark mass of branches near water level. "We'll get lost in those trees!"

The river was high enough from the spring rains to have reached the middle limbs of the trees, whose leafy branches seemed to embrace the canoe, scraping noisily along its aluminum sides. Nudger prayed the shrill, hollow sound wouldn't carry.

Gripping branches for leverage, he and Lacy pulled and paddled the canoe farther into the backwater until they were near shore.

When they thought they were well concealed, they sat very still.

The sound of a boat's motor came nearer . . . faded . . . came nearer again. Nudger thought he saw the beam of a searchlight playing over the river. Once he was sure he heard men's voices.

Then the sound of the boat receded and he could hear only the lapping of water around the limbs and trunks of the trees, up against the sides of the canoe.

Lacy used her paddle, and Nudger clutched branches hand over hand, and they worked the canoe to river's edge. Then they climbed out, waded through water only a few inches deep, and wrestled the canoe up onto dry land.

Incredibly, Lacy was gasping and giggling at the same time. "Jesus, wasn't that fun!" she said, almost choking. "Great, great fun, Nudger!"

"You're crazy!"

"Could be. What a rush!"

Nudger's knees were watery. He felt as if he'd just stepped ashore after the Battle of Midway.

"Let's get out of here," he said.

Lacy didn't argue, but it took her a while to stop giggling. Nudger cut her some slack, attributing her behavior to nervous reaction.

When they found their way to the road, Lacy began walking in the opposite direction from where the Granada was parked.

It took Nudger only a moment to see where she was going. Near a bend in the road was a red neon sign that said STEAMBOAT RESTAURANT.

"We can call a cab there," Lacy said. "That way we can ride back to your car without walking past the Hart estate. After we get your car, we can drive back for the canoe."

"Good plan," Nudger said. He was still shaking and his legs were wobbly. "But I'm going to make another call."

"Who to?"

"Hammersmith. About that kid in the pool."

CHAPTER THIRTY

You need more than what you saw, Nudge," Hammersmith said, when Nudger called him from the Steamboat Restaurant. It was a tiny place with paneled walls covered with photographs of celebrities. Most of the photos were autographed. Nudger couldn't believe any of those people had ever eaten here. The signatures must be forged. "Not that I don't agree with you, but from a legal standpoint, lying around nude while a kid swims isn't exactly child molestation. Then there's the fact you were trespassing on the guy's property."

Nudger hadn't mentioned breaking and entering. He remained silent, staring at Steve McQueen, who stared sullenly back at him above "Loved your Steamboatburger— Best wishes."

"Then there's the fact that Hart has money and influence and a herd of attorneys," Hammersmith continued. "You have none of those things. As I see it, Nudge, if you really push this, you might wind up paying a fine and seeing prison time."

"Life not being fair," Nudger said, "you're probably right."

"If you do get something solid on Hart with the kid, let me know. I mean that."

Nudger said that he would, then hung up, frustration wringing his stomach into tight knots.

He left the phone and sat at a table with Lacy near a window. They were both exhausted and said little as they sipped diet Cokes and waited for the cab.

"Police gonna move on Hart about the kid?" Lacy asked.

"No. They can't."

"Thought that was how it'd be." She sounded bitter and resigned.

They sat and sipped, depressed and staring out at the darkness. Life not being fair.

After returning to the Granada by cab, they drove back to where they'd left the canoe near the half-submerged trees. There was no way to get the car close, so Nudger and Lacy had to drag and wrestle the canoe to where he'd parked the Granada twenty feet off the road.

Nudger was puffing hard by the time they'd hoisted the canoe upside down onto the roof of the car and lashed it down with ropes, strung through the rolled-down windows and across the inside of the car, so it wouldn't blow off on the highway.

"Can we return this boat tomorrow?" Nudger asked, as he settled down behind the steering wheel and started the engine.

"Canoe, Nudger," Lacy said beside him.

"What?"

"It's a canoe, not a boat."

Nudger didn't think it was time for a lesson in nautical

terms. He steered the Granada back onto Peterson Road and accelerated. "I'll drop you off, then I'll leave the canoe tied to the roof of the car out in front of my apartment. Nobody will steal it."

"Somebody might." She sounded irritated. The night's tension had passed and she was emotionally played out.

Well, Nudger was played out and irritated himself. If Lacy hadn't bought that stupid, block-long convertible that looked like something Elvis had traded in, the boat—canoe—would be lashed to the top of her car. "Then how about when I drop you off," he said, "we take the canoe down from the car and leave it at your—"

He stopped talking when he noticed brightness and saw headlights looming larger and larger in the rearview mirror. He was aware of Lacy turning around in her seat to look behind them.

"Nudger—"

The headlights were suddenly blinding. Nudger's head snapped back and bounced off the headrest as whatever was behind them slammed into the rear of the Granada.

The steering wheel writhed in his hands and the car swayed and bucked as the right front wheel left the road. Trying to keep his grip on the sweat-slippery plastic, he fought the steering wheel, yanking it hard to the left.

The Granada bounced back onto the road and was suddenly up on its two left wheels. It crashed down with a teeth-rattling jolt and thunked level again, then finally straightened out. But the headlights grew brighter as whatever was behind them closed in again at high speed.

Nudger stomped on the accelerator. The Granada's engine snorted and rattled, but the headlights in the mirror remained the same. They were high off the road and widely spaced. He saw the dark form of what looked like a pickup truck raised to a towering height on jacked-up suspension and oversized tires. It was the kind of vehicle that might roll right over the Granada, crushing it into something unrecognizable as a car.

Nudger's stomach manufactured acid that rose into his throat. He mashed his foot down harder on the accelerator, but the headlights behind them stayed close.

"I don't need this!" he screamed. "I don't need this!"

"Shut up and drive!" Lacy snapped. "They're getting closer!"

"It's one of those monster trucks!" Nudger shouted over the roar of the engine and the wind rocketing through the open windows.

"Stamp on the accelerator! Give the car more gas!"

"I am! We have to stay on the road!"

"More gas!"

"We can't outrun it, Lacy."

"We should have brought my car!"

"We couldn't see where we were going, with a boat over our heads!"

Which gave him an idea: couldn't see where we were going.

"Canoe!" Lacy said.

"Yoo-Hoo!"

"What?"

"There's a Yoo-Hoo bottle rolling around on the floor on your side. Pick it up and toss it out the window so it hits the truck's windshield! Maybe we can blind them!"

"Very good, Nudger!" She bent low, groped around, and came up with the empty Yoo-Hoo bottle.

"Wait till they close in again, so you can't miss!" Nudger instructed.

But there was no need to wait. The big truck's engine roared angrily behind them like a beast pursuing prey, and the headlights rushed toward them.

"Aim carefully!" Nudger shouted.

Lacy extended her right arm out the window, craned her neck to keep an eye on the truck, and deftly and decisively flung the Yoo-Hoo bottle up and behind the Granada.

Immediately the truck's headlights withdrew. For an instant, in the rearview mirror, Nudger could see its windshield.

Damn! It looked okay.

"Missed!" he shouted.

"I hit it, Nudger!" Lacy corrected. She was twisted around and could see the truck directly through the rear window. "You just can't see it in the mirror. The bottle cracked the hell out of the truck's windshield!"

"Not enough!" Nudger yelled. "The driver can still see out well enough to drive. And right over the top of us."

"Then see if you can get this junk you drive to go faster!"

"Dunker Delite!"

"Huh?"

"There's a very stale, very hard Dunker Delite on the floor in a sack. Take it out and see if you can score another hit on the truck's windshield."

"That's only a doughnut, Nudger!" Lacy said incredulously.

"A Dunker Delite isn't only a doughnut, Lacy!"

She bent forward, came up with the crumpled and greasy paper bag, and removed the Dunker Delite. "This thing really is hard and heavy," she said. "It must weigh several pounds."

The mirror reflected brilliant light from closing headlights.

"Here they come again!" Nudger yelled.

Lacy repeated her maneuver, this time with the Dunker Delite instead of the Yoo-Hoo bottle.

The truck made contact with the Granada, causing it to careen as Nudger fought the steering wheel for control.

But when he glanced in the rearview mirror, he saw the headlights falling back and could see that the truck's windshield had become milky white, its shatterproof glass fragmented but still in its frame. The Dunker Delite missile had done its job and finished what the Yoo-Hoo bottle had started.

"Wha-hoo!" Lacy yelled.

Nudger got the car going in the direction of the road and accelerated. The headlights behind them fell back then veered out of sight.

"We got 'em!" Lacy shouted.

But the headlights were behind them again, distant and drawing nearer, only not so fast.

"They can't see much," Nudger said, "but they're still back there, and traveling fast."

"Let's feed 'em the damned boat!" Lacy said.

"Canoe."

She wrested her pocketknife from her jeans and opened it, then got on her knees on the front seat facing backward and began sawing at the taut ropes holding the canoe to the roof despite the wind that whirled beneath it.

"Hold on to the rope on your side," she said, and started sawing on the ropes strung through the front windows and across the inside of the car inches beneath the headliner. "They'll come at us again."

"We've gotta do this right!" Nudger said, clutching the cut rope and feeling the windblown canoe yank at it and test his grip. He slowed the car a few miles per hour.

The driver behind them took advantage of the slackened speed and a straight stretch of road. The truck speeded up. Nudger tapped the accelerator as if trying to escape another attack. They needed to be traveling fast, but not too fast.

"Let go the rope when I say!" Lacy shouted. She was holding the rope end on her side of the car with both hands, craning her neck to watch the truck close in.

Nudger built up more speed.

The truck kept coming.

"Now, Nudger!"

They released their grips on the ropes simultaneously. Nudger heard a metallic scraping sound on the car's roof as the wind beneath the canoe lifted it and momentarily held it airborne. He caught a glimpse of it in the rearview mirror, spinning sideways.

There was a loud crash behind them and the truck's headlights went dark.

On her knees again, facing backward, Lacy was bouncing up and down on the seat. "Wha-hoo!" she screamed again. "That stopped the bastards!"

Nudger's entire body was shaking.

"Game point!" Lacy yelled jubilantly, slapping the back of the seat.

Game? Nudger's heart was slam-dancing with his ribs as he kept his speed up on the dark river road, trying to put as much distance as possible between them and the disabled monster truck. His stomach was pulsating and he was nauseated. He fumbled for his roll of antacid tablets, but his hands were trembling so he couldn't remove them from his shirt pocket.

"You gotta admit it, Nudger," Lacy crowed, jabbing him in the ribs with her elbow, "that was a major rush! It was goddam great!"

Nudger admitted nothing.

"Now we don't have to return the canoe!" she said. She began laughing insanely.

What have I gotten into? Nudger wondered, concentrating on keeping the car on the dark, curved road.

Where is it taking me?

CHAPTER THIRTY-ONE

Nudger was in a canoe over Germany. Below him Berlin blazed. Tracer bullets flashed by him and Messerschmitt fighter planes roared past in tight formation and winged into a steep turn to make another pass. He put his canoe into a dive, but the canoe wasn't as fast as the Messerschmitts.

The German planes were behind him, diving faster and closing the distance, about to open fire and blast the canoe out of the sky. A terrified Nudger knew he would either be killed in the air or plunge into the dark ocean below and die on impact. He wondered which would hurt most. One of the Messerschmitts honked its horn and roared past him, its pilot, Wayne Hart, looking over at him and grinning. "Wear some clothes, you bastard!" Nudger screamed into his radio mike, and futilely hurled a Yoo-Hoo bottle at the German plane. Hart was saying something back. Nudger suddenly realized a Messerschmitt was on his tail, and he didn't have a parachute. The canoe's phone was ringing.

Nudger awoke and groped for the receiver, his eyes still closed.

" 'Lo," he muttered thickly into the phone. He found he couldn't open his eyes; they seemed to be sealed shut with gluelike mucus. " 'Lo," he said again, pressing the cool plastic receiver hard against his ear. There was a roar, and he thought the German planes were returning. That got his eyes open.

His bedroom was bright with morning sunlight swirling with dust motes. He heard the roar again, and he knew it had been made by a bus on Sutton Avenue beneath his window.

There were no German planes. He sighed with relief at not having to cope with airborne Nazis.

"Nudge? You okay?"

Hammersmith. Not Göring.

"Okay," Nudger said, rubbing his eyes with the knuckles of his free hand. "You woke me up, is all." He looked over at the clock on the nightstand and saw it was a few minutes past nine.

"I wanted to catch you before you did anything rash," Hammersmith said. "I did some more checking on Wayne Hart. He's a leading donor to Mizenty House."

"What's Mizenty House?" Nudger asked, trying to get his tongue moving so his words weren't slurred by sleep.

"Charity that helps pregnant teenagers. Some of the wealthiest people in the area support it. That could explain the young girl you saw in Hart's swimming pool."

"She didn't look pregnant," Nudger said.

"You don't look like a tough private eye."

Okay, Nudger thought, looks could deceive.

"What you saw might have been perfectly innocent," Hammersmith said.

"Not a chance."

"Be sure, Nudge. I figured I better call before you went charging in someplace and regretted it. Guys like Hart can hold a grudge."

"He was sitting around in front of the kid nude," Nudger said. "Wasn't even wearing any clothes in his plane."

"Huh?"

"Nothing. I'm saying that what I saw didn't look innocent."

"And I'm saying maybe it wasn't, but you can't do anything about it. Every year, Hart has a big fund-raising party on his estate, takes some of the big-shot donors out on the river in his boat. The fund-raiser's coming up soon. That might be why that young girl was in his pool. She might have a role in the proceedings."

"C'mon, Jack!"

"I'm just being devil's advocate, Nudge. Hart would probably say she was going to be this year's Mizenty House poster girl or some such."

"He was naked. This is St. Louis."

"Maybe you made a mistake and he had on skimpy swim trunks. Or maybe even one of those flesh-colored trunks, you know, string bikinis or whatever, that you might not have been able to see from your angle."

"Okay," Nudger said, defeated.

"Devil's advocate," Hammersmith reminded him. "I'm only trying to help you."

"I know. Thanks for the warning."

"Another thing. It looks like we got an ID on the guy who did a job on you and Lacy. He's a Serbian refugee named Ratko Djukic." Hammersmith diligently spelled the last name for Nudger. "Been in this country about six months, which is why we didn't have much on him. Still nothing official on him, but the word from the Feds is that he's a war criminal, only it can't be proved."

"How and why did he find his way to this country?"

"The how is that he was probably sponsored by someone with money and pull. I can't tell you the why, because I don't know it."

"Do the Feds know Dju—Ratko's—sponser?"

"Nope. I checked on that one myself. I didn't mean an official sponsor, Nudge, only someone who wanted Ratko in this country."

"I can guess who," Nudger said.

"But you can't prove it."

"Not now, I can't. But maybe later."

"Don't poke anything anyplace where it might get cut off, Nudge," Hammersmith warned.

"Remember Eileen?" Nudger asked. But Hammersmith had hung up.

Nudger lay back in bed, listening to traffic down on Sutton and thinking about Wayne Hart and the young girl. About Ratko the pointy-headed giant and his bowie knife. Had he been the driver of the killer truck last night? Monster truck, monster driver?

Awake and afraid and angry now, Nudger climbed out of bed. He felt helpless and probably was helpless; modern man in the modern world, aligned against goons in the employ of the untouchable, entangled in misapplied laws and facing phalanxes of attorneys with briefcases.

He showered, got dressed, and found that he was out of coffee. Decided to have orange juice instead with his buttered toast. Burned his toast so badly it was inedible. Dribbled orange juice on the front of his white shirt. Felt not at all better.

"You look like something the dog drug in, Nudge," Danny said, when Nudger entered Danny's Donuts.

"Cat," Nudger corrected, sliding onto a stool at the stainless-steel counter.

"You say black?" Danny asked, drawing a cup of sludge-like coffee from the complex, hissing steel urn.

"Yes," Nudger said, surrendering. He'd had no coffee this morning. Even Danny's would be better than . . . no, it wouldn't, but he'd drink some of it, now that it was before him on the counter like hemlock he couldn't refuse.

A few stools down from Nudger sat a very tall blonde woman who worked in one of the office buildings across the street. There was a folded *Post-Dispatch* in front of her, but she was staring morosely beyond it and dipping a Dunker Delite in a cup of acidic coffee. Nudger wondered what she'd think if she knew a similar doughnut had been used last night to help shatter a windshield. At the opposite end of the counter sat a bearded homeless man wearing a grimy red T-shirt, denim overalls, and a Cardinals baseball cap. He was simply staring at his Dunker Delite as if it puzzled him but it was food and he owed it to himself to eat it. Nudger had seen the man searching through trash receptacles along Manchester in the early morning and thought his name was Herb but wasn't sure.

"Give me six of these to go," the tall woman said, shocking Nudger.

Danny got half a dozen Dunker Delites from the display case and put them in a white paper sack that immediately became spotted with grease. A seventh Dunker Delite was plunked onto the counter on a napkin in front of Nudger.

"On me, Nudge."

Oh, God! Nudger thought.

The woman paid Danny and walked out with the sack in one hand, her purse in the other, as if to equalize the weight. She'd left her newspaper behind. Nudger stretched to the side, managed to get a hand on the folded paper, and dragged it over to him.

He sipped at his coffee and pretended to nibble at the Dunker Delite while searching through the paper.

There was no mention of a truck colliding with a canoe on Peterson Road. The result of the collision must not have been serious. Nudger didn't know if he should be disappointed.

"I'm not gonna eat this damned thing," Herb said suddenly and decisively, then climbed down off his stool and stalked out.

Danny, busy replacing Dunker Delites in the display case, didn't seem to notice.

"Got a lid for this coffee?" Nudger asked. "I'm gonna have to eat breakfast while I drive this morning."

"No problem, Nudge."

While Danny fitted a plastic lid on the foam cup and slid the Dunker Delite into a paper sack, Nudger stared out at the sunny morning beyond the shop's grease-smeared window. It seemed that not much harm could come to a person on a morning so bright.

Still, before leaving the doughnut shop, he used the pay phone to call Hammersmith and tell him where he was going.

"I know better than to try to dissuade you," Hammersmith said. "You're like a puppy tugging at a rag caught in a railroad track. That a train might be coming doesn't seem to concern you."

"The train concerns me."

"Not enough," Hammersmith said. "Phone me when you come back and let me know what happened. If you can." He let the receiver clatter in its cradle as he hung up. So annoyed with Nudger.

Nudger called Lacy at the Hostelo Grandioso. Her phone rang ten times before she picked it up. She said nothing, but he could hear her breathing.

"It's Nudger, Lacy."

222

"Did we kill the goon?"

He assumed she meant the driver of the monster truck. "Nothing in the morning papers about it, so I guess we only caused enough of an accident to stop him."

"Damn!"

"Hammersmith finally got an ID on the goon. He's one Ratko Djukic, and he wasn't in the local computer or VICAP files because he's new to the country, from Serbia."

"How'd he get to this country?"

"Somebody more or less sponsored him, is the best guess I've heard. He's also rumored to be a war criminal."

"Sounds like a sound rumor to me."

"I'm driving out to see Hart," Nudger said. "Can you meet me there in half an hour?"

She was silent again for several seconds. Then: "You still bothered by that kid we saw?"

"Among other things."

"You *are* something, Nudger. That Claudia doesn't know what she has hold of."

"Can you be there?"

"Can you keep me away?"

He didn't have to answer before hanging up.

Glancing again at the bright morning for reassurance, Nudger carried his coffee and Dunker Delite out to his car and drove toward Wayne Hart's estate.

Whenever he came to railroad crossings, he stopped and carefully looked both directions before driving on.

CHAPTER THITY-TWO

When Nudger used the intercom next to the wrought-iron gate to announce himself and Lacy at the Hart estate, there was no reply. They stood next to their cars in the morning heat and listened to the drone of insects. Two cars and a van swished past on Peterson Road. Nudger felt a bead of perspiration make its way down the side of his neck.

Then an electric motor purred and the iron gate slid to the side to admit them. They got back in their cars and drove up the long driveway toward the house.

A wiry, grinning man about fifty, wearing a neat blue suit with a small white carnation in its lapel, greeted them at the door and ushered them through a hall lined with paintings, then through an expensively furnished den and into a spacious office overlooking the pool. The paintings were mostly landscapes, with a few modern works that Nudger didn't comprehend. None of them featured prepubescent girls. They'd bypassed the room Nudger and Lacy had broken into last night.

Wayne Hart, taller than Nudger had imagined and not nude today, was standing behind a large mahogany desk. It and the rest of the furniture in the office had the patina of valuable antiques.

Twenty feet off to the side was another, smaller desk. A middle-aged woman in a beige business suit sat at it working at a computer. Despite the severe cut and shoulder pads of the suit, she appeared very round-shouldered, as if she'd sat hunched over detail work for decades.

Hart was wearing dark suit pants, a white shirt, blue suspenders, and a paisley tie. He was fat, but in the manner of a ruined athlete, with a barrel chest and wide shoulders suggesting great strength. His chubby face was puffed into a constant smile, and his eyes were made small by padded fat. Nudger wasn't surprised to see that he wore a diamond pinky ring on each hand.

"You're lucky you caught me at home and not at my downtown office," he said in his raspy, high-pitched voice. "We were preparing the guest list for next week's party."

"I thought we should talk," Nudger said.

Hart seemed to consider the suggestion, then nodded. "Willa, why don't you go to the kitchen and tell Aaron to fix you a little brunch. I'll buzz when I need you."

Willa smiled and stood up from her desk, then left the office. She was slim and held herself as erect as possible when she walked, as if trying to compensate for her rounded shoulders. Obviously not expecting to be gone long, she'd left her computer on, with its monitor displaying whatever she'd been working on when she was interrupted.

Hart didn't invite Nudger or Lacy to sit, and remained standing behind his oversized desk. "I'm not familiar with the lady," he said, nodding toward Lacy.

Lie number one, Nudger thought. He said, "She and I are partners."

"Oh? In what sort of enterprise?" Continuing the dumb act.

"Private investigation."

Hart's puffy smile widened. "Ah, what a romantic occupation! It's inspired so much great literature. Are you a Raymond Chandler fan?"

"I've read him. I'm a lot like Philip Marlowe."

"And are you like Miss Marple?" Hart asked Lacy.

"More like Mike Hammer."

"Hmm." Hart rubbed his chins.

Lacy began to wander about the spacious office, staring at objects with blatant admiration. "You're in a more lucrative business than ours, Mr. Hart. What I wouldn't give for a computer like this! How much RAM does it have?"

Hart laughed. "You'd have to ask my assistant. She's the computer genius."

Nudger helped himself to a chair that was angled to face Hart's desk. It was leather and its fat cushion hissed when he sat down. "Can I be direct?"

"It would help. Willa and I have to finish composing and printing out our guest list."

"For the Mizenty House charity affair?"

Hart looked surprised. "No, this is for a private party. Personal guests."

Nudger assumed Hart meant the Close Calls employees' annual fete that Derek at West Gallery Mall had referred to.

"Then there will be no minor-age girls at this party?"

Hart put on a puffy, puzzled look. "Whatever do you mean?"

"I think you know what I mean, or you wouldn't be bothering to talk to us."

"What I'd like to do is listen. What did you mean about minor-age girls?"

"You said the guest list had nothing to do with Mizenty

House donors, so I figured there wouldn't be any prepubescent girls present."

"I see." Hart pretended to be mollified. He had to know that Nudger and Lacy had been on his grounds and in his house last night. And he had to wonder what they might have seen. Maybe there'd been a lot to see, and that was why this conversation was allowed; Hart couldn't know how much Nudger and Lacy knew. And Nudger and Lacy couldn't know how much, if any, leverage they had on Hart.

"You mentioned being direct," Hart said, and glanced at his gold wristwatch.

"Several months ago," Nudger said, "a woman named Betty Almer died. A short while later, her father, Loren Almer, was killed in a house fire. Later still, Betty Almer's fiancée died in an auto accident. Last week, a woman named Lois Brown left me a message saying she was in danger, and shortly thereafter she died."

"Some sort of plague?" Hart asked.

"That's what we were wondering."

"Were any of these deaths suspicious?" Hart asked, frowning and feigning interest.

"Depends on who you ask. What brings us here is that in some of these deaths, including Lois Brown's, your name came up during our investigation."

"You already called me about . . . I believe his name was Brad Millman. His company put in swimming pools, and he gave me a bid."

"But you already have a pool," Nudger said, pointing behind Hart out the window toward the swimming pool, whose still, blue water was glittering in the sun.

"I didn't ask Millman's company for a bid to install a

pool," Hart explained. "I needed to have the present pool repaired. Tiles and concrete were cracked beneath the waterline and it was suffering serious leakage."

"What about Lois Brown?"

"The name doesn't strike a chord. I know nothing about her, I'm sure."

"Your name and number were in her possession, concealed as if she didn't want anyone else to see them."

"The woman sounds paranoid."

"She said she was in danger. Next thing I knew she was dead."

"One of the natural or the accidental deaths?"

"Maybe neither." Nudger decided to take a chance. "Do you know someone named Ratko Djukic?"

"Will you repeat that last name?"

Nudger did, but it came out different from his last pronunciation.

"I'm sure I've never heard of the man."

"How did you know we were talking about a man?" Nudger asked.

Hart looked at him. "Would you or anyone else name a daughter Ratko?"

"Maybe as a nickname."

Hart gazed at him with those tiny, flesh-narrowed eyes. He looked bored. He was tired of this game. Then he stood up and smoothed his tie. "Look, Mr. Nudger. Miss . . . ?"

"Tumulty," Lacy said. Nudger had almost forgotten she was in the room.

"Anyway, the two of you," Hart said. "I'd like to help, but I really am busy. I honestly know nothing about these unfortunate people or why they were aware of my name or the name of my company. But I'm a well-known person in this city. My company is well known. Couldn't you simply be looking at pure coincidence here?"

"It isn't likely," Nudger said. "I was hoping you could explain."

Hart lifted his beefy shoulders in a shrug. "Well, I can't. You seem to think there's some thread running through these accidental or natural deaths, somehow connecting me to them. It simply isn't true. And frankly I don't have time to keep telling you so." The expression in his recessed, porcine eyes hardened. "We had a break-in here last night, so I got off to a late start this morning and have a lot of work to catch up on. I'm truly sorry, but you're going to have to excuse me."

Nudger stood up from the leather chair. It hissed at him again as its cushion expanded.

"It's been a pleasure talking to you," Hart said. "If there's some way I really can help you in the future, don't hesitate to call on me." He extended his hand.

Nudger shook it. It was warm and moist. He watched while Lacy shook hands with Hart.

"There is something else," Nudger said, hesitating at the office door that had been magically opened by the same wiry man who'd ushered them through the house. "Do you know anything about a young girl . . . skinny, blonde hair, likes to swim?"

"That doesn't narrow it down very much," Hart said, his smile stuck firmly to his plump face.

"Likes to swim in your pool," Nudger amended.

Hart didn't change expression. "Could be Tanya, a distant niece. She was visiting here until this morning, but she's returned to her family in the east."

"Someone would probably notice if she came back," Nudger said.

"I would hope so," Hart said behind him, as Nudger and Lacy left the office. He sounded amused, taunting them.

When they were back outside, Lacy said, "The bastard's guilty as Adam with that girl."

"Let's drive to the Steamboat Inn and talk about it over coffee," Nudger suggested. "Even the flowers might be bugged around here."

"All of the daffodils *are* pointed toward us," Lacy observed.

"They might simply be aghast at the sight of your car."

Lacy was smiling as she climbed into her ostentatious and dated pink Caddy.

As he started the Granada and prepared to follow her back out onto Peterson Road, Nudger was glad to see that her car had left a large oil spot where it was parked in Hart's driveway.

During the drive along Peterson Road, Nudger couldn't help glancing into his rearview mirror from time to time, almost expecting to see the monster pickup truck perched high on its huge tires and charging toward him again.

But danger was far away. This was broad daylight, and there was considerable traffic moving in both directions. Witnesses to call the police. And the Steamboat Inn would no doubt have other customers.

Feeling relatively safe, he relaxed and kept and eye on the towering pink tail fins of Lacy's Caddy, wondering how she'd gotten the car past its state air pollution inspection, the way it belched oily black smoke.

"My friend wants two hundred dollars for the loss of his canoe," Lacy said, when they were seated in a Steamboat Inn booth over steaming cups of coffee.

"Sounds like a bargain," Nudger said.

"I told him a hundred. That thing wasn't much more than a hammered-out tin can. It wasn't safe to take out on the river."

"That's not how you talked about it last night."

"You on my side or his?"

"Negotiate some more. Offer him a hundred and fifty."

"That's the plan." She added more cream to her coffee and stirred it. "He'll accept it. What I need from you is a check for seventy-five dollars."

"I'll write you one soon as we leave here."

She gazed out from beneath her bangs and smiled at him, a hardened and material waif made happy by the prospect of money.

"You didn't say much in Hart's office," Nudger remarked.

She withdrew the spoon and placed it on the table next to her cup. "I didn't think you invited me along to contribute to the conversation."

"I'm not complaining," Nudger said. "It just isn't like you to be so reserved. I almost forgot you were there."

"So did Wayne Hart," Lacy said. "That's how I managed to steal the disk from his assistant's computer."

Nudger watched her take a sip of coffee.

"I want a receipt from the canoe guy," he said.

CHAPTER THIRTY-THREE

At Hostelo Grandioso, Nudger stood behind Lacy and looked over her shoulder. She'd inserted the stolen disk into her laptop computer and was trying to figure out how to view its files.

The little cabin's air conditioner was clattering and gurgling away, but Nudger was still sweating. As he watched the computer's flickering screen and listened to Lacy curse in frustration, he wondered where the pointy-headed giant with the bowie knife was keeping himself. Nudger's hope was that the man had been driving the monster truck, and the collision with the canoe had at least injured him enough to keep him out of commission for a while.

"She scores!" Lacy yelled, as she broke the code, causing Hart's guest list to appear on the computer screen.

Nudger leaned forward and with Lacy studied the names and addresses. Lacy paged down without asking Nudger if he was ready, and another five names appeared on the screen. The next to last one was Warren Tully.

"Seventeen names in all," she said. "Not so large a party you'd need an assistant to organize it."

"Hart probably uses an assistant to do anything he doesn't absolutely have to do himself," Nudger said. "And remember, some of the seventeen might bring guests."

"Still not a big party," Lacy said. She sounded disappointed at not being invited.

"Can you print out that list?" Nudger asked. "We need to check out the names."

"No printer here. I can print it out at home."

"Not worth the chance," Nudger said. "Let's copy the list in pencil, then destroy the disk. Hart probably knows it's missing by now, and knows who took it."

Lacy found a pencil and some Hostelo Grandioso stationery with a caballero-lariat logo on it. Nudger used his pen, and he and Lacy sat for about ten minutes copying the names and addresses from the computer screen onto paper.

"I'm going to get on-line and work on these names from here with my computer."

Nudger thought that was a good idea. He and Lacy each took half the names on the guest list.

"I'll go to my office and work the phone, see what I can find on these guests," Nudger said, "then I'll call you."

"Or I'll call you. With the computer, I bet I can get to a lot more information than you can using old technology like the phone."

Nudger, soon-to-be man of the previous century, thought she was probably right, but he said nothing as he folded his list of names and poked it into his damp shirt pocket.

"You better get with the high-tech world, Nudger," Lacy persisted, plugging her computer into the telephone jack near the bed. "Technophobes, guys like you who are afraid of computers, are gonna be as obsolete as Beta VCRs before long."

"I'm not a technophobe," Nudger protested.

"Like Nixon wasn't a crook." She smiled up at him. "I'd

let you stay here and work the phone, but my modem will have the line tied up."

"My office is better anyway," Nudger said. "It's hot in here. It'll run up my phone bill, but it's worth it."

"Wherever we are together," Lacy said with a wink, "it's gonna be hot."

Maybe it was because of that last remark, or maybe because it made more sense to be with Claudia than in his office, but as he turned the Granada left out of the Hostelo Grandioso's parking lot, Nudger decided to do his phone research from Claudia's apartment.

By noon the next day, Nudger and Lacy had most of the available basic information about the guests on Wayne Hart's list. Lacy was right—in a limited time and via her computer, she'd garnered much more information about the guests on her list than had Nudger about those on his. They exchanged information by fax. Nudger received and sent his faxes at Double Play, a small copy shop on Grand Avenue not far from Claudia's apartment. Lacy used the fax machine in the Hostelo Grandioso's office.

Nudger was impressed by Double Play's fax machine, and how easy it was to send and receive. After initial confusion, then brief instructions from the teenager behind the counter, he'd easily mastered the machine.

He felt like a bona fide citizen of the technological era as he walked back to the Granada with the still-hot faxes in the briefcase he'd borrowed from Claudia. He'd always thought that the generation ahead of his own, the one that had endured the Great Depression then World War Two, Korea, and the Cold War, was the most impressive American generation of the twentieth century. Behind Nudger lurked Generation X, whose members had grown up with and smoothly adjusted to the microchip world that befuddled Nudger and his ilk. It seemed to him that people between the ages of forty and sixty were stuck in the middle. Well, he would cast his lot with Generation X, even if he was thick through the midsection and breathed hard after taking a flight of stairs. He even liked Natalie Merchant, Hootie and the Blowfish, and thought Madonna could act a little. Eyes to the future!

"What do you think of Hootie and the Blowfish?" he asked Claudia, settling down on her sofa and preparing to read the information faxed to him by Lacy.

"I like Sinatra and Gershwin," Claudia said.

So did Nudger. That was a fact. All of a sudden he felt old again, like Generation Rx.

Claudia had brought in the potted plants from the balcony off the kitchen that overlooked the building's small rectangular backyard. She was pruning and watering them inside, where it was cooler.

While she busied herself with the plants, Nudger leaned back in the soft sofa, sipped Budweiser from a can, and began to read Lacy's faxes. He found himself humming "That's Why the Lady Is a Tramp."

Two hours later, when he phoned Lacy, he said, "Notice what I noticed about the guest list?"

"I did," she said. "Of the seventeen invited guests, five are like Warren Tully: within the past year they were the beneficiaries of the wills or insurance policies of men or women who died accidental deaths."

"So what does it mean?" Nudger asked.

"Couldn't tell you, Nudger. But I bet it means something." She waited for him to say something. When he didn't, she said, "What do we do with this information, take it to the cops?"

"It would interest them," Nudger said, "but not so much they would or could do anything about it."

"Even so, Nudger, you should tell Hammersmith."

"I should," he agreed. "And I will. What do you think about choosing two of the five beneficiary guests and putting loose tails on them?"

"Why only two? I know three cops who'll work off-duty tailing the other three on the list."

"We'll have to pay them," Nudger said.

"Not much, Nudger. These are guys who'll do anything for me. You might say they've been paid in advance. Not to mention that some of them are married."

Lord, Lord! Nudger thought. "City cops?"

"Two of them, yeah."

"Does Kerner know about them?"

"Kerner?"

"Dan Kerner. The Third District cop you gave the gifts to for his birthday. You remember, tiger-striped underwear, ski mask. That Kerner."

"Kerner doesn't have to know this part. Neither does Hammersmith."

"You deal with our three operatives," Nudger told her. "I don't want to have to lie to Hammersmith."

"Omissions aren't lies." She sounded annoyed. "Don't be such a superior son of a bitch, Nudger. Your inferiority complex is what I like about you."

"I'll stay just the way I am," he assured her, and hung up.

Immediately he called Hammersmith at the Third and told him about Hart's guest list, though not how it had been obtained.

"Odd," Hammersmith said, after thinking over what Nudger had said.

"More than coincidence, Jack."

"Yeah," Hammersmith agreed, "but maybe it's something easily explained. There could be something we don't know that connects these people. Maybe those beneficiary folks all have the same law firm, and the attorneys are also on the guest list."

"Seems unlikely."

"The entire world I see every day seems unlikely. Is unlikely. But I live in it. It's my reality. You really only have a hunch there's something more than coincidental about Hart's guest list. I can't sit back fat and happy like you and decide what is or isn't a hunch before I act."

"I'm not fat!" Nudger said, amazed anew by the obese Hammersmith's audacity in calling attention to someone else's weight problem. Not that Nudger had a problem yet.

"It was only a figure of speech, Nudge." But there was a gloating note in Hammersmith's voice.

"All right," Nudger said, annoyed that he'd let Hammersmith get under his skin. "The point is, I think this is more than a hunch on our part."

" 'Our'?"

"Mine and Lacy Tumulty's."

"Gee, the company you keep, Nudge. You should have stayed in the police department."

Obviously Hammersmith was having one of his off days and wanted to argue, but this time Nudger was determined to ignore the bait. And he didn't want to defend Lacy, considering how she was recruiting three of Hammersmith's officers. "My situation doesn't have anything to do with this, Jack," he said reasonably.

"If you'd stayed a cop, Nudge, you wouldn't have eaten all those doughnuts."

"I told you I wasn't fat! And I don't have an inferior—"

Click, buzz.

Hammersmith had hung up.

Arrogant bastard! Nudger thought.

But he knew better. There was probably a sound reason for Hammersmith's agitated state and protective sarcasm. And abrupt termination of phone conversations was simply a Hammersmith eccentricity. Like his toxic green cigars. Anyway, Nudger didn't have time to be petty and bear a grudge.

He hung up the phone, then scooped up the faxes and his own information and carried them into the kitchen.

"You look irritated," Claudia said.

"I'm not."

"Um," she said.

"There's something interesting here," he said.

Claudia was standing over a pot with geraniums and ferns in it that was sitting with some other potted plants on a sheet of newspaper on the kitchen floor. She brushed soil and clippings from her hands into the pot. She was barefoot, wearing shorts and a green-and-white striped cotton blouse with a pocket ripped halfway off. Her regular gardening clothes.

"Wait a minute, Nudger," she said, stooping and lifting the geranium pot. "Let me set this one back outside."

He watched her step back onto the balcony. It wasn't in the shade, and its concrete floor would be hot on her bare feet. She'd come back in soon.

He caught a glimpse of her head, her long dark hair, moving suddenly vertically and thought she was bending down with the pot.

Then he realized her head, her upper body visible through the kitchen window, had moved *straight* down.

And he heard the loud crash of iron and concrete as the balcony pulled away from the building and struck the walk below.

CHAPTER THIRTY-FOUR

Nudger dropped the faxes and bolted for the old glass double doors that led out onto the balcony. He shoved them open and almost stepped out into space two stories above the hard and jagged debris heaped against the side of the building. Here and there green plants were visible among the twisted iron and chunks of concrete.

But no body!

No Claudia!

"Nudger!"

The voice came from below him, to his left.

He craned his neck to look down and saw Claudia clinging to a bent, steel reinforcing rod protruding from the building several feet beneath where he stood.

"Don't let go, Claudia!" He lay flat on his stomach on the floor and extended his left arm toward her.

He couldn't reach her.

"I can't hold on much longer, Nudger!" She sounded exhausted and terrified.

He was rocked by a mental image of her on the unforgiving wreckage below. "Hold on! Please!"

He scrambled to his feet, his mind careening from idea to idea, none of them good enough to save Claudia before her grasp loosened on the rusty steel rod and she fell. In the true and terrible core of his mind was the unthinkable question: Did she want to live enough to hang on?

He opened the cabinet beneath the sink and found nothing other than bottles of cleanser and dishwashing detergent, a miniature plunger whose handle wasn't long enough to make up the distance he was short of being able to clasp Claudia's hand and wrist and pull her to safety.

"I called them!" someone yelled from the backyard below. "I called the fire department!"

Nudger knew the fire department wouldn't get here in time. They dealt in minutes, not seconds.

Then he noticed the spray nozzle protruding from the back of the sink near the faucet handles. He grabbed it and pulled hard. Its rubber hose unreeled about four feet. More than long enough! With a mighty yank, he broke the hose from its moorings. Water sprayed from the sink toward the ceiling.

Carrying the hose and nozzle, Nudger returned to the gaping space beyond the open double doors. He lay down again on the floor, feeling the coolness of water beneath him now. Leaning as far out as possible, he swung the nozzle end of the rubber hose toward Claudia. She released her grip on the rod for a moment with one hand and caught it.

"Wrap the hose around your wrist!" Nudger told her.

When she'd done so, he crammed his shoulder against the door frame and slung his body sideways, bracing with his right foot on the opposite side of the door. He didn't want to fall out himself. He looped his end of the thick rubber hose around his right hand, then clutched it with both hands.

"Okay!" He shouted, summoning his strength. "Let go of the rod with your other hand and I'll pull you in."

"You sure, Nudger?"

Half a dozen people, one of them a man he recognized who lived downstairs, were standing in the yard staring up at them. "Better do what he says," the man said. "We'll try and catch you if you fall."

"That won't work," a teenage boy said. "She'll bust like an egg."

Jesus! Nudger thought.

"Nudger?"

"Let's try it, Claudia. Claudia?"

Abruptly she released her grip on the rod and her entire weight swung beneath him on the length of rubber hose, almost pulling his arms from their sockets. His body slid on the wet floor and he thought he might slip into space and fall with Claudia. Desperately he shoved with his foot and shoulder, stiffening his body and wedging himself tighter in the doorway.

He stopped sliding. Claudia hung suspended on the taut, stretched hose. Motion ceased.

He began to pull on the hose.

Beneath him, Claudia braced her bare feet against the building's brick wall and began to climb as he drew up the hose hand over hand, each time wrapping it around his right wrist that was by now numb.

"Can't make it, Nudger!" Claudia gasped, when she was only a few feet beneath him.

"Can, too!" Nudger shouted at her. He tugged harder at the hose. "Can, too!" He could see her bare feet bleeding from contact with the rough concrete where the balcony had torn away from the building, the blood red and vivid.

Her left hand slipped an inch or two down the hose, and frantically he pulled harder, drawing her toward him.

"Hang on, dammit!"

She said nothing. He could hear her desperate, rasping breathing.

One of her hands found his wrist and tried to wrap around it, but her fingers slipped off and she almost dropped.

"Claudia!" He made his right arm rigid, released the hose with his left hand, and grasped her right wrist as she clutched his.

This time she held.

He shifted his body, felt her left hand close around the hose near where he was gripping it.

"Pull, Nudger!" There was fire and determination in her voice now. She had a chance to live! She wanted to live!

He gritted his teeth and braced himself harder. Heard himself whimper as he used all his remaining strength and will to draw her to him, up, up to safety.

Up!

Up and in!

Her body was lying across his now, most of her weight pressing down on him. She released his wrist, moved her hand quickly and grabbed the edge of the door frame. She pulled, kicking with both legs, while he rolled to the side to help her.

And her weight shifted over him.

And they were both inside, lying on the edge of nothing.

"Wow! Maximum!" shouted the kid below. "Just like on TV!"

Then everyone down in the backyard was yelling. Suddenly they started to applaud.

Nudger didn't have the strength to take a bow even if he'd wanted to. He lay next to Claudia, between her and death now, and listened to the shrill, approaching sirens of the fire department emergency crew.

They were too late, but who could blame them? Probably they didn't even know what kind of call they were answering. Where's the fire? they were probably wondering, searching the sky for smoke. Where's the fire?

In my chest, Nudger thought, struggling to catch his breath.

An air horn sounded and an engine roared as the hook and ladder unit racketed around the corner onto Wilmington.

Nudger sat next to Claudia's bed in Incarnate Word Hospital and listened to the nurse's squeaky soft-soled shoes as she bustled about and arranged covers and medical paraphernalia. Claudia lay propped up on two pillows. There was a white disposable ice pack on her forehead. Beneath the thin sheet, her feet were bandaged where she'd kicked and scraped her toes against rough brick and concrete. Her right hip was badly bruised where she'd banged it against the wall, and one of her hands was cut and bandaged, injured from gripping the rusty concrete reinforcement rod that had saved her life.

"She'll be fine," the young, sincere nurse said to Nudger, then *eep-eeped* out of the room.

Nudger had been assured of the same thing half an hour ago by the doctor who'd treated Claudia. No serious injury, but something had struck her in the head, or she'd given it a bad bump, though there was no concussion. And the X rays of her bruised hip were inconclusive and had to be taken again. So they wanted to keep her overnight.

"Head hurt?" he asked softly. His voice didn't seem to carry well in the cool room.

"No." Her dark eyes shifted to look at him from beneath the soft white edge of the ice pack. She was on pain medication and not thinking exactly straight. "Nothing hurts. You saved me, Nudger."

"We did it together," he said.

"You're modest."

"Yeah, I guess I am."

"Don't be nauseating, Nudger."

"Whatever you say."

"I say I'm woozy. How long they plan on keeping me in here."

"Overnight at least."

"Tha's 'kay with me."

"What did they give you for pain?"

"Don' know. Like it, though . . ." She closed her eyes.

"Claudia?"

"Be here when I wake up, Nudger . . ."

"I was going to tell you I would be."

Her chest rose and fell evenly beneath the sheet and she began snoring lightly.

Other than that, it was quiet in the room except for the faint background rush of traffic out on Grand Avenue. Sounds of people living out their lives. The way Claudia and Nudger would be able to live out theirs.

Nudger stood up, stretched, then wandered out into the corridor.

He stopped and stood just outside the door to Claudia's room. The huge, fleshy form of Hammersmith was advancing on him. Hammersmith moved with the odd grace of fat men who had once been thin and possessed underlying strength; he seemed almost to be gliding through the air, only touching down to steer with his comparatively small and shiny black shoes.

"How's she doing, Nudge?" he asked, when he was close to Nudger.

"Okay. She isn't seriously hurt, and she's asleep. They've got her on some kind of pain medication that acts like opium."

"Can I look in on her?"

"Sure, but she won't know it."

Hammersmith poked his head into Claudia's room, jutting his rounded rear end out, then backed away and closed the door. Nudger remembered when Hammersmith had been slim and sleek and could charm female suspects into confessions or informing on lovers or cohorts. Too many years ago. He and Nudger had both changed, inside and out.

"The fire department says the balcony broke away because the concrete was old and cracked around the rerods," Hammersmith said.

"Rerods?"

"That's what construction guys call those round reinforcing rods, like the one Claudia grabbed onto. Over time, the concrete gets weathered or chipped away around them, and if they're used for structural support, they can bend or lose contact, and whatever they're helping hold up can come down. Remember when the Kingshighway viaduct collapsed a few years back?"

Nudger nodded. At two in the morning, fortunately when no one was around to be killed or injured, tons of concrete had suddenly roared down. It had taken the city months to dispose of the rubble, and now there was a new Kingshighway viaduct, improbably but beautifully lined with countless decorative street lights.

"Same thing," Hammersmith said. "Old concrete structure, and its time came." He squinted at Nudger with his cop's cool gray eyes. "There's nothing suspicious about this, Nudge. The other balconies on Claudia's building are the same way, real safety hazards. The owner's gonna have to remove or rebuild them all."

Nudger wiped his hand down his face. He was perspiring even after sitting in the cool hospital room with Claudia. "You really believe that balcony collapsed by itself?"

"In an official capacity, I have to believe it."

"What do you believe in an unofficial capacity?"

"I doubt that this had anything to do with anything, Nudge. Accident's occur."

"Sounds like a bumper sticker."

"Bumper stickers are the philosophy of our age, Nudge. And Claudia's building is old enough to have developed structural problems. It was built in nineteen twenty-five."

"With those balconies?"

"Well, that I don't know. Maybe they were added later. Say, during the depression." Hammersmith fingered three of his horrible green cigars protruding in cellophane wrappers from his white shirt pocket. "But if you isolate this incident, it has every earmark of being an accident."

"I don't believe it."

"You don't have to. You're a private citizen, Nudge. You can believe it was a ray from a UFO did the deed."

"I'll at least check and see if there was a sighting nearby," Nudger said. "Got time for a cup of coffee?"

Hammersmith glanced at his wristwatch. "Sure, as long as Claudia's asleep. She going home tomorrow?"

"It looks that way."

"It wouldn't hurt if she stayed here a couple of days. For her own protection."

"I thought you said the balcony collapsing was an accident."

"I think it was, Nudge. But nothing in life is sure. Dracula never really died, and we have the option of going to prison instead of paying taxes."

"Are you operating on a hunch instead of the facts?" Nudger asked, remembering their earlier phone conversation.

"On friendship," Hammersmith said, shaming him.

Nudger bought two cups of coffee from a vending machine in a nook down the hall and was quiet. He figured Hammersmith must have been on some kind of debating team in school.

When Hammersmith had gone and he was sure Claudia was safe and down for the night, Nudger left the hospital.

Before driving home, he stopped by his office and picked up the day's mail. He drove with one hand and riffled through the stack of bills, coupons, and advertisements with the other. A square, dark blue envelope near the bottom of the pile made him pause. He remembered a stack of such envelopes on Willa's desk, in Wayne Hart's home office.

When Nudger opened the envelope and examined its contents in the light of the traffic signal at Manchester and Sutton, he was surprised to find he'd received an invitation to Wayne Hart's party.

CHAPTER THIRTY-FIVE

The invitation mailed to my apartment doesn't say party," Lacy told Nudger the next morning over the phone, "it says soiree."

"That just means they'll serve croissants." Nudger turned up the air conditioner in the window near his desk, then settled back in his chair.

"Are we going?" Lacy asked.

"After what happened yesterday, we're definitely going." He told her about Claudia almost being killed when her apartment balcony gave way.

"She gonna be okay?" Lacy asked, sounding genuinely concerned.

"The doctors say so."

"You think the balcony collapse was a murder attempt, Nudger?"

"I don't know for sure. What do you think?"

"Don't know. Maybe we can gain some insight at Wayne Hart's soiree. Though we should be insulted; we weren't on the original guest list, so our invitations were mere afterthoughts. And since the party's tonight, I don't have much time to find something attractive to wear that'll conceal a gun."

"Stop trying to talk like you're Kinsey Milhone."

"Who's that?"

"A character in a series of books Claudia reads. Female private investigator."

"No kidding? There are more of me?"

"No," Nudger said, "not of you. Have you talked to anyone at National Triad about them saving half of Millman's life insurance money and splitting it with us?"

"Sure. I told you, leave that to me and don't worry about it. I've been with a young exec there name of Lance Cintamon and I know we can work a deal."

Nudger wondered just what Lacy meant by 'been with' but didn't ask.

"You going to see Claudia today?"

"Soon as I hang up," Nudger said.

"Tell her I hope she'll be okay."

"I will." He was surprised by this bit of civility from Lacy.

"Better not tell her we've got a date tonight."

Lacy was laughing when she hung up.

Incorrigible.

Claudia was sitting up in bed eating breakfast when Nudger entered her room at Incarnate Word.

"They want to keep me another day," she said, around a mouthful of scrambled eggs.

"Good idea."

She took a sip of what looked like tea. "I feel good enough to go home. Besides, I'm not sure my insurance will cover another day."

"I'll talk to the doctor about that," Nudger said.

"Talk to him about me going back to my apartment." She sounded adamant. He knew he had a problem.

"We'll see what he says. They look at those X rays of your hip again?"

"Not that I know of."

"Then you should stay here. For all you know, you've got a hairline fracture."

"It's probably just a bruise." She finished her eggs and wiped her lips with a napkin.

"You look beautiful," Nudger told her, "even without makeup and with bruises."

"You sound like a sadist. Go see if you can find that doctor—Shirehap or something is his name—and tell him I'm ready to be checked out."

"You've got it backward," Nudger said, concerned about her, sure, but at the same time getting a little aggravated by her attitude. "It's the doctor who tells *you* if you're ready."

"I know how I feel."

And he knew the uselessness of arguing with her. He stood up from his chair and tucked in his shirt where it had worked out above his belt at his sides. "I'll go see about those X rays."

"Nudger?" she said, her voice softer. "I'm sorry about my mood, the way I talked to you, but I really do feel better."

"Good." He walked over and kissed her on the forehead, as she had a bit of scrambled egg stuck to her lower lip.

"You want me here because you're worried about me, right?"

"Of course."

"I mean, you think my balcony falling might not have been an accident."

"I have my doubts," he told her.

She stared at him as if seriously considering his position.

"I still need to get out of here," she said.

He left to see if he could find the doctor.

One of the nurses directed Nudger to a small nook with a chair and a potted plant in it and he heard her page a Dr. Sirak. He sat and waited, watching patients in varying degrees of pain or discomfort pass in their hospital robes, sometimes aided by visiting friends or relatives. A man with a heavily bandaged head was rolled past on a gurney, his eyes closed and a peaceful expression on his face. The nurse and uniformed attendant pushing the gurney were smiling as if they'd just shared a joke. Nudger wondered if the man had died and they hadn't noticed.

Within five minutes a dark-haired man with sensitive brown eyes, wearing a rumpled green surgical gown and carrying a sheaf of bulging file folders, approached Nudger. On the breast of the gown was a plastic name tag that said he was DR. JOSEPH J. SIRAK, JR.

Nudger stood up from the chair and introduced himself. Dr. Sirak waited patiently for him to get to the point.

"I'm a friend of one of your patients, Claudia Bettencourt."

"I recognize you now from yesterday," Dr. Sirak said. "Do you want to know her condition?"

"Something more than that, Doctor. You see, there's good reason to think she's safer here in the hospital than at home. The accident that injured her . . . well, it might not have been an accident."

Dr. Sirak regarded Nudger calmly with unblinking eyes. "Have you reported this to the police?"

"Yes, of course. They, uh . . ."

"Don't believe you?"

"Not exactly that," Nudger said. "It's more that there's insufficient evidence. At least as far as they're concerned."

Sirak sighed and shifted his weight. He smiled at Nudger. "You're obviously very much concerned about Miss Bettencourt," he said. "What exactly do you want, Mr. Nudger?"

"For you to convince her she should stay in the hospital for another day."

"All right."

Nudger was surprised. "Huh?"

"I was going to keep her over anyway, Mr. Nudger. The new X rays on her hip are inconclusive. Probably she's fine, but it would be wise to take precautions."

"A third X ray?"

"No, that isn't necessary. I want a specialist I know to interpret both sets of X rays."

"Will there be any problem with her insurance?"

"Tell her not to worry. I'll take care of that."

Nudger grinned and pumped Dr. Sirak's hand. "I appreciate this, Doctor. It takes a lot of worry off me."

Dr. Sirak shook his head. "Don't think I'm varying my treatment of a patient because you asked me to, Mr. Nudger. I wouldn't keep her over if I didn't think it desirable."

"Of course not." Nudger resisted the urge to wink.

"I'm serious. We're dealing with medical insurance here. Nobody diddles Blue Aide."

"Wouldn't want to," Nudger said hastily.

Dr. Sirak tucked his chin in and looked at Nudger the way a traffic-court judge once had, after Nudger pleaded innocent to reckless driving and explained that he'd swerved his car to avoid running over a stray kitten.

It had been true, but Nudger had been found guilty and had to pay a fine.

"I'll go talk to her now," Dr. Sirak said, and walked away in the direction of Claudia's room.

Nudger stayed the rest of that day with Claudia, slumped in the chair near her bed, reading the same *People* and *Reader's Di-*

gest over and over. Claudia slept most of the time. He suspected the nurse had given her a sedative to keep her from being restless and demanding.

He didn't leave the hospital until five that evening, when he drove to his apartment to shower and dress for Wayne Hart's soiree.

When he walked into his apartment his phone was ringing. He picked it up, said hello, and found himself talking to Lacy.

Or rather, listening.

"No sense taking two cars tonight, Nudger. Want me to swing by your place and pick you up on the way to Wayne Hart's?"

Nudger cringed, seeing himself and Lacy arriving at Hart's plush party in her haughtily finned pink Cadillac convertible.

"I'll pick you up," he said.

"Okay, great! I can hardly wait."

He didn't like her tone. "This isn't a teenage date, Lacy."

"Claudia doing okay?"

"She's better, thanks."

"I think you're gonna love my dress, Nudger."

Nudger chewed an antacid tablet after he hung up. He could never be sure if Lacy was putting him on.

People like that dealt in the unexpected.

They were like throw rugs waiting to be tripped over.

They made him uneasy.

CHAPTER THIRTY-SIX

When he pulled up in the Granada in front of her decrepit cottage at the Hostelo Grandioso, Lacy must have seen him through the window. The door opened immediately and she stepped outside.

She was wearing an impossibly tight black dress made out of some kind of crinkly material. On her feet were black spike-heeled shoes that made Nudger wonder if she'd need her cane again to walk. The dress had a low neckline and a high hemline. Her short dark hair was fashionably mussed, and she'd made a pass at elegance with a simple string of pearls around her neck.

"You look nice," Nudger said, when she got in the car, thinking she looked as if she might be on her way to practice the oldest profession.

She thanked him for the compliment and scooted over on the seat, showing a lot of leg, so she could close the door.

"Like the dress?" she asked, as he made a left turn out of the parking lot.

"Sure." He was telling her the truth, in a way; what he especially liked about it was that it made it clear there was no place she might be concealing a gun.

"You look nice, too," she said. "At first glance the spots on your tie aren't noticeable. And isn't it a little warm for a corduroy sport jacket?"

"The spots on my other jacket, along with the ones on my tie, might be too busy."

They drove in silence for a while.

Finally Nudger said, "Claudia's coming home from the hospital tomorrow morning. She might have a slight problem with her hip, but she probably only has some cuts and bruises that will heal within a few weeks."

"Claudia who?" Lacy asked.

Nudger was sure she was going to cause trouble tonight.

A white-jacketed security guard stood by the black wrought-iron gate to the Hart estate. He stared dubiously at the rusty Granada, but after Nudger gave him their names and showed the invitations, the guard used a sender on his belt to make the gate glide open.

Nudger drove the Granada along the driveway toward the house until he ran out of room and had to park at the end of a line of cars. Some of the parked cars were luxury models, Mercedeses, BMWs, and Cadillacs unlike Lacy's. But others were almost as old as Nudger's car, though they were sporty models and were in much spiffier condition.

He and Lacy got out of the Granada and followed another uniformed security guard's directions along a lighted flagstone path to the back of the sprawling house, where a white canopy was erected over an area where about twenty people were standing around talking, munching on hors d'oeuvres and sipping drinks from a bar set up at the far end of the canopy. Everything was illuminated by soft floodlights that for some reason attracted no insects. The women were dressed up, and all of the men had on suits or sport jackets. Nudger saw that his was the only corduroy coat there, all right. Music for elevator listening was seeping softly from concealed speakers.

"I'm glad you two could come," a high, raspy voice said.

Wayne Hart was suddenly standing in front of them. He was wearing a dark blue suit, black shirt and a red and blue ascot, and, incongruously, blue-and-white Nike jogging shoes. In his pudgy right hand was what appeared to be scotch or bourbon mixed with water in a heavy glass with a pebbled base.

"It's beautiful here," Lacy said. "I've never seen it at night."

Hart smiled as if in pain. "The reason for my invitations was to settle whatever suspicions you might have about me and this place. You seem to have gotten the idea that something illicit is going on here, and it simply isn't so."

One of the security people caught Hart's eye and motioned to him.

"Excuse me," Hart said. He put on a fat-padded smile. "Help yourselves to something to eat and drink. Mingle and talk. Enjoy. Please."

He hurried away to attend to host duties.

"There's one of the beneficiaries," Lacy said, pointing toward Warren Tully as Nudger and Lacy walked beneath the shelter of the taut white canopy. The music was louder there, but still unobtrusive.

"It's not so much the five beneficiaries who interest me," Nudger said, "it's the other twelve names on the guest list."

"We'll have a chance to see them here," Lacy said, "along with their guests."

A waiter approached them with a tray of hors d'oeuvres. Lacy took a miniature sandwich, Nudger a spiced meatball skewered with an oversized toothpick. As they made their way toward the bar, nodding and smiling at people, he increased his estimate of the number of guests to about twenty-five. Several men did an admiring double take when Lacy and her dress passed by. Several women gave her different kinds of looks. Nudger didn't know whether to feel proud or ashamed to be seen with her.

He and Lacy got glasses of white wine at the bar. Beyond the bar, the lawn sloped away. There were lights and activity down at the dock, and lights on the big cabin cruiser were glowing.

"Let's separate and mingle," Nudger said.

"I'll mingle," Lacy said, "but I prefer to stay in one piece."

While Nudger was thinking about that, she walked away from him. He wished she wouldn't wriggle so much, but maybe it was her injuries, causing her to limp slightly in the preposterously spike-heeled shoes.

He wandered about and introduced himself, engaging in self-conscious small talk; the night was perfect, the grounds were beautiful, the spicy meatballs were delicious, though somehow he'd spotted his tie with their sauce. He shook hands with a man named Craighower, whose fingers were calloused from his work as a carpenter for one of the big residential building firms in town. After Craighower he met Jim Partridge, who he knew was a former arson investigator who'd been dismissed by the city five years ago, suspected of stealing from the debris of burned buildings. A bespectacled man with a full gray beard and a tweedy coat as out of season as Nudger's jacket introduced himself as Clyde Bolton and was exactly what he appeared to be, a retired physics professor.

Nudger saw Lacy talking to a group of five men, who were all grinning and staring at her as if she were a delightful alien who'd just dropped from the sky. They were flirting furiously with her; Nudger knew she was only pretending to flirt. Well, he hoped that was the case . . .

The innocuous music suddenly ceased. "We set sail in ten minutes," declared Hart's raspy voice over the speaker system. "More drinks and hors d'oeuvres on board."

"Will that boat hold all of us?" Nudger heard a woman ask.

"Sure," a man said. "*Blue Destiny* is an oceangoing yacht. Hart sometimes takes it all the way downriver and out into the gulf."

Nudger was relieved to hear that. The boat didn't look all that large to him, either. But maybe there was a deceptive amount of room below deck.

He and Lacy made their way down toward the dock.

Before descending the rough-hewn wooden steps, she stopped and touched Nudger's arm.

"I'm not going," she said softly.

"Lacy—"

"We don't want to argue about it here," she said, stepping aside to let a man and woman pass. "As far as you know, I'm on board the boat."

Before he could say anything else, she drifted off into darkness.

He caught sight of her for just a moment, crossing a lighted area of yard up near the house. He recognized her slight limp, but she appeared to have removed her spike-heeled shoes.

Not liking this turn of events, he boarded the big cabin cruiser. Hoo-boy! Nudger's stomach became queasy even though the boat was still moored and merely bobbing gently at the dock.

On deck level, just below the bridge, was a surprisingly large lounge with a bright blue carpet and curtains, and a gleaming mahogany bar at one end. Most of the guests had found their way into the lounge and were standing about, some of them talking and laughing as they eased toward the bar, where a brawny man in a white jacket was filling their orders for drinks.

A ship's bell bonged three times. Apparently that was some kind of joke known to some of the guests, because a few of them laughed about it. Then almost all of them laughed; wanting to be among the in people. The bell was also a signal that the boat was pulling away from the dock. What had been a low rumble became louder as the powerful diesel engines churned water with their twin screws. The lounge tilted slightly as the boat's bow lifted, and Nudger's stomach lurched. He was afraid of what might happen when the boat got well out into the river.

Music began seeping from speakers mounted around the lounge. Johnny Mathis began to croon. Nudger found himself standing by the bar and ordered a club soda, hoping it would help settle his stomach. After a couple of sips, he felt sicker.

Craving fresh air, he elbowed his way through the crowded lounge and went back on deck. Half a dozen others were out on deck, leaning on the rail, watching the lights on shore glide past as the boat made its way downstream. The big diesels were rumbling softly again, letting the current do the work. Ahead of them, off to the right, Nudger could see a glow in the sky that must have been the lights of downtown St. Louis.

Next to him, a woman remarked on what a neat ship Hart had.

"It's a boat," the man with her said. "The way you can tell a ship from a boat is that a ship is big enough to carry a boat. This one is towing a dinghy."

"Dinky?" Nudger asked, curious.

"Dinghy," the man said with mock patience. He was a chesty guy with a bald head and seemed eager to show off his superior knowledge in front of the woman. "It's a little boat, like a rowboat, towed by a bigger boat like this. It's used to explore small tributaries or to go to shore wherever this boat can't dock because of its size."

Nudger looked far back into the night and saw a small boat riding the water at the end of a long tow line.

"We're going to explore a tributary in that dinky?" the woman with the bald man asked.

He turned away from Nudger, putting his arm around the woman's waist. "Dinghy," he corrected. Then he leaned closer and whispered something in her ear and she giggled.

The diesels continued their steady rumble and the river rushed and slapped against the hull as the boat gently rocked. And rocked and rocked.

Hating himself for this—becoming seasick not even on an ocean but on a river—Nudger leaned with both elbows on the rail. He took deep breaths of the river air, trying to settle his stomach.

Nausea assailed him in ocean-sized waves. Along with fear, because his seasickness incapacitated him.

He knew there were no sharks in the river. But he also knew there were some *on* it, as ravenous and vicious as their ocean counterparts.

And he stood among them.

CHAPTER THIRTY-SEVEN

Lacy stayed concealed behind some bushes near the corner of the house and watched *Blue Destiny* veer away from the dock and head downriver. For a minute or so she could hear music wafting from it, then the sound faded on the river breeze, and the boat's lights passed beyond a bend.

She wasn't sure what she might find in the house, but she *was* sure this was the ideal time to look. Everyone other than the caterers, dutifully cleaning up, was out on the boat. And after the last time she and Nudger had entered the house, Hart wouldn't imagine either of them had the nerve to try again so soon.

She left the cover of the foliage and walked toward the patio and French doors where she and Nudger had tried to enter the last time they were here. If anyone from the catering company happened to notice her, they wouldn't see anything suspicious, merely one of the guests, the attractive—Lacy smiled—woman they'd no doubt noticed in the sexy black dress, strolling along the grounds.

The French doors were locked this time, too.

But Lacy was sure that with all the guests and help wandering around the estate this evening, the alarm system would be turned off.

She removed the contents of her little sequined black handbag—tissues, chewing gum, a pen light, and a package of condoms—and fit the tiny purse over her fist like a glove, then punched out the pane of glass near the latch. It was the first time she'd found one of those glittery little evening bags really useful.

Without hesitation, she reached in, unlocked the doors, and pushed inside the house.

Despite her pounding heart, she was happy to breathe cooled air and feel some of the perspiration start to evaporate on her damp skin. When she was sure she was alone, she stuffed her small and scant possessions back into her evening bag and tried to see where she was.

The room was dark, like most of the house, and she didn't dare switch on a light. Avoiding the hulking shapes of furniture and what looked like sculpture, she made her way across the room, then out into a dark hall. There she fished her penlight out of her bag and flashed its narrow yellow beam around.

This was a different hall from the one she and Nudger had been in during the last break-in. The vast house must be a labyrinth.

Shielding the beam with her hand, she moved slowly along the corridor, trying one closed door after another.

Each door was locked, which was odd.

But one of the doors, near the end of the hall, had at its base a horizontal bar of light. Half of the bar dimmed, then brightened again.

Someone was in that room.

Lacy approached the door carefully and tried the knob.

This door was locked like the others.

She pressed her ear to the door and could hear voices.

At first she thought there were several people in the room, talking excitedly, interrupting each other. She strained to hear.

Then she recognized one of the voices as belonging to Wilma Flintstone.

And there was Fred.

Yabadabadoo, she thought.

She had an idea who might be inside the room. She knocked softly on the door, hoping it wasn't an adult nostalgia buff watching the Flintstones.

The voices died and there was only silence for a long time.

Lacy knocked again.

"Who is it?"

A young girl's voice—Lacy was sure. Very young. "Tanya?"

"What?"

"I need to come in and talk to you," Lacy said softly.

"You can't. It's against the rules."

"Unlock the door," Lacy pleaded. "Please!"

"That's against the rules, I told you."

"Is anyone in there with you?" Lacy was reasonably sure there wouldn't be, with the door locked.

A pause. Then: "No."

"Then break the rules," Lacy urged. "Neither of us will ever tell. I want to help you, Tanya. Do you understand?"

"I don't have a key. I can't unlock the door."

Lacy thought about kicking the door open, but her legs were still unsteady, and she might reinjure her heels. By the beam of her penlight, she examined the door. It was an old six-panel creation, not particularly thick and strong. And its hardware would be old and weak, possibly fastened with rusty screws.

Possibly.

"Stand back away from the door," she instructed softly.

There was no answer.

Hoping the girl was out of the way, Lacy drew a deep breath, stepped back against the wall opposite the door, and flung herself at it.

Bounced off it.

"Damn!" she said, holding her shoulder.

But through her pain she'd felt the door give slightly, and she hadn't made much noise.

She picked up the narrow runner on the hall floor and folded it several times. Using it for a pad over her still throbbing shoulder, she ran at the door again.

It gave again.

Lacy tried again.

Again.

And the door flew open.

The girl who'd been at the pool was standing near a large-screen TV that was now silently playing a *Flintstones* cartoon video. She was wearing a yellow T-shirt, white shorts, and pink rubber thongs. The room held a canopy bed, a white dresser and vanity, pink curtains, and a doll collection in a tall bookcase. A girl's room.

"Are you a relative of Mr. Hart?" Lacy asked, making herself smile at Tanya, who up close looked about ten or twelve years old.

Tanya didn't appear afraid. Her expression was neutral, as if she might be in mild shock. And her eyes didn't look quite right, her pupils slightly enlarged. Lacy wondered if she was drugged.

"Do you live here?" Lacy asked.

"Right now I do. I . . ." Her gaze wandered and she looked confused. Lacy recognized that unblinking hesitancy. She was sure the girl was drugged.

She moved toward her to hug her. "I want you to come with me, honey."

"I don't think so," a deep voice said.

Lacy turned to see the pointy-headed giant, Ratko, standing in the doorway. He was wearing faded Levi cutoffs and was shirtless and shoeless. His eyes were bloodshot and swollen, as if he'd just awakened. There was a large gauze bandage taped over his right side, and his left arm was in a sling. So he had been driving the monster truck the night of the attack on Peterson Road.

"Have an accident?" Lacy asked, backing away.

The giant didn't say no thanks, just had one. Lacy lost some respect for him, but the memory of what he'd done to her was still vivid and crippling. On quaking legs, she backed away from him.

Grinning with his peculiar pointed teeth, he reached around to a sheath at the small of his back and drew his huge bowie knife.

"I'm going to cut farther up this time," Ratko said. "And farther in." He had an accent but spoke English well enough to be easily understood.

He stepped past Tanya, who was standing and staring with her mouth open, and casually shoved her back against a wall. She sank to the floor and curled up tightly, staring down at the carpet.

"I know you don't have a gun anywhere on you, in that dress," Ratko said to Lacy. He blatantly leered at her.

"Don't underestimate an American woman," she warned.

He shrugged. "It means something special that you're an American?"

"Yes."

"So, you're patriotic. That makes no difference. Where I come from patriotism is a disease—people catch it and almost always they die."

"Get out of here!" Lacy yelled at Tanya. "Run, honey!"

The girl didn't move.

"She only does what she's told," Ratko explained. "She's been well trained. Not like you at all. Now I'll show you what happens to women like you who think they are special because they're patriotic."

He lowered himself into a crouch and moved to the side, cutting off any hope Lacy had of reaching the door.

What she reached was a Suzy Doll on the shelf near the bed. She recognized Suzy from when she was the hottest-selling toy two Christmases ago. Suzy had big hair and big boobs and was, all in all, a healthy, hefty girl. Lacy hurled her at Ratko's injured arm.

He grinned wider and spun away, but not quite fast enough. Suzy struck his bandaged ribs.

The grin disappeared and he grunted in pain.

"For that you will pay," he said.

Lacy hurled another doll from the collection at him and he danced aside, causing her to miss. That was okay. She'd only wanted to distract him for a moment while she hiked up her skirt and bent to tear loose the gun that was taped snugly against her inner thigh.

Ratko appeared stunned when he focused his gaze on her again and she was aiming a gun at his bare chest.

Then he grinned, letting her know the gun made no difference and he was still in control. He deliberately dropped his knife on the floor so that he was unarmed, then spread his huge arms wide.

"I don't think you want to use that gun," he said, slowly advancing on her. "You are a beautiful and gentle woman who could never harm an unarmed human being. I can tell that from the lilt in your voice and the softness in your eyes."

Gee, he was convincing, a giant with the soul of a poet.

"I know that look," he continued. "My mother had that same softness and goodness on her face and in her heart. She could deliberately hurt no one. As you can't. The gun is heavy and shaking because you are one of the lovely and compassionate lambs of the world, not one of those who would inflict pain. You can't change what you are. You're trembling. It is impossible for you to squeeze that trigger." He smiled and extended his hand for the gun.

"You guys who can turn it on and off amaze me," Lacy said, and shot him six times.

CHAPTER THIRTY-EIGHT

Feeling not at all better, Nudger straightened up from the rail. He saw that the lights of downtown St. Louis were closer now, and he wondered when Hart was going to turn the boat around and head back upriver.

The river seemed rougher out here in the middle, and Nudger didn't think he'd be able to stand his seasickness much longer without doing something embarrassing. He pried another antacid tablet off the roll he'd brought with him and popped it into his mouth and chewed. It didn't seem to help. Nothing seemed to help. His stomach continued its nauseating rock and roll.

If only he knew that soon the boat would be going back, he could find comfort in anticipating the end of his agony. Bumping into the fat bald man with his arm around the girl, Nudger pushed away from the rail and ignored their hostile glares. He lurched along the deck toward the lounge, hoping to find Wayne Hart or a bathroom, whichever came first.

But he could find neither.

Finally a man in a white uniform, whom Nudger assumed must work on the boat, grinned at him and pointed toward a small passageway. "Head's down there," he said, and hurried on his way.

Nudger wondered what the man had meant. 'Head man,' maybe. Hart.

He ducked low and made his way along the passageway.

Soon he was overjoyed to find a bathroom. But before he could enter, a woman in a blue dress smiled at him and squeezed in ahead of him.

Nudger stood swaying out in the corridor, or passageway, or whatever. He wasn't in the mood to guess at nautical nomenclature. He put his right arm out and braced himself against the motion of the boat. To his left was a narrow door labeled LIFE PRESERVERS. That was clear enough. He saw that the door was unlatched, opened it, and found a tall, narrow cabinet—empty.

His mind began to turn despite his seasickness. Fear found its way into his discomfort. Or maybe it was his nausea that was keeping him from thinking clearly. Maybe he was being an alarmist.

Still, he couldn't ignore the possibility that the terrible thought that had crept into his mind like an unwanted, dangerous stranger might be right. Too many signs pointed to it: the missing life preservers, the guest list, the nighttime excursion, even Hart's uncharacteristic and impractical dark suit on such a warm night.

Forgetting about the bathroom, he made his way back up on deck, then to the boat's stern. He gazed back into the night.

He knew then that he was right about Close Calls, about

this party, about the guests, about why they'd all been invited, then herded onto Blue Destiny.

The music was still playing, and everyone was chatting and drinking and having a grand time. No one noticed that Nudger had climbed up on a hatch cover until he shouted over the sound of the music and laughter.

"Hart's gone!" he yelled. "There are no life preservers on board! The dinky's gone!"

Everyone was silent, still, staring at him.

"Dinky?" a woman said.

"Don't you understand?" Nudger shouted in frustration. "The dinky's gone!"

"Too much drinky for him," a man said.

Everyone laughed. They turned away from Nudger and resumed their conversation and their drinking. The fat bald man was passionately kissing the woman he was with now, pinning her against the far rail.

"The dinky's gone!" Nudger yelled again.

He was ignored.

He stumbled down off the hatch and almost fell. Caught his balance and leaned against the rail.

The throbbing diesel engines stopped. The vibration of the deck ceased. Blue Destiny was drifting downstream with the current.

Nudger grabbed a padded vinyl seat cushion from one of the benches near the hatch cover. Then he climbed up on the rail, balancing himself and clutching the cushion to his chest, and jumped over the side.

The current was swifter than he'd imagined, and the water was cold despite the warm night. He was carried swiftly away from the boat, aware of people standing at the rail staring at him. "Hey!" a man yelled, sounding very close as his voice bounced off the water.

Nudger held onto the cushion with all his strength and kicked to guide himself toward shore, but it didn't seem to be working.

The water around him was suddenly orange, brighter and brighter. Then the explosion rocked him and he felt the rush of the concussion as the river shoved him several feet and spun his body around.

He turned and saw the stark silhouette of Hart's boat for only a moment at the base of a huge orange fireball that was rising and unfolding into the night sky. Within a few seconds, small pieces of debris began plunking into the water.

His stomach so tight that he could barely move, Nudger hugged the seat cushion to him like a lover and let the river take him. He was still sick, and now he was trembling. He closed his eyes.

Though he didn't lose consciousness, he did lose track of time.

"Grab hold the line! Grab it!" a man's voice was calling urgently.

Nudger was wet, shivering. He opened his eyes and saw the vast size and bright lights of a riverboat only twenty feet away from him. There was a large, rectangular lighted opening below the lower deck, and several men were standing in it as if posed on a backlit stage.

"Grab it this time!" one of the men shouted again, and Nudger saw him contort his body and hurl a line toward him.

The thick rope plopped into the water ten feet in front of Nudger and began drifting away with the current.

Nudger kicked with his feet and gained on it, stretched out an arm, and gripped it.

Reluctantly, he let go of the floatable seat cushion and grabbed the line with both hands.

"Wrap it around yourself!" one of the other men yelled.

Nudger managed that, and they drew him toward the boat.

"What is this?" Nudger asked, as they dragged him on board. He was dripping water and had lost his remaining shoe. "Where am I?"

"The *Casino Queen* gambling boat," the man who'd tossed the line said. "Tonight, you're the luckiest one on board. Don't know how you survived that explosion."

"There's somebody else out there," Nudger said, "a man in a dinky."

"The Coast Guard's on its way," another man said. "We'll radio them and they'll pick him up for sure, whatever he's in."

"His luck finally ran out tonight," Nudger said, and was sick.

CHAPTER THIRTY-NINE

It was like you thought, Nudge," Hammersmith told Nudger the next day in Claudia's apartment. "Close Calls was much more than a phone retailer."

Nudger had spent the rest of last night with Claudia, after the hospital emergency room had examined him and he'd given his statement to the police. Now he was sprawled on the sofa and she was in the kitchen, preparing breakfast. Nudger was no longer seasick; the scent of frying bacon and eggs was making him hungry.

Though he'd been up much of last night, Hammersmith had dropped by on his way in to the Third for the day shift. Nudger assumed he'd already had breakfast.

"You want coffee, Jack?" Nudger asked.

"Sure."

Nudger got up and went to the kitchen, kissed the nape of Claudia's neck, and poured two cups of coffee.

He carried the cups back to the living room, handed one to Hammersmith, and sat back down on the sofa. Hammersmith remained standing.

"Wayne Hart ran a unique and profitable business, using Close Calls as a front," Hammersmith said. "Close Calls' primary business wasn't phones, it was to arrange for so-called accidental deaths. Once a client was obtained, Hart's expert employees, the ones who died in the boat explosion, would ingeniously rig the intended victim's house or other environs so within a short period of time, an accident would be almost inevitable. On the surface the house wouldn't change, but an oven's gas line would be made faulty, or a basement step loosened, or a washer or dryer's wiring made dangerous, or the wrong size bulb would be placed in a socket, or an outside concrete step would be angled so that when it was icy the victim might slip and fall. Subtle but dangerous alterations that could be put down to wear or original design. Nothing even the victim would notice— until it was too late."

274

"Devious," Nudger said, feeling an unwilling admiration for Wayne Hart's evil concept.

"And lucrative. First a large advance was paid by the client, then Close Calls received a percentage of the insurance settlement. And of course, Hart had some built-in security safeguards. After a reasonable time had passed following the victim's death, the client also met an accidental death at the hands of Close Calls' careful craftsmen. That way loose ends were always being tied. There was plenty of money in this for everyone involved, only the clients didn't have much time to enjoy theirs."

"It might have gone on for a long time," Nudger said, "considering Hart had a method of cleaning up after himself."

"It was you and Lacy who spooked him," Hammersmith said. "Not only were you closing in on what Close Calls was really about, but you stumbled onto Hart's personal vice."

"Young girls," Nudger said.

"Yeah. Very young. So he decided to liquidate his business and move on, and the safest way to do that was to arrange for a final, grand accident that would eliminate the possibility of any of his latest clients, or his employees, talking into the wrong ear. So he threw his party and rigged the boat explosion. Afterward, he was going to remain officially dead until he could be sure no suspicion was attached to the explosion."

"Did you learn all this from Hart himself?" Nudger asked.

"Nope. You and he weren't the only survivors last night,

Nudge. A woman who worked for Close Calls as an electrician, specializing in small appliances and replacing good wiring with worn, realized what you meant when you were yelling about a missing dinky. She jumped overboard a few seconds after you did. The Coast Guard fished her out of the river before they found Hart safe in the dinghy."

Nudger remembered the woman standing with the fat bald guy by the rail on the boat, the look on her face. She was probably the survivor. The bald guy hadn't made it.

"The woman told us about a body that's supposedly buried near Hart's estate, that of a woman named Gloria Brand, from Omaha. She was another of Hart's employees he couldn't afford to leave behind. She would have been on the boat with the others, only he couldn't have her at the party with you and Lacy because you knew her as—"

"Irma Millman," Nudger finished for him. "Brad Millman's so-called sister."

"You and Lacy were where you shouldn't have been when she met you," Hammersmith said. "But no need to go into that now. She went to Millman's condo to find and remove anything that might implicate Close Calls or Hart in Millman's death. You and Lacy were lucky to get there first."

And lucky to leave the condo alive, Nudger thought, with a twitch of his lower intestine. These were dangerous people he and Lacy had stirred up. "What about Tanya, the kid Lacy found in Hart's house?" he asked. "She okay?"

"Lacy's seeing to it," Hammersmith said. "Some sort of maternal instinct seems to have stirred in her."

"Hard to imagine," Nudger said.

"Think she-wolf with cub, Nudge."

"Ah!"

Tired of standing, Hammersmith lowered his bulk into a chair, ignoring the loud protest of springs and frame.

"What about Lacy?" Nudger asked. "She get hurt in her mix-up with Ratko?"

"Not a scratch on her. The county police answered her call and found her standing over Ratko with an empty gun. His knife was still clutched in his dead hand. Self-defense."

Nudger wondered where Lacy had concealed her handgun beneath the dress she'd been wearing. Wondered about the real circumstances of Ratko's death. "There are a lot of ways to die," he said.

"Wayne Hart knew it, and made a fortune out of it." Hammersmith knitted his white eyebrows in a frown. "What Lacy's steaming mad about for some reason is a guy named Lance Cintamon double-crossing her, costing her a lot of money in some kind of insurance deal he backed out of. Says she doesn't trust any man and shouldn't have lowered her guard and thought with her hormones. You know anything about that?"

"Only that I'm not surprised," Nudger said.

"Jack," Claudia called from the kitchen, "do you want to stay for breakfast?"

"I could be talked into it," Hammersmith said, absently patting his protruding stomach.

But not talked out of it, Nudger thought.

"Hart will be held without bail while prosecutors continue adding up how many counts of murder to charge him with," Hammersmith said.

"Hard to convict someone with all that money."

"Not in this case," Hammersmith said. "No matter how

many attorneys Hart has or who they are, eventually he'll be convicted and he'll die by lethal injection."

Nudger wasn't so sure about that. He *was* sure, at least, that Hart would never again live outside prison walls. Reasonably sure, anyway. Which was all you could expect in this uncertain world.

"Even if Hart somehow escapes the needle," Hammersmith told Nudger, "like you said, there are a lot of ways to die. Slowly, inside prison, is one of them."

The kitchen table was too small for the three of them, with Hammersmith's bulk, so they ate at the larger table in the dining room.

No sooner had they sat down when Hammersmith knocked over his orange juice and soaked Claudia's tablecloth. Embarrassed, he broke out in apologies and awkwardly tried to soak up the liquid with his napkin.

"Not to worry," Claudia assured him, "it was an accident."